THE MOUTH OF THE CROCODILE

THE MOUTH OF THE CROCODILE

Michael Pearce

This first world edition published 2014
in Great Britain and 2015 in the USA by
SEVERN HOUSE PUBLISHERS LTD of
19 Cedar Road, Sutton, Surrey, England, SM2 5DA.
Trade paperback edition first published 2015 in Great Britain
and the USA by SEVERN HOUSE PUBLISHERS LTD.

British Library Cataloguing in Publication Data

Pearce, Michael, 1933- author
    The mouth of the crocodile. – (A Mamur Zapt mystery)
    1. Owen, Gareth Cadwallader (Fictitious character)–
    Fiction. 2. Murder–Investigation–Sudan–Atbarah–
    Fiction. 3. Egypt–History–British occupation,
    1882-1936–Fiction. 4. Detective and mystery stories.
    I. Title II. Series
    823.9'14-dc23

ISBN-13: 978-0-7278-8463-3 (cased)
ISBN-13: 978-1-84751-566-7 (trade paper)
ISBN-13: 978-1-78010-614-4 (e-book)

All Severn House titles are printed on acid-free paper.

Severn House Publishers support the Forest Stewardship Council™ [FSC™],
the leading international forest certification organisation. All our titles that
are printed on FSC certified paper carry the FSC logo.

FSC	MIX
FSC www.fsc.org	Paper from responsible sources FSC® C013056

Typeset by Palimpsest Book Production Ltd.,
Falkirk, Stirlingshire, Scotland.
Printed and bound in Great Britain by
TJ International, Padstow, Cornwall.

ONE

All night the drums had been beating in the village across the river.

'Someone must be dead,' said Pollock.

In the morning they learned that the death had occurred on this side of the river. A man had gone into the water to wash his face, as many of the Sudanese usually did. The water was cool and the river more convenient than the wells and pumps which were the townspeople's only other source of water. Jamie saw them on his early-morning walks with Bella, their big Alsatian dog. He would throw dom nuts into the river and Bella would retrieve them. The nuts were as big as pears and had a hard shell, but inside there was a cotton-like material which made them float easily.

But he didn't throw the nuts just where the man had died and the people were washing. He preferred to walk along the dry, dusty bank, past where a herd of goats was tethered, and throw them there. Pollock, whom he sometimes met on his walks, said that the Sudanese didn't like to wash where the dog had been. But the water would have moved on, wouldn't it, by the time the men were washing, so what was Pollock on about? All the same, Jamie kept downstream to do his throwing.

The men – it was always men washing in the river, never women, so what did the women do? Get water from the pumps, probably; he had seen them carrying their wooden buckets into their houses. And sometimes they put water into their big clay pots and carried them home on their heads. Jamie had tried carrying a pot on his head but it wasn't as easy as it looked.

But why didn't they wash in the river, as the men did? Pollock said that they preferred to wash in private. It was more decent that way. But why should that matter for the women and not for the men? Pollock said he would understand when he grew up. Jamie did not think that was a satisfactory answer.

Anyway, the women washed at home and the men came down to the river. They would walk out into the water – the river was shallow at this point – and splash water over themselves. That's what the man must have been doing that morning. He must have gone out too far and stepped over the side of the bank. It fell away steeply after a few yards. Jamie had been out there himself with his father when the swimming pool was out of action. They had been careful not to go too far, even though Jamie could swim.

In fact, he was a good swimmer, better than most of the Sudanese, who splashed around but did not really swim. However, Jamie's dad was quite sticky about his swimming in the river. Crocodiles sometimes came to this side and Dad said you had to be careful.

Once, looking down into the water, Jamie had thought he had seen a crocodile, a big dark shape, quite close in. But his dad had said that they didn't come over to this side, so it was probably something else – *um suf*, perhaps, a bundle of floating reeds. Although, thought Jamie, usually they floated on *top* of the water.

But that morning Jamie was not the only one who thought of the possibility of crocodiles. A group of Sudanese huddled anxiously at the edge of the water peering down into its depths, not even going in to wash. Some sort of debate was going on. Pollock said that they were talking about recovering the body. Apparently, you had to do that for legal reasons as well as religious ones. The religious ones were the most important to the Sudanese, Pollock said, but if there was a question of inheritance, the legal ones became pretty important, too.

'How are they going to get the body up?' asked Jamie.

'In the end someone will have to dive for it,' said Pollock. 'But no one's keen to do that. Especially the dead man's brother. On whom the duty in the end falls.'

Some of the Sudanese were poking about in the water with long poles.

'I don't think that will do much good,' said Jamie.

'No, it won't,' agreed Pollock. 'They're waiting for some fishing lines with hooks on them. Then they'll go up and down in a boat.'

Jamie didn't think that was very promising either.

'No,' Pollock agreed. 'In the end someone is going to have to go down there.'

Jamie would have liked to stay and watch that bit but he had to get home for breakfast. Already he was late and there would be trouble. And it might take hours, Pollock said, while the brother plucked up courage.

'It seems a bit daft,' said Jamie, 'to just walk over the edge. I mean, if you're doing it every day . . . Surely you would know the ground falls away?'

'That's what they're saying,' said Pollock.

'Then . . .'

'They think he must have been pushed,' said Pollock.

Actually, Jamie found this quite believable. Sometimes when the men were washing themselves they fooled around, splashing each other, playing games and generally larking about. When they were milling around like that it would have been only too easy for a push to go the wrong way. Only the week before, Jamie had himself been pushed. Quite deliberately, he felt. He had nearly fallen over. And not very far from the dangerous edge, either. But when he had looked up angrily to find the culprit, everyone was looking the other way.

It had been serious enough, however, for him to make the mistake of telling his parents.

His mother had flown off the handle and told him to keep well away from the river in future when the banks were crowded with people washing.

Jamie had demurred, saying what about Bella's walks?

His mother had hit the roof and had come pretty close to banning the walks altogether.

'That's hardly necessary,' his father had objected mildly. 'It was obviously an accident.'

'Was it?' demanded his mother.

'Of course it was!'

'An English boy?'

'Come, Jane. It's not like that. You know it's not like that.'

In the end Jamie had had to agree to keep well away from the water's edge in future when the bank was crowded. And, since he couldn't face the prospect of his mother blowing her top yet again, he had kept religiously to his promise, staying high up on the river bank, far, as Pollock put it, from the milling crowd.

Which was why he couldn't quite make out what the people down by the water were saying and he had to ask Pollock.

Pollock would probably have gone on for ever but at the top of the steps Jamie could see Mohammed signalling agitatedly.

'You'll be in trouble!' he said, when Jamie got there. 'They've been waiting for you for ages!'

Jamie hurried out on to the veranda, where the breakfast things

were laid. But he need not have worried because he found his
parents talking to a visitor and seemed, fortunately, to have forgotten
entirely about him.

The guest shook hands with Jamie and said his name was Gareth.

'Gareth?' Jamie repeated.

'It's an unusual name, I know,' the man said. 'That's because
it's Welsh.'

'You can call him Mr Owen,' his mother said.

The man waved a deprecating hand.

'I'm going to call you Jamie,' he said. 'Not Master Nicholson.
If that's all right with you.'

Jamie said it was. People didn't go in for master or mister much
in the Sudan. They usually called men like his father 'Effendi'.
Sometimes when Jamie went down to the market they called him
Effendi, too. More often it was 'the young Effendi'.

'What brings you down here, Gareth?' his mother asked.

'Escort duties.'

'Escort duties?' said his mother, wrinkling her nose. 'That sounds
a bit lowly for you!'

'Special request from the Khedive.'

'Are you allowed to tell us what it's all about?'

'No. But I will. A Pasha was attacked on the train coming
south.'

'Can't the police handle it?'

'He was a very special Pasha. A Royal Pasha. And a member of
the Khedive's household. Not to mention his Cabinet.'

'Oh, I see.' She hesitated. 'Even so . . .'

'He was on his way to Khartoum. Probably to a meeting. They
tried to snatch his briefcase, but he hung on to it. It was empty
anyway.'

'Well . . .'

'They obviously thought it wasn't.'

'Was he hurt?'

'Dreadfully. He says.'

'But you don't think . . .'

'I think he'll survive. But he's making the most of it.'

'But why are you involved? It's a bit late, isn't it?'

'He thinks they might try again on the way back. And it might
not be empty this time.'

'Oh, I see. And it's even worth sending you down . . .?'

'It was an important meeting. And the papers could be important.'

'Very. If they're sending you down . . .'

'I don't think they quite intended that. They just asked for an escort. And they were a bit taken aback when the Old Man insisted on sending me. "A member of the Royal Household?" he said. "We can't have that. We must see that you get home safely." They weren't too pleased.'

'I would have thought they'd have been flattered!'

'But who knows what I might get up to on the way? I might even like a peek into the briefcase myself.'

Jamie's father laughed.

'I would not be surprised,' he said.

Jamie was quite shocked.

'Are you a sort of . . . spy?' he said.

'Not exactly.'

'He's the Mamur Zapt,' said Jamie's father.

'Gosh!' said Jamie. The Mamur Zapt. Head of the Khedive's Secret Police. Here!

'It still sounds like spying,' he said.

'Well, in a way it is. But it's not just that. More intelligence work in general.'

'I know,' said Jamie. 'Like Kim.'

He had just been reading this new book about a boy in India, at that time still a major part of the British Empire. The book had only just got to Egypt. His grandmother had sent it on to him, thinking, correctly, that he would enjoy it.

'Are you like Kim?' Jamie demanded.

'More like Creighton,' said the Mamur Zapt.

Jamie was impressed. He even knew the book.

'Finish your breakfast, Jamie!' his mother directed.

Jamie took up his knife and fork again. This was big. The Mamur Zapt in his house! He would have to tell the fellows at school. But then he thought: perhaps he shouldn't tell the fellows at school. This was obviously top secret.

But he had to tell someone. He had a flash of inspiration. He would tell his grandmother! He would put it in a letter. He still hadn't, he thought guiltily, thanked her for the book. He would write to her now and mark the letter *Confidential*. If he could remember how to spell it.

He was mulling this over when he heard shouts in the yard.

A man suddenly rushed in. He was an Egyptian, an Effendi wearing the pot-like red hat that government employees wore in Cairo and in a posh silk suit that people certainly never wore down here in the Sudan. His face was sweating and he seemed very worked up about something.

'Captain Owen! Captain Owen!' he cried agitatedly.

The Mamur Zapt rose from the table. 'Why, Pasha, what's happened?'

'Another one!' he almost screamed.

'Another . . .?'

'Attack!'

'Outside?' said the Mamur Zapt crisply. And in a moment he was gone.

'No. Not outside. At least . . . Yes, I suppose it was outside!'

'Are you hurt, Pasha? Whereabouts?' said Jamie's father. Because, as Jamie told himself, and everyone else who would listen later, there was no sign of blood anywhere.

The Pasha put his hand on his heart. 'Water!' he gasped dramatically.

Mohammed, watching all this with goggle eyes, rushed off to fetch some.

'Sit down, Pasha. Do sit down.'

Jamie's mother drew up a chair.

'Sit down, Pasha. You're all right, now. You're safe!'

The Pasha gulped down some water.

'Some coffee?' asked Jamie's mother, pushing a cup in front of him and pouring the coffee pot.

'Please, yes!'

He drank thirstily. He smacked his lips and held out the cup for some more.

'Would you like to lie down, Pasha?' said Jamie's mother solicitously. 'Shall I call a doctor?'

'No, thank you. That will not be necessary.'

The Pasha looked around and seemed to realize where he was. He got up hastily. 'You must be Madame Nicholson.'

He bowed formally and then, to Jamie's amazement, kissed his mother's hand. 'I beg your pardon! Rushing in here in such an unmannerly way.'

'Not at all, Pasha. Glad to be of assistance.'

'I was just coming to your house, to find Captain Owen, when . . .'

'You were attacked?' said Jamie eagerly.

The Pasha noticed his existence for the first time. 'Well, not exactly,' he admitted. 'At least, not quite exactly. I was coming along the river bank, that seemed the shortest way, when, suddenly, people were shouting. Someone had been attacked!'

'But not – not you?' said Jamie's father.

'It was meant for me,' said the Pasha darkly.

'But how . . .? You're sure?'

'Quite sure. They'd tried before. On the train. But I fought them off.'

'Good heavens!'

'And then they attacked you again on the river bank?' asked Jamie's father.

'Not me. One of my people. But it was meant for me.'

'You know that?'

'Oh, yes. They were out to get me. There can be no doubt about it. They had tried before, and now they were trying again.'

He looked around.

'The Mamur Zapt,' he said. 'He was supposed to be protecting me. I was expecting to meet him here. Where is he?'

'He was here, Pasha. He was here all the time. Don't you remember? He went out when you walked in. To see if he could catch the people.'

'Locking the stable door after the horse has gone!' said the Pasha bitterly.

'But you are safe, Pasha,' said Jamie's mother soothingly.

'Just,' said the Pasha. 'It was a close thing.' He sat down beside his chair. 'Where is it?' he said, panicking. 'Where is my case? I had it with me. They told me to always keep it with me. They even wanted to chain it to me. To me! To put a chain on me! "I am not a slave!" I said. "Of course not, Pasha," they said. "The briefcase is the slave. If it is chained to you it will be safe." "But suppose they steal me with it," I said. No, no. No chain, please! It is unbecoming to a Pasha. "All right then, but guard it with your life," they said. "You can count on that," I said. But now it has gone!'

The Mamur Zapt came up the steps from the garden at this point, carrying a briefcase. 'Yours, I think, Pasha,' he said, handing it to the Pasha.

'My dear fellow!' the Pasha said, clutching it with relief.

'Where did you find it?' asked Jamie's father.

'On the ground. Where His Highness had dropped it.'

'When I was attacked!' said the Pasha.

'Tell me about the attack,' said the Mamur Zapt.

'They were all around me! Pushing and pulling. Some even struck me. I fought them off. And in doing so, I must have dropped my briefcase. I had to. To defend myself.'

'Of course, Pasha. Of course.'

'They had already killed my man. Sayyid, his name was. Poor fellow! He died for me, you know. I was the one they really meant to kill. Sayyid must have gone down to the river to wash himself, and they killed him. The swines!'

'Just a minute, Pasha,' said the Mamur Zapt. 'A man was actually killed on the river bank, you say?'

'Yes!' said Jamie. 'I saw it!'

'You saw it?' said the Mamur Zapt, turning towards him.

'Well, not exactly,' Jamie had to admit. 'But pretty nearly!'

He told them what he had seen.

'Jamie . . .' his mother began.

The Mamur Zapt held up a hand. 'No,' he said, 'let him finish.'

'And I was pushed,' said Jamie. 'Deliberately.'

'I hardly think so, Jamie,' said his father.

'Me too,' said the Pasha.

'Your man, I think you said?' said Owen.

'That's right. Poor Sayyid!'

'But, forgive me, Pasha – what was your man doing on the water front?'

'Washing.'

'Your man? In the river? Forgive me, Pasha, but I would have expected for your man to have other facilities available to him.'

'Well . . .' The Pasha waved an airy hand.

'Did he come down with you in the train?'

'No, no. Of course not!'

It emerged that the Pasha had estates nearby and that the dead man had come from one of those estates.

'He was meeting me here,' said the Pasha.

'On the river bank?' said the Mamur Zapt incredulously.

'Why not?' said the Pasha. 'At least everyone knows where it is. Even in this benighted spot!'

'And what was to be the subject of this meeting?' asked Owen sceptically.

'That is hardly relevant.'

'Oh, but I think it is. If it were connected with an attempt on your life.'

The Pasha obviously couldn't think of a way out of this one. His mind appeared to wander off. 'I should never have come down here,' he grumbled to himself. 'I should have let someone else do it. But the Khedive was particularly insistent. *Not*, as that mischief-maker Nahas claims, because it is far away from Cairo, but because the issues require sensitive handling. The Khedive himself said so. "I need a man I can trust," he said, which he certainly couldn't if he had sent Nahas.'

'It is obviously an issue of importance,' murmured Owen.

'Well, it was. The whole Cabinet agreed. And when I saw the papers, I understood why.'

'You saw that at once?'

'I certainly did!'

'Would that be obvious to anyone who read them?' asked Owen.

'Oh, yes. Why do you ask?' said the Pasha suspiciously.

'Because it has implications for the way we look after you. Clearly, we mustn't let the papers fall into the wrong hands.'

'Indeed not! That would be terrible!'

'I was wondering if we should put you in a special carriage.'

'What?' said Jamie's father, waking up with a jump.

Such privileges were guarded jealously by the railwaymen, reserved only for very special people on very special occasions – or, of course, for themselves when they wanted to get around the Sudan on business. It was justified by the lack of hotels or even Rest Houses, indispensable if you wanted to be sure of a good night's sleep before going on to your next meeting. To ensure this, senior railwaymen made use of special coaches which they called saloons. Each coach was fitted out with a kitchen, a place for the cook and another servant, a bedroom and a sitting room where you could work.

Jamie's father had one and he had promised that the next time he went out he would take Jamie with him.

Jamie's father pulled himself together. 'Of course, Pasha. I will see what I can do. It won't be easy. All our suitable saloons are heavily worked.'

The Mamur Zapt smiled. 'Do your best,' he said. 'The Pasha has had an exhausting time and we need to look after him.'

'Well,' said the Pasha, gratified, 'that would be very nice. Very nice, indeed.'

'You could have my own,' said Jamie's father.

'What?' said Jamie. 'But . . .'

Jamie's father kicked him under the table.

Jamie nursed his wrath. His father had promised him that the next time he went out, he could go along too. Jamie saw no reason why he should renege on his promise just because of a fat old Pasha! An occasional sortie in the special saloon was one of the highlights of Jamie's existence, not to be easily forgone. He kicked his father back.

'On second thoughts,' said his father smoothly, 'possibly I can do better. We happen to have the Royal Coach in the yard; it's just been having some work done on it but it's all ready to go out on the line. We were going to give it a trial run anyway.'

'Just the thing!' said the Mamur Zapt enthusiastically. 'Give it a trial run with the Pasha on board! I am sure that the Khedive wouldn't mind. He would want to see it properly tried out before he went in it. And I am sure he wouldn't object to one of his most faithful and distinguished servants being given the honour of testing it out first.'

'I'm sure he wouldn't,' said the Pasha, smiling happily.

'And what we can do, too,' said Jamie's father, 'is tack my saloon on behind it. I've got to go up to Halfa anyway. And the Mamur Zapt can go in it and won't be far away from the Pasha should the need arise.'

'An admirable idea!' said the Pasha. 'Right next door would suit me best.'

It could not be done at once, however. The coach would have to be given a thorough checking in the workshop first. Then it would have to be brought up from the yard. And, finally, the Chief Suffragi insisted it should be given a good cleaning and dusting before being released on to the line. Although it would be carrying a mere Pasha, it was the Royal Coach, after all, and needed to be seen as a reflection of the Khedive's glory.

It would all be done, the Chief Engineer and the Chief Suffragi assured them, by the following day. Owen had his doubts about this and Jamie's father substituted for the following day the day after, but they were all confident about that.

It suited Jamie too. At first he had taken it for granted that he would be the one to miss out, but his father said no. The Mamur Zapt wouldn't mind if Jamie went along with them. Jamie's father could move into the dining room to sleep and Jamie could make up a bunk alongside him.

'Then I'll be able to keep an eye on him,' he assured Owen. 'It's likely to be a more onerous task than yours.'

The Mamur Zapt said that it might be best if he was the one to sleep in the dining room because he would be moving about during the night anyway. It was important to check that no one was climbing aboard at one of the train's frequent stops. It was a favourite trick, he said, not just of those wanting to steal things but also anyone wanting a free ride. And, given the presence of the Pasha on board, there was an extra need for vigilance.

So Jamie would have his ride after all and it would be even more exciting than usual because the Mamur Zapt would be on board fending off potential aggressors, in which task, thought Jamie, he might himself be able to provide modest help.

And, said Jamie's mother, both the Mamur Zapt and the Pasha could stay that night with them. This would mean Jamie vacating his bedroom but he didn't mind that. At this time of year they normally slept outside on the lawn anyway, where it was cooler. The Pasha, however, was going to sleep inside. He preferred to retain city customs.

'And a mosquito net, please.'

Which could easily be provided. They didn't usually bother about nets themselves. Jamie's father claimed that where there was movement of the air, mosquitoes did not come. Jamie knew that this was untrue because he had been bitten several times when he was sleeping outside but he didn't mind much. Only once had he had malaria and his parents usually shrugged it off.

'It's just like a bad cold,' his mother said.

The Pasha, however, seemed to envisage it as being eaten alive. It was yet another of the things that made him anxious to get back to Cairo.

Before then, however, he had an important duty to perform: attending the funeral of a relative. In the Sudan, as in Egypt, disposal of the remains had to follow on quickly after death. Within twenty-four hours, it was prescribed. Bodies decomposed rapidly in the heat. The funeral of the drowned man was therefore going to take place the very next day and the Pasha was going across the river to the village on the other side to visit the relative's family house. The Pasha himself was, of course, a distant relative and was under a certain obligation to attend. He would not himself be performing any of the rites – that role was reserved for those closer in relationship to the dead man – but the presence of so senior a figure was itself an honour both to the dead man and to his family.

The body was found that afternoon. It had been carried some fifty yards downstream by the current and it would probably be more had it not stuck in a protruding arm of the bank. Once dislodged it had floated to the surface of its own accord and the men had washed it ashore, taking care not to touch the body, both for reasons of respect and because there were fears that the body might burst open. That sometimes happened, said Pollock, because of the force of the gases trapped in the abdomen. Jamie would have liked to have seen that happen but his mother had hustled him away. In any case, Pollock told him afterwards, it didn't happen this time.

When Jamie rejoined the people on the bank, the action was over. The body had been put in a boat and transferred to the dead man's village on the other side of the river.

There were still groups of mourners left on the bank. There was only the one boat ferrying people across and it was a small old boat with a square, patched sail and none of the graceful lines of the sleek feluccas. It was used mostly for ferrying the poorer people across the river to the market on the other side. Even now, along with the unusual number of passengers, it carried chickens which busied around under people's feet, pecking up the grain which had been dropped from the big bags of durra it often carried. With such a load on board the boat sat very low in the water and wobbled uncertainly away from the bank.

At the last moment, the Pasha appeared with a group of followers. The boat was already full indeed, beginning to push away from the bank and, despite peremptory shouts from the Pasha's retainers, was unwilling or probably incapable of turning back. After more shouting to and fro it proceeded on its way, leaving the Pasha and a sizeable group of people to await its return.

Among the mourners was the Mamur Zapt, who stood talking to the Pasha, and others in the crowd, including the chief of the local police, again an Englishman, named Crockhart-Mackenzie.

Jamie noticed that the Pasha was not carrying his briefcase. Had he forgotten it? Or did he think it was safe to leave in Jamie's house?

There was still a long time to go before the boat got back. The Nile was nearly half a mile wide at that point and the sail power the native boat could muster was very limited.

Jamie suddenly became aware that the Mamur Zapt had slipped away. He saw him going up the steps into the house. Was he going to pick up the briefcase for the Pasha? What was he going to do with it? Put the papers somewhere else?

The Mamur Zapt flitted quickly around the room, pulling open drawers, looking under pillows, moving Jamie's things. Jamie didn't mind. His mother had emptied the drawers when she had learned that they were having the Pasha to stay the night. They were still empty.

'So what has he done?' said the Mamur Zapt to himself. 'Put the papers somewhere else? Has your father a strong box?' he asked Jamie.

'Yes,' said Jamie, 'but it's only a little one. He uses it to keep money in.'

He showed Owen where it was.

Of course, they could not open it. They could hear the few coins there were inside rattling.

The Mamur Zapt put the box down. 'I don't think so,' he said. 'He would want to keep the papers close to him. On his person, I expect. The briefcase is a bit too obvious.' He shrugged. 'Well, we'll see. Meanwhile, we had better get down to the river again. The boat will be back soon.'

He had said 'we', so Jamie took it that he was included in the party. In any case, he got into the boat with the others.

First there were the professional mourners, wild-looking men with their gowns torn and their hair straggling down unkemptly over their shoulders to demonstrate their grief. Some of them were carrying *tars*, a sort of instrument rather like a tambourine, which they plucked and struck with the flat of their hand, all the while keeping up a mournful chanting.

And then behind them were some small boys, dressed up for the occasion with stiff, bemused faces.

Behind them came the crowd, swelling all the time, extending now right across the square in front of the mosque. Somewhere in the mass of people, probably near the back, would be the bier. Yes, Jamie thought he could see it now: a sort of litter, or flat bed, held up high above the crowd on people's shoulders, with the dead man lying on it in full view of everybody. It wavered a bit as it came through the crowd, quite close to Jamie. There were people dancing around it, tearing at their clothes and beating their chests, and in front were two men, *fikis*, reciting verses from the Koran. Jamie tried to make out the words. He spoke passable Arabic, at the kitchen level, that was, where he had grown up playing with Mohammed's children, but he couldn't make out these ones at all. Something about a turban? That couldn't be right, surely?

He looked questioningly at his father, standing beside him.

'Turban?'

His father nodded.

'To show his standing,' he said. 'Head of the family. And a prominent figure in the community.'

'I thought he was just a lowly clerk in the offices,' said Pollock.

'Well, they always try to make much of a chap when he's dead,' said Jamie's father.

'Perhaps it's because the Pasha is here,' said Pollock.

They could see the Pasha near the bier, beating his breast along with everyone else.

The procession halted in front of the mosque. The crowd was far too big for everyone to get in. Instead, people gathered in front. There was a slight delay and then the crowd parted and the bier went on into the mosque.

A small group went on into the mosque, too. Among them was the Pasha.

And beside him was the Mamur Zapt. However, the Mamur Zapt stopped outside the entrance to the mosque and did not go in. Jamie suddenly realized that from where Owen was standing, at the open door of the mosque, he could see inside.

He went on standing there until the bier emerged again into the sunshine and then slipped back.

The Pasha, who had come out just after the bier, went across and stood beside him.

A low murmur went up from the crowd and then, as the bier moved away, it began to get excited. People pressed in on the bier, crying out and weeping.

The Pasha did not follow them.

'Enough is enough,' Jamie heard him say to Owen.

Owen nodded. 'I think respect has been shown,' he said to the Pasha. 'The family will appreciate it, I am sure.'

'One has one's responsibilities,' said the Pasha.

'A big turn out,' said Jamie's father as they stepped back into the boat.

'Surprisingly so,' said the Mamur Zapt.

Jamie's father looked at him. 'You think so?'

'If he was, as you say, just a clerk in the offices.'

'It's the fact that the Pasha was there,' said Pollock.

'That, too, is a little surprising. Pashas don't usually bother much about lowly relatives. And I wouldn't have thought that this particular one was the sort to make exceptions.'

'More to it than meets the eye?'

'I wouldn't be surprised,' said the Mamur Zapt.

The Pasha sat at the front of the boat. He seemed pleased with himself. From time to time he gave a little smile.

TWO

Jamie sat up in bed and reached down for his sandals. He shook each carefully to make sure there were no scorpions in the toes, put them on and then padded across the lawn, avoiding the fishing line that his father had put out overnight. One end of the line was tied to a leg of his bed and the other led away across the lawn and down the steps to the river. Every morning Jamie's father pulled the line in and on the end of it there was usually a fish. Other fathers didn't do this and Jamie's mother regularly remonstrated with him. One day, she predicted, there would be not a fish but a crocodile on the end of the line and it would pull his father and, probably, the bed too, into the river. Jamie rejected this but did not entirely discount the possibility and every morning he checked to see that the bed was still in place.

It was this morning and so was his father, sleeping peacefully beneath the orange tree.

Bella came across the lawn to greet him, carrying a dom nut in her mouth, ready for action.

Jamie went down the steps on to the river bank, which at this time in the morning was nearly always deserted. The washers came down later.

Not entirely deserted, however, for there by the water's edge were two figures, one of them that of the Mamur Zapt, the other that of the Atbara Chief of Police, Crockhart-Mackenzie.

'Morning, Jamie,' said Crockhart-Mackenzie. He reached down and patted Bella on the head. 'Morning, Bella,' he said.

'Morning, Jamie,' said the Mamur Zapt.

'You're up early,' said Jamie.

'Always am,' said Owen. 'Can't go on sleeping once the sun gets in my eyes.'

In Cairo, when the nights were hot, he slept on the roof of his house and was woken by the sun. Zeinab had moved her bed precisely so that she wouldn't be woken by it. If the baby stirred, it was Owen's job to move it into Zeinab's bed so that mother and baby, soothed by each other's warmth, could sleep on a little longer. Owen, meanwhile, liked to walk to the edge of the roof and look out over the Nile below and the little public garden along the edge when the doves were just waking up and beginning to gurgle softly. He enjoyed that part of the day, when everything was quiet, before the city exploded into noisy, febrile life. Even here, where it was certainly quiet – quiet enough to hear the *sageeyas*, the waterwheels, creaking in the distance, and the Nile, here as in Cairo, peacefully making its path towards the sea just below him – he didn't feel as much at ease as he did back there.

He wondered why that was. Was it that deep down he knew there was work to do and he had already switched on? Or was it the new thing that had suddenly thrust itself into his and Zeinab's life, the uncompromising arrival of the baby? Yes, he decided, it was that. It was amazing how soon they had got used to it, how quickly they had come to take it for granted, how every morning he looked forward to the first snuffly, moist embrace. He was missing that. And even the early-morning beauty of the Nile, with the sun beginning to glint on the water, and the bundles of *um suf* curling and uncurling in the current, and the birds beginning to stir in the garden behind him, didn't quite make up for it.

'I was pushed,' said Jamie.

'Tell me about it.'

'I was down there,' he pointed. 'Just picking a dom nut out of the water to throw for Bella, when somebody pushed me. Hard. I nearly fell over. It wouldn't have mattered if I had fallen over, because I was sufficiently far back not to have fallen over the edge, but all the same it wasn't a nice thing to do. Dad says it was an accident but I don't think it was. I think it was deliberate.'

'Why do you think that, Jamie?' asked the Mamur Zapt.

Jamie hesitated. 'Because it wasn't a bump, it was a push. A definite push. People are always bumping into you at that time in the morning down there. There are a lot of people and they mill around. They get water in their eyes, I think, but this wasn't like that.'

'Did you see the man who did it, Jamie?' asked Crockhart-Mackenzie.

'Not really. I looked round but by the time I turned, he was gone. It was a big push and I nearly fell over and by the time I had got properly on my feet he was back in the crowd.'

'That sounds a bit nasty, Jamie,' said Owen sympathetically.

'I suppose it didn't really amount to much,' conceded Jamie. 'Not really.'

'But it was distinct enough for you to mention it,' said Owen.

'Yes, that's right. I wouldn't ordinarily have mentioned it but this was – well, so definite.'

'Better not go down there again,' said Crockhart-Mackenzie. 'Not for a day or two.'

'Does this sort of thing happen often?' asked Owen.

'No. Not really,' said Crockhart-Mackenzie.

'No,' agreed Jamie. 'That's why it stood out.'

'What was Bella doing?' asked Owen.

'She was in the water. Waiting for another nut.'

'She didn't bark?'

'She's a bit of a dope in the early morning,' said Jamie.

'I'll ask around,' said Crockhart-Mackenzie. 'We would not want this sort of thing to be repeated.'

'It's probably nothing,' said Jamie. He didn't want another fuss like the one his mother had kicked up.

'All the same, I'll ask around,' said Crockhart-Mackenzie. 'At the very least, it will remind people to watch what they're doing when they're larking about.'

Further along the bank, the boat was pulling in. The boatman threw some hens over the side. They squawked indignantly and then splashed their way to the shore. A couple of black-gowned women scrambled out after them. The boatman pulled in the sail and then pushed the boat up on to the bank.

'Hello, Mustapha!' said Jamie.

The boatman raised a hand in greeting. Then he went back into the boat, took out a dom nut from inside the hull and threw it into the water. Bella plunged after it.

The Mamur Zapt and Crockhart-Mackenzie turned to go.

'I'm catching the train out tonight,' said Owen. 'There are one or two things I'd like you to do for me.'

'Of course!'

'Can you check up on the man who was drowned? Find out what you can about him.'

'I know about him,' said Crockhart-Mackenzie unexpectedly.

'You do?'

'I've had my eye on him for some time.'

'How's that?'

'There was a bit of trouble in the works and we received a tip that he was one of the trouble makers. It came to a head when the Royal Coach was brought in.'

'The one that's being done up? In readiness for the Khedive.'

'That's right.'

'The one we're taking out this morning?'

'Yes. The one you ordered.'

'I just asked for a coach. Nicholson suggested this one. A good idea, I thought. It's cheered up the Pasha no end.'

'Oh, it's a good idea. And it's probably worked to our advantage.'

'How so?'

'It means that people won't have time to do anything to it.'

'Vandalism, you mean?'

'Worse. Possibly. It's the Khedive's coach. And not everyone loves the Khedive.'

'So they might . . . try to arrange that something goes wrong?'

Crockhart-Mackenzie nodded. 'That's what our informant said.'

'And this chap, the chap who was drowned . . .'

'Was involved. Part of a group we suspected might try something like that. There were others more directly involved, who worked in the workshop. But this chap, Sayyid, was their contact in the programming office. Or so we were told.'

'He would know when the coach was going out?'

'They had been doing it up. It needs a proper servicing and they thought while it was in they could give it a freshener. Paint it up a bit. Touch up the gilt. So this group thought they might take advantage of that and really do something to the coach. The undercarriage, I suspect. Anyway, we got tipped off that something like that was going to happen, and I've been keeping an eye on them.'

'I take it they don't like the Khedive?'

'You take it correctly. Or so it would appear. But we don't know much about the group. We've had the tip-off only very recently. And I don't think they're quite ready yet. So this request of yours may have forestalled them. I'll get some reliable men to do a double check on the saloon before it goes out. And on the train as well. So you should be all right.'

'And the men,' said Owen, 'keep an eye on the men. And let me know if you find out anything.'

'I will,' promised Crockhart-Mackenzie. 'I will.'

'And continue digging on Sayyid. I'm still puzzled. If he was on their side, why kill him?'

'If they did kill him,' said Crockhart-Mackenzie.

'If they did,' Owen agreed.

'I still think it was an accident,' said Crockhart-Mackenzie.

The Royal Saloon was brought up from the yard at about five o'clock, its new paint sparkling golden in the late sun. It lay in a siding with a guard mounted on it. Owen went through the saloon himself to be quite sure. He peered at the undercarriage, although, as he himself would be the first to admit, if there was anything mechanically wrong with it, he was not one who would spot it.

When he had finished, the cook and the boy moved in. There was room for a couple of servants in the saloon and although the journey was a short one, it was important to guard against the contingencies, and poisoning was one. Jamie heard Owen telling his father that the arrangement of the saloon, the royal one and then the one which carried Jamie and his father, would make it easy for Owen to act as Royal Taster, a post, he said, which, given the sumptuousness of the food, he had always rather fancied. 'A job to die for,' he said.

'Just make sure that you don't!' said Jamie's mother, who, trusting neither the railway staff nor her own husband, was conducting her own check.

Another person who was surveying the saloon, albeit less critically and with far greater satisfaction, was the Pasha.

'It is only right,' he said, 'that when the Khedive's servants are travelling on their duties, they should be afforded the same privileges as their Royal Master.'

More to the point, the fans were very good and were already working. The temperature outside was in the nineties, as it often was in the Sudan – another thing which increased the Pasha's anxiety to return to Egypt. He lingered in the saloon, testing the bed.

Jamie meanwhile was conducting his own survey. The train from Khartoum to Cairo had now come in and the two saloons, the royal one and Jamie's father's one, were being attached. There were saloons for the benefit of first-class passengers and Jamie decided to take a look at them. They were pretty good, he decided, although not, of course, up to the standard of the royal one. Taking advantage of the Mamur Zapt's inspection, and the Pasha's recumbency, he checked on the facilities. Gold paint and tassels everywhere. The wood of best quality and finely polished. Little standard lamps on the table of the finest silk – like the ones he had seen on the Pullmans, only even better. Soft carpeting on the floor. In Egypt and the Sudan you didn't usually put carpets on the floor, you put them on the walls. That was not so easy in a train but Jamie noticed with approval that an attempt had been made.

'Jamie, shake the sand out of your sandals,' commanded his mother.

The Pasha didn't wear sandals. He wore shiny leather boots. Must be hot, thought Jamie.

There was the smell of new leather through the saloon. It was like going into one of the big shops in Cairo – Andelaft's, say, or Joseph Cohen's. But the distinctive smell of leather was everywhere, that and sandalwood.

He thought that the Khedive might not be too pleased at the comparison.

But what pleased Jamie was the softness of the seats. In his view the Arab did not really understand about seats. For a start, there were many of them. You usually sat on the floor, admittedly on cushions, but that wasn't quite right. Where did you put your back? And where there were chairs, at the dining table, say, they were usually without upholstery and after a time became pretty hard.

But the seats in the Royal Coach weren't like that. They were low and soft, so that you sank into them, and they were covered with a sort of red velvet. Occasionally you caught a whiff of cigarette smoke, which Jamie didn't like, but Egyptians did. Still, it was different from English smoke, which Jamie also did not like. He had once seen a very elegant Greek lady smoking a cigarette in a long turquoise holder which went with her dress. The smoke from that had a strong, heavy scent and Jamie had not minded that. People said that Madam Toapatelis was very racy. Jamie wasn't sure what racy meant but looking at her slim body he thought she might be better at races than most of the women around.

Jamie's father came upon him at this point and hustled him off back to their own saloon, which usually seemed like magic to him but today was a bit of an anti-climax. The other carriages had been hitched on by now. Among them was a couple of first-class saloons which Jamie thought might be worth a look.

Coming out of one was an Egyptian girl about his own age.

'Who are you?' she said.

'Jamie.'

'You're not with the Pasha?'

'No, I'm with my father.'

'Who is he? An official of some kind?' she asked, slightly disdainfully.

'A senior one,' said Jamie, not to be put down.

'My father is with the Treasury,' she said, as if playing the Ace card.

'Oh!' said Jamie weakly. He was not sure how that stood *vis à vis* his father. He had an uneasy feeling that he ought to play this one carefully.

'Have you come from Khartoum?' he asked, seeking to distract.

'Yes. And a horrid place that is, too.'

'I'm from Atbara,' he said.

'There? Well, I am sorry for you.'

'It's all right,' said Jamie, outflanked.

'I'm going to Paris when we get home,' she said.

'I'm going to London.'

Which wasn't true, but surely London outranked Paris?

'Oh, London!' She didn't seem impressed.

'It's a big place.'

'Very bourgeois,' she said dismissively.

Jamie wasn't at all sure what that meant. 'It suits me,' he said defiantly.

'It would!' She started to go past him.

'You can't go that way,' said Jamie. 'That's the Khedive's coach.'

'I know.'

'The Pasha is there.'

'Oh, what a bore!' said the girl.

'Resting,' said Jamie.

'He's always resting!' said the girl. 'It's the bits between resting that he finds difficult.'

'You know him?'

'We were with him in Khartoum. They kept going to meetings. And sent me to look at the zoo! The zoo! I ask you!'

Jamie had quite liked the zoo.

'When I get to Paris, I'm not going to any zoos, I can tell you!' She made for the door to the Khedive's apartment, then stopped irresolutely.

'We could poke our heads in,' suggested Jamie.

'Yes, we could. You poke first.'

'All right.'

He went through cautiously.

'No one here,' he reported.

'He's walking about outside. I can see him.'

They went in and looked around.

'I don't think much of the taste,' said the girl.

'No?'

'Overblown!' she pronounced. 'Rather too decadent for me. Do you think the British chose it? Or the Pasha?'

'I expect the Khedive chose it.'

'Ah! That explains it!'

Owen came into the saloon through the door at the other end. He gave Jamie a wave.

'Who is that?' demanded the girl.

'The Mamur Zapt,' said Jamie, hoping thereby to recover some of his ground.

'Ah! The enemy of the people!'

'Not *all* the people!' said Owen, overhearing.

Another man, an Egyptian, came into the saloon and stopped. 'Aisha! What are you doing here?'

'Having a look round,' said Aisha, somewhat sulkily. 'This is my father,' she said to Jamie.

And then, trying to put everyone in their place: 'Father, this is the Mamur Zapt.'

'I know,' said her father. He shook hands with Owen. 'Mahmistry el Zaki has often spoken to me about you, Captain Owen.'

'A great friend!'

'Of mine, too.'

'You are in the Parquet?'

The Parquet was the Department of Prosecution of the Ministry of Justice – the ministry's cutting edge, as it were.

'I was. Still am, really. But nowadays I am mostly attached to the court.'

'A legal advisor?'

'Less and less. More a diplomatic dogsbody.'

Owen laughed. 'That must mean you're getting somewhere,' he said. 'If only!'

'Mahmoud must be envious.'

'I don't think he is, actually. Half of him is envious. The other half shudders and shrinks away.'

'He is too good a man to be locked up in the court – sorry, I didn't mean it quite like that!'

'Oh, but you're right! I feel that, too. In my own case that is, with far less justification than Mahmoud. You see what looks like a higher rung in the ladder and go to it and then you find that it is not all that it is cracked up to be. But you don't find that yourself, I am sure.'

'I quite like my rung on the ladder.'

'I quite understand that. But, you know, you puzzle us, Captain Owen. Every other Mamur Zapt in history has used the post to enrich himself. Whereas you . . .'

'Am as poor now as I always was!'

'Mahmoud admires that greatly. He says that is what the country needs. He is still puzzled, however. He says that the English, while they are here, do not on the whole enrich themselves; they just enrich their country at our expense.'

'More than a grain of truth in that,' said Owen.

They both laughed.

'Aisha,' her father said, 'you have been here long enough! Take yourself back to our coach. Take your friend with you. You are coming on the train, I take it?' he said to Jamie.

'To Halfa,' said Jamie.

'Aisha will be glad of your company.' He hesitated. 'And you are . . .?'

'Jamie.'

'Nicholson Effendi's son,' said Owen.

'Ah! I didn't know him well but I've certainly met him. And your mother, too. Please give them my regards. And now, once more, Aisha . . .'

Aisha reluctantly led the way out.

Owen had placed her father now. He must be Yasin al-Jawad, another of the Parquet's bright young men. The Parquet was a breeding ground of such men: able, ambitious and impatient. The new men, the coming men. The Pashas, like the British, viewed them askance. They were as much a threat to them as they were to the British. They knew about modern ideas and about the way things were done abroad. Especially about the way they were done in France.

The Egyptian legal system was based on the Napoleonic Code, following the French-leaning sympathies of an earlier Khedive and the effects of the French occupation of Egypt earlier in the century. French, not Arabic, was the language that they habitually worked in and with the language came other things, a liking for French culture and for all things French. Their wives shuddered at the thought of the *burka* and followed the styles of Paris. When they wore veils they were the flimsy half-veils of the sophisticated Parisienne and not the long, all-concealing veil of the Arabs. Their husbands had a thirst for French books, French ideas which did not always sit comfortably with traditional Egyptian culture. And their daughters were brought up as little French girls rather than invisible Arab ones.

They tended to be nationalist rather than Islamic in their political allegiances. Which, of course, did not make them any easier for the British to deal with. Owen's role as Head of the Khedive's Secret Police was a heavily political one. Murder, robberies and things of that sort were not for him; they were for the ordinary police and the Parquet. The Parquet lawyers took over the role of detectives in the British system. The police reported crimes and the Parquet investigated them and compiled a case which they presented to the courts. Anything political was the concern of the Mamur Zapt.

In practice this meant that he had a great deal to do with the Parquet. Which was how he had come across the name of Yasin al-Jawad, who had started as ordinary Parquet lawyer and then drifted upwards to become, as he had said, a general political dogsbody to the Khedive.

So what was he doing here? He had been attending a meeting in Khartoum, according to Aisha. Was it the same meeting as the Pasha had been attending with his briefcase? It seemed unlikely that there were two meetings on at the same time in a small city that the Khedive had been sending people to. Owen wondered again what had been the business of the meeting – a meeting which on the one hand had led to the attack on the Pasha, but which Yasin al-Jawad had felt so relaxed about that he had brought his daughter with him.

Jamie followed Aisha as she went out through the saloon and then jumped on to the ground. Although Atbara was a main station, there was no real platform. You descended straight on to the sand. If you were joining the trains there were porters to lift your luggage up into the carriage. Only a few of the carriages were saloons – that is, carriages with bedrooms and a small kitchen. The others had simple plain seats. Ordinary passengers sat on those, and sometimes, in the coaches at the end, brought their livestock with them. Hens scuttled around under people's feet.

Most of the passengers already on the train had got out to stretch their legs. Those joining had brought their friends with them and were standing talking. There weren't many passenger trains each day, perhaps two in the morning and one in the evening. Most of the passengers were for Khartoum or Cairo. A branch line went up to Port Sudan on the coast.

The engine, a big steam one, had been uncoupled and was taking on water down near the marshalling yards. It needed a lot of water for the desert crossing, although there were watering points between here and Wadi Halfa. Most of the passengers were ordinary Sudanese in long gowns and turbans. There was the occasional woman among them, squatting down on the ground, sometimes with a chicken underneath her skirts. There was, too, the occasional effendi, in a smart linen suit. If he was a civil servant he usually wore a red, pot-like fez. If he was just a businessman he wore the suit but not the fez.

There were no other children. The local children would have come out of school now and gone home for their evening meal. From the houses around the station came little columns of smoke and the smell of frying, usually mixed with a strong whiff of garlic.

Actually, there weren't many children at all. European children, at this time of year, were away at school in England. A few went to schools in Khartoum. Jamie was between schools – a school he had attended in Khartoum, and the school in England that he would be going to in the autumn. There were no other English boys in Atbara at the moment. And no girls.

This one didn't count as she was just passing through. She probably went to school in Cairo.

'Where do you go to school?' he asked as they walked along the train.

'Cairo.' She made a face. 'There's not much in the way of schooling for girls there,' she said. 'I shall probably have to go to Alexandria. That's where most of the Parquet send their children. It's more European.'

'More European?'

'It's by the sea. Cooler. My father is unhappy about it, though.'

'About it being cooler?'

'No, no, no. About it being European. In the wrong way. He says it's too much like the Riviera. The Parquet wives all go there in the summer and have a good time. Beaches, parties – that sort of thing.'

'And he doesn't like that?'

'He gets bored. My mother likes it, though. Lying on the beach and looking beautiful. I *quite* like it, but only quite. It gets boring after a time. I can see what my father means. I'm a bit like him, you know.'

'You are?'

'Yes. He says it's because I have a brain and most Egyptian women don't. It's because they're not allowed to have one, he says. That's the trouble with Egypt, he says, and that's why I want to go to France.'

'England's pretty good,' said Jamie.

'No culture,' said Aisha. 'That's what my father says. And my mother. Although I think that what she means by culture is not the same as what my father means.'

'What does she mean?'

'Shops.'

'And what does your father mean?'

'Work. It's a pretty depressing look out if you're a girl in Egypt.'

'I think work would be all right,' said Jamie. 'If it were interesting.'

'Ah, but that's the problem. It's not easy to find an interesting job if you're a girl in Egypt. What does your mother do?'

Jamie hadn't thought about this. He could hardly say she looks after the children, because there was only him, and he didn't need looking after.

'Gardens,' he hazarded.

'Gardens!' said Aisha, astounded. 'Haven't you a gardener?'

'Oh, yes,' said Jamie hurriedly, 'but someone has to tell him what to do.'

'Doesn't sound much of a job to me!' said Aisha.

Dusk comes early in the Sudan and night falls quickly. Even while they were standing there, lights began to come on in the marshalling yards.

Engines began to fade into the darkness like big slumbering ghosts. Jamie always liked this bit. Everything became sort of mysterious. Just beyond the yards was the Nile and that, too, was mysterious, once the hard light of day had gone. You began to see palm trees outlined against the sky, and the sky was as clear as on a frosty night in England. Yet the warmth of the sun still drifted upwards from the ground. There was no need even for a jacket, although some of the effendis travelling on the train affected to find it chilly and kept their coats on. At this time of day Jamie's mother sometimes threw a cardigan around her shoulders.

She wasn't coming with them in the saloon, although she often did. She said that with the Mamur Zapt on board, and doubtless with an entourage, the saloon would be getting rather crowded. Not having his mother with them meant two eggs, not one, for breakfast. It was a little treat that he and his father and the cook shared. He wondered what Aisha did. Probably no eggs at all, just a crust. Or was it a rusk? That's what made Parquet women keep so slim, as opposed to Egyptian ladies in general, who tended to put on weight. Or so Pollock said.

Aisha, though, was thin as a pencil. Jamie wondered what her mother was like. Thin or fat? Thin, too, Jamie imagined. She wasn't with them. She said, according to Aisha, that the last thing she wanted to do was sit on a train for hours and hours. Even with the fans going. Aisha said it was a relief to get away from her. And perhaps her father felt the same. Anyway, she had been left behind.

The station was emptying now as the passengers climbed back into their places. In the saloons the table lamps began to switch on. He heard someone calling for drinks. That must be an Englishman. Muslims didn't drink alcohol. Much.

Jamie's father came rushing up at the last moment carrying an armful of papers. He got into their saloon. Jamie thought he wouldn't interrupt him yet. He was probably working.

The Mamur Zapt and Crockhart-Mackenzie came along the train looking under the carriages for stowaways. Jamie once had considered stowing away himself and then jumping out to surprise his father. However, on reflection, he had thought his father might not be too pleased. Boys were always stowing away and then falling off and getting injured. Anyway, under the carriages it was dirty and greasy and the sand blew up in your eyes and mouth. Once he had seen a boy who had stowed away and then fallen off. He was covered with sand and bleeding and there was something wrong with his leg.

Jamie considered telling Aisha about this but thought she might not be interested. You never knew with girls.

Not that Jamie knew much about girls. You never saw Arab girls – not to talk to, at least. Aisha was, actually, the first Arab girl he had ever talked to.

He put that to Aisha. She considered for a moment and then said that he was the first English boy she had ever talked to. But she had talked to lots of French boys. Or so she said.

Jamie didn't believe her. He thought she was putting it on. He considered saying *that* to Aisha but didn't quite dare.

'Time to get on board,' said Crockhart-Mackenzie.

'See you in Cairo,' said Aisha.

She wouldn't, of course. He was getting off at Wadi Halfa.

The Pasha was sitting in the Royal Saloon looking morosely out of the window as the last houses went by. Once they had gone there was just desert. The Pasha didn't like open spaces. He was a city man – more than that, a Cairo man, through and through. And Cairo was still a long way away.

Owen knocked on the door and came in. 'Hello, Pasha. All's well, I hope?'

'In so far as anything can be said to be well in this dreadful country!' muttered the Pasha.

'And yet you yourself have connections with the Sudan,' said Owen. 'Or, at least, relations here.'

'Best forgotten,' said the Pasha.

'Distant relations, I imagine.'

'Very distant.'

'It was good of you, then, to go to your relative's funeral.'

'I was just doing my duty,' said the Pasha modestly.

'Of course! He was from your estate, I think you said?'

'One of them,' said the Pasha loftily.

'I think you said that he was one of your men,' said Owen.

'One of them, yes.'

'Even though he worked for the railway.'

'I hire them out,' explained the Pasha. 'My overseer says we make more money that way.'

'But still they are your men?'

'Oh, yes. Forever.'

'And you still use them from time to time.'

'From time to time, yes.'

'When you come down to the Sudan.'

'Very rarely, I can assure you.'

'But you still keep in touch?'

'At arm's length,' said the Pasha. 'Very much at arm's length.'

'You were meeting someone, I think you said?'

'Did I?'

'On the river bank.'

'Really? I don't remember that.'

'You must have been on your way to the meeting when it happened.'

'Fell into the water. When he was washing. Foolish fellow! Should have taken more care. I never fall into the river when I am washing.'

'Well, no, you wouldn't . . .'

'Should have watched what he was doing.'

'Did it inconvenience you?'

'Why should it?'

'Not being able to hold the meeting. After you had gone to the trouble of arranging it.'

'Or was it he who had arranged it,' said the Pasha, with indifference.

'Surely not! It is not for the likes of him to arrange your meetings.'

'That is true,' admitted the Pasha. 'Perhaps he was doing it for someone else?'

'Was he?'

'I really don't recall. And I resent you asking these intrusive questions, Captain Owen.'

'Oh, I am sorry, Pasha! I was only asking in your interest.'

'In my interest?'

'An attempt was made to murder you. And we don't want another one, do we?'

'We certainly don't!'

He was quiet for a moment. Then he said: 'But what is that to do with these questions?'

'I am looking for a pretext for the attack on you, Pasha.'

'No pretext is necessary,' said the Pasha grandly, 'for an attack on someone in the Khedive's service. The Khedive has enemies everywhere. And it is your job, Mamur Zapt, to search that out!'

'And to protect the Khedive's loyal servants when they are doing their duties,' said Owen.

'Quite so. Most definitely.'

'Which I am doing. And that is why I am interested in the circumstances of any attack on you.'

'As long as your inquiries into the circumstances do not take you too far into the Khedive's private business.'

'On that, Pasha, I shall rely upon guidance from you!'

'You couldn't do better,' said the Pasha.

THREE

The train started with a jerk. It gathered speed and then the houses were slipping by. They had disappeared into what had become the darkness of the town and they were travelling through the desert. The only shapes now were the clumps of thorn bushes. Now they were slipping along the bank of the Nile. The water stood out strangely in the darkness. You could see it quite clearly, even the sandbanks low in the water, and the reeds. You would have thought they would disappear first but they didn't. And the palms. You would have thought they would soon slip away into the gloom but you went on being conscious of them for quite some time, the lofty fronds dipping as the train went past. Then they, too, slid away and all you could see was the greyness of the desert, an occasional patch of thorn, and the gleaming ribbon of the river.

Jamie always liked this bit. There was a kind of magic to it, as the very shapes came and went. First you could see them quite distinctly and then you couldn't. They became vague and wavy, before disappearing altogether. And then there was just the continuing greyness of the sand, which gradually became silver as the moon came up. When your eyes became used to the darkness it seemed as clear as day. Now every shape, every bush, every telephone pole, every water tank – it seemed as if you could pick them out from miles away.

Mohammed, the cook, came in with a very white table cloth over his arm. Jamie's father cleared away his papers and Mohammed spread the cloth and went away to fetch the cutlery. Jamie liked this bit very much. Mohammed spread the cloth every night at home, usually out on the verandah, when it was dark and insects made a buzzing halo around the lamp, which Mohammed insisted on moving away from the table. Sometimes the insects, especially the moths, singed their wings against the light and fell fluttering on to the table. And on to the food if you weren't careful. There were fewer insects in the saloon than there were on the veranda and somehow the napkins were brighter and everything was lifted somehow and it was the beginning of the journey and it was exciting.

The table in the saloon had been laid for three and after a while the Mamur Zapt came in and joined them.

'How's the Pasha?' asked Jamie's father.

'Beginning to regret he's not having dinner at the Semiramis.'

'He's doing all right here, isn't he?'

'Dying to get home. At least, I hope he is not *dying*.'

Jamie's father laughed. 'That's up to you, isn't it, Gareth?'

'The Pasha hopes so.'

'Well, he'll be all right, won't he, as long as the train keeps going?'

'While it keeps going, no one nasty can get on board. And Crockhart-Mackenzie has checked the train very thoroughly before it got going.'

'I saw you with him,' said Jamie.

'He does this sort of thing better than I do. He does it more often.'

'Does anyone know where the driver is going to stop for water?'

'I like to think the driver does. But sometimes he might make a mistake if someone else has been at the water.'

'Does that happen often?'

'Yes.'

'Can't you stop them from doing it?' asked Jamie.

'It's not easy to,' said his father. 'We try to clamp the lid but the Bedu have wised up to that. And, anyway, they shoot holes in the boiler or tank.'

'But then it would all run away!' cried Jamie.

'We have crews out checking two or three times a week,' said his father. 'The thing is that somehow the tank gets raided between the checks.'

'Couldn't you make the tank stronger?' said Jamie.

'Bulletproof, you mean? You could. But it would cost more. And after a while people back at home would wonder if it was worth running the railway at all.'

Jamie pondered this. Surely people wouldn't be so daft as to close the railway down? Just because they couldn't find the money for it?

'You'll be all right for a bit yet,' said the Mamur Zapt reassuringly. 'There's talk of war.'

And *that* seemed daft, too, thought Jamie. To rely on war to save the line! Why, if that went, the country would go, too. There were no roads. They could go by boat, he supposed. Plenty of boats went

up and down the Nile. All the same . . . It would be going backwards, thought Jamie. He was a staunch believer in progress.

The Mamur Zapt and his father fell into talking about war. Or
was it *the* war? There wasn't a war on at the moment but they both
seemed to think one was imminent. Although Jamie was very interested in the conversation – he liked hearing adults talk when they
were not wasting their time talking about silly things – he found it
hard to follow the detail. And his mind kept drifting off . . . what
would he do if there *was* a war, for example. Would he fight? he
wondered. What would it really be like? It was hard to imagine. He
would ask the Mamur Zapt sometime. He had been a soldier in
India before coming out to Egypt. He would know. But by this time
he had lost the thread of the conversation.

'Your eyes are closing, Jamie,' his father said. 'We'd better get
the beds ready.'

But Mohammed had already got the beds ready. There was a sort
of bunk bed in the dining part of the saloon which could be folded
down and Jamie usually slept on that. This evening, though, he was
going to let the Mamur Zapt have that, so that Owen could get
around if he needed to, without disturbing anyone, and Jamie was
going to sleep in the sleeping part with his father.

He pulled up the blind before actually getting into bed and looked
out. It was all desert, as he had known it would be, and would be
for miles. But it looked different from the way it usually did, perhaps
because the moon had somehow disappeared. Usually, with the clear
sky above and the soft grey sand below, you could see quite clearly.
Tonight everything was sort of subdued. It was definitely darker.
Perhaps that was just because the moon had gone in.

But it hadn't. He could still see a patch in the sky where the
moon was shining, dully but definitely there. Then something moved
across it, and gradually everything became darker, and there was a
sort of thickness in the air. And a sort of funny taste in his mouth.

He snuggled down into his bed. Even with just the single sheet
on, it was hot. He kicked it off. He felt sleep coming over him,
blending in with the rhythm of the train.

What was it someone had said? About the Pasha? He'll be all
right, as long as the train keeps going.

The train did keep going but at some point during the night its rhythm
changed. Jamie, even asleep, picked up the change and stirred. The

rhythm became broken, slowed, faltered, then finally stopped. He waited, still half asleep, for it to continue. It did, but only for a few moments. Then it slowed and finally stopped altogether.

Jamie sat up in bed. There was a queer half-light in the compartment. He looked at his new watch. It showed half past one; this was all wrong. First of all, he shouldn't be waking up at this time. Second, it should be dark, not half-dark like this. He pulled up the blind and looked out. It was dark all right, but a sort of muddy dark. There was no proper light. The moon had either not come out or had come out and then disappeared again.

Outside, there were people's voices and lamps. He looked across the compartment. His father's bed was empty.

He felt for his sandals. When he put them on they felt different from normal. They were not full of sand but there was sand in them. This again was unusual. Every night he carefully tipped out whatever sand was in them. There usually was some sand; it accumulated as you went through the day. But this morning it was thicker, there was more of it. And when he put his bare feet on the floor of the saloon, it was thicker there, too. You could feel it quite distinctly under your feet.

There was some on the bed, too, and on his pile of clothes. It must have come in during the night, even though the windows were closed. Sometimes he slept with them open but last night he had closed them, because of the thickness in the air.

In the light of the lamps outside he could see sand swirling quite thickly. At times it covered up the lamps entirely.

Jamie was used to sandstorms and didn't like them much. The sand got into everything, into your eyes – you mustn't rub them, that was the key, as it would make them sore. You just had to put up with it. Put your head down and wait for it to stop.

When it got really bad you wrapped your head up in a towel. That wasn't very nice, though, because the sand somehow still got through. It got into your mouth and up your nose and it wasn't easy to breathe.

He heard his father open the door.

'Are you all right, Jamie?'

'Is it a *haboob*?' he asked.

'Yes. It's blocked up the line. We'll have to dig it out.'

'Will that take long?'

'It depends how thick it is. If it was just a little bit of sand we could work our way through it, but it looks a bit thick for that.'

'So what do we do?'

'Keep digging. It will stop blowing soon and we'll be able to see where we are. If there's a lot of it, too much for us to shift, we'll just have to sit here and wait. I'm going back to lend a hand now. You stay put.'

'Can't I go out?'

'You can go out, but don't go very far from the train.' He went out and then popped back.

'By that I mean, don't go far enough from the train to the point that you can't see it. We've got better things to do than go looking for a boy in a *haboob*.'

Jamie did go out. When he put his shirt on it was all bristly and grainy inside. The particles rubbed against him unpleasantly. He would have put a clean shirt on but the sand had already got every-where and even in the drawer there was a thin film over everything. He remembered that that was how it was in a *haboob*.

When he put on his shorts, sand fell out of the pockets.

It would be his hair next.

Should he put on his helmet? He didn't normally bother, just against the sun, but against the sand it was different. It kept it out of your hair. A bit. Until it got really bad.

He stepped down on to the sand. He could tell at once that it was thicker. You had to sort of wade through it.

And the wind was blowing all the time. It whipped up the sand and sent particles stinging against your face. He pulled his helmet forward over his face. That protected his eyes but now it was hurting his ears. Jamie always got sand just behind his ears. If you tried to rub it out that just made them sorer. It was utter misery.

Towards the front of the train, in the light of the lamps, he could see people digging. Some he could recognize: Mohammed, the cook, his boy, and the guard. He could make out his father and some of the passengers. But not the Pasha. Nor Aisha. Nor, come to think of it, the Mamur Zapt. But suddenly there he was, helping the diggers but never moving too far from the Royal Saloon.

A sudden flurry sent the sand stinging into Jamie's eyes and he flinched away, turning sideways into the train. But that didn't seem to do any good, for the wind shifted and sent the sand skidding along the saloon.

He climbed back up into the train. He held the door open for less than a minute but even in that time a pile of sand accumulated in the doorway. A sudden shift spilled it all over the inside of the saloon.

He went and sat down at the table and tried to look out. All he could see was sand swirling. He could even hear it, a kind of howl. The surface of the table was covered with sand and when he rested an arm he left an imprint. There was sand on his lips, too. It had got in at the corner of his mouth and when he tried to clean it up with his tongue it seemed to make it worse. He thought about wrapping his head up in the towel but that seemed silly: indoors, and cowering away from the wind! He went on sitting there, keeping his hands still on the table, so that he wouldn't bring sand on to his face.

The howl of the *haboob* gradually died away. The sand seemed to swirl less. He began to be able to make out shapes, people.

A figure went by the window and raised an arm in greeting. With a shock Jamie realized that was his father. He was covered in sand, all over. It was like a suit: lips, chest, face, sun helmet.

The men at the front of the train had stopped digging and were standing talking.

His father went past again, then turned to walk down the train. From time to time he went inside, stayed for a moment or two, then climbed down and continued his walk. Mohammed and the boy, not used to the physical labour, crouched down on the step and rested their heads in their arms.

The guard and *his* boy came walking back.

The few passengers who were still outside came climbing in. The last to do so was Aisha's father. He stopped for a moment outside the Royal Coach, then shrugged his shoulders and went on.

The Pasha came through the door.

'Drive on!' he said grandly.

The Mamur Zapt was with him.

'What!' he said incredulously. 'I don't think you appreciate the situation, Pasha. You *can't* drive on. The line is blocked.'

'Unblock it, then!'

'That is, actually, what we have been trying to do. There's too much of it – sand on the line. There are great drifts. You can't actually see where the track should be. And it seems to go on like that. For hundreds of yards. With the few men we've got it's impossible to clear the line.'

'So what are you going to do, then?' said the Pasha petulantly. 'I can't stay here forever.'

'I'm afraid you'll have to stay for a while. They'll be sending out an engine with a sand scoop from Halfa soon.'

'How soon? I cannot hang around here indefinitely!'

'You'll have to, I'm afraid, Pasha. It will take some hours to get here. If, indeed, it can. It depends on how extensively the sand has drifted.'

'What's all this about a scoop?'

'There's an engine with a sand scoop at Wadi Halfa, Mr Nicholson tells me. It will already be in action. But if the sand is heavy it will be some time. Men may even have to dig a way for it. But it will get here, Pasha, eventually. Don't worry. But you'll have to be patient.'

'I think it's a disgrace, Captain Owen. And I shall certainly speak to the Khedive about it.'

Owen laughed. 'I think even His Royal Highness does not control the desert, Pasha.'

The Pasha retreated back to his own coach, banging the door behind him, and Jamie thought he saw Aisha behind him.

Jamie's father came up the saloon wearily, followed by Mohammed.

'When you feel up to it,' his father said, 'a cup of coffee would be most welcome!'

'How about breakfast?' said Jamie.

Other people were clearly thinking the same thing. People got out of the carriages with mugs in their hands. Among them was Aisha.

'Pretty grim, wasn't it?' said Jamie.

'I don't know why I didn't listen to my mother,' muttered Aisha gloomily.

'They're sending an engine with a sand scoop on it,' said Jamie. 'From Halfa.'

'All we need is donkeys!' said Aisha. 'Allah, this is a backward place!'

'It won't take them long to get through.'

'And, meanwhile, I have to sit here with sand in my hair and in my mouth, and just wait!'

'It won't be for long,' said Jamie encouragingly.

'Long enough!' said Aisha.

She took her mug and walked back to her saloon, opened the
door and pushed the mug inside. Then she came back. 'Sand everywhere,' she reported. 'Even in my bed!'

'It's getting light now,' said Jamie. 'Properly light, I mean.'

'Is this the dawn?' said Aisha. 'You can keep it!'

'I usually go down to the river,' said Jamie.

'Why?'

Jamie couldn't think of an answer immediately. 'I just do. It's
nice first thing in the morning.'

'It's nicer to stay in bed,' said Aisha.

The *haboob* seemed to have passed but it had left ruin in its wake.
Sand had built up around the carriages until you could barely see
their wheels. Ahead there were great drifts of sand. The railway lines
had completely disappeared. The engine, too, had almost disappeared,
into a great drift of sand. It looked as if it was a mole or something
burrowing down into a hill. Only the rear, where the coal tender was,
stood out above the sand. Sand had buried the engine almost up to
the top of the driver's cab.

There would be no getting out of this in a hurry, thought Jamie.

The driver and his mate had got down out of the cab and were
standing waiting for something to happen. Jamie's father was talking
to the guard and to a group of men who had got out of the carriages.

Jamie and Aisha walked along the train. Doors were opening and
people were brushing sand out on to the ground.

The sky was now quite clear but the wind was still blowing, quite
gently but enough to send sand-devils chasing over the desert.
Occasionally there was a flurry and the sand whirled up and stung
your knees. Then it died down but you could see a layer of still-
active sand swirling about at about knee height. At least it was not
in your face, thought Jamie.

Aisha pulled her veil over her face, not so much from modesty
as for protection. The particles of sand still had the capacity to sting
painfully when a sudden puff shot up.

He hadn't seen Aisha wearing a veil before. Perhaps she was saving
it until they got back to the city. Jamie thought that if she were
wearing a veil he would have much less sense of her as a person.

'I was getting fed up just sitting there,' she said. 'I sat there all
night.'

Jamie nodded. 'I had gone to sleep,' he said. 'Then I woke up
and the *haboob* was blowing.'

'I wanted to go outside but the wind was blowing so hard, I couldn't open the door.'

'I went outside a bit,' said Jamie. 'But it wasn't very nice, so I came in again.'

'I didn't stir,' said Aisha. 'My father told me not to.'

'But you did stir,' he said, thinking back.

'No, I didn't!'

'You walked around a bit in the train.'

'I certainly did not! My father told me to stay exactly where I was.'

'In the train,' insisted Jamie. 'I saw you in the Khedive's saloon.'

'You didn't!'

'I definitely did. You were standing right behind him.'

'No I wasn't.'

'I'm sure I saw you.'

'Well, you were wrong. I never left my place in our saloon.'

'Perhaps just for a bit?' suggested Jamie.

'Not at all!' she said definitely.

'The Khedive's saloon.'

'The Khedive's saloon? What do you think I am?'

Suddenly she flared up. 'What do you think I am?' she demanded again. 'What are you saying?'

'I'm not saying anything. Except that I saw you.'

'You didn't! You couldn't have. Because I was in our saloon all the time.'

'But . . .'

'What a nasty thing to suggest!'

'Nasty?'

Jamie had no idea what she was talking about.

'To even think of it!' she stormed.

'Look, all I said was that I thought I had seen you when the train stopped. You were walking just behind the Pasha . . .'

'What a disgusting mind you have!' said Aisha.

'Disgusting? Look . . .'

'Either that, or you are a very silly little boy!'

She stamped off back to her saloon.

Jamie was completely bewildered.

When Owen dropped in on the Pasha he found him talking to Yasin. They appeared to have been talking business for there were papers spread on the table in front of them.

'Hello, Owen!' said the Pasha. 'Had a good night? I didn't!'

'I think few of us did, sir.'

'What a night!' said Yasin.

'Frightful!' said the Pasha. 'The sooner we get back to Cairo, the better. When will that be, do you think?'

'Hard to tell. A couple of days, possibly.'

'Two days!'

'Or even three. The driver has walked on up the line and he says it is completely blocked. You can't see the rail, he says. And it's like that for at least another couple of miles. Behind us it's no better. Nicholson Effendi says they will have sent an engine up behind us, but the guard has been back and he says it may take days for it to get through.'

'But that means . . . We can't just stay here!' said the Pasha, aghast.

'It looks as if we'll have to.'

'But this is quite unacceptable! I have to be back in Cairo. The Khedive . . .'

'I'm sure His Highness will appreciate our difficulties.'

'But I have things to do!'

'Me, too,' said Owen.

'And me,' said Yasin.

'But . . . but . . . important things to do!'

The other two nodded.

'It is most unfortunate,' said Owen.

'It is absolutely impossible!' said the Pasha.

'People will be working hard at both ends,' said Owen.

'Have we adequate supplies?' asked Yasin.

'Nicholson Effendi has been looking into that. He thinks we should be all right. There's a question about water but he thinks that if we are not extravagant we can manage for up to four days.'

'Four days!'

'Rescue really should have reached us by then.'

'Four days! Cut off in the desert! What a primitive country this is!'

'There is just the one track, of course. But there is also the river.'

'Yes, the river!' cried the Pasha, brightening up.

'Unfortunately, just here, that is some distance away too. But it's helpful to know that it is there in an emergency.'

'But this *is* an emergency!'

'A little hardship, Pasha. But not really anything to worry about.'

The Pasha shuddered. 'This is a vile country!' he said.

'We'll win through. Both Egypt and Britain will be moving all their resources into this.'

Yasin looked sceptical.

'Someone as important as the Pasha . . .' murmured Owen.

'The trouble is,' said the Pasha, 'that once one is out of Cairo, somehow one counts less.'

'Don't worry, Pasha. They'll soon be here.'

'We'll just have to make the best of things,' said Yasin.

'Quite so, yes,' said the Pasha doubtfully.

'An example must be set!' said Yasin. 'And with you, Pasha . . .'

'Yes, yes, I suppose so,' said the Pasha, even more doubtful. 'But you're right,' he said suddenly. 'It behoves a member of the Royal Court to set an example to the people at large.'

'The Khedive would expect no less.'

'Very well, I will, then. I'll walk along the train encouraging people. We are in difficulties, I shall say, but we'll come through them. Yes, that's what I will say. Stick my head in and encourage them to show a bit of fortitude.'

He stood up and walked to the door. And then stopped.

'Will it be all right?' he asked anxiously. 'Just walking down the train? Will it be safe?'

'Safe?' said Yasin.

'There have been some . . . unexpected eventualities,' said the Pasha. 'I was attacked on the train. On my way down. And a faithful servant of mine was murdered.'

'Murdered!'

'Died, at any rate,' said Owen.

'Isn't dying enough?' said the Pasha tartly. 'I think it would be a good idea if the Mamur Zapt came with me.'

'Glad to, Pasha,' said Owen. 'But I think you'll be safe on the train.'

'I wasn't before,' was all the Pasha said.

For a while after the *haboob* had blown itself out, the day was fresher. But soon the heat began to mount. In the Sudan it was always hot. On an average day the temperature was over 70 Fahrenheit. But the heat was normally a dry heat and seventy or eighty degrees was not felt to be so oppressive. In the desert, though, the sun seemed to pick out the train particularly. The woodwork burnt your fingers; the metal, you wouldn't dream of touching. Jamie, back in Atbara, had once left his bicycle out in the sun and when he came back the metal had blistered his fingers.

As the morning wore on, the temperature inside the train soared. In the saloons the fans did not seem to be working. The Pasha, used to the cool shops of Cairo, and perhaps the cool Palace, and certainly his own house, complained bitterly.

'What a ghastly country!' he said again and again.

After a while, unable to bear it, people came out of the carriages and walked up and down searching for shade, even the shade afforded by the carriages, but gradually as the sun rose higher, even that dwindled.

Aisha did not appear. Perhaps she was still cross with Jamie, although why, he could not think.

He put it down to mood. Many of the English complained about moods. By all accounts they emerged out of nothing, blew up from somewhere in the desert, maybe, and hit you like a touch of malaria. Maybe this was what Aisha was suffering from. Or maybe she was just prone to sulks. He had not forgiven her calling him a silly little boy. Jamie in his life had been called many things and 'silly' was by no means the worst of them. All the same, it rankled. Or perhaps it was the 'little boy' that rankled. He was quite glad she didn't appear. Although by the end of the morning he was feeling bored and even a silly – yes, that was right, silly *and* sulky – girl would have been welcome.

Owen and the Pasha came back from reassuring the passengers.

'*Were* they reassured?' asked Jamie's father.

'Not very,' admitted the Mamur Zapt. 'Just resigned, and a bit cross.'

The Pasha at once took to his bed. He stuck his head out once to ask if the fans could be turned up. When he was told that unfortunately they couldn't be, he shook his head wearily and went back inside.

At one point, walking up and down outside, Jamie thought he heard Aisha's voice inside the Royal Saloon. It made him cross. Why had she made such a fuss before when he had said he had seen her there? She had said she had been in her own saloon the whole time. Well, she hadn't been. She had lied to him, and for no reason at all. The next time he saw her he would tell her. And if it made her cross again, so much the better!

The heat built up and the train slumbered inertly in the sand. There were fewer signs of life. Jamie's father had portioned out food and water. There was as yet no shortage of either and he reckoned that however slowly the rescue trains went, they would be here within two days, three at the most. There was really no crisis. All the same, he checked what stores there were and had them all under his control. He did not want there to become a crisis, he explained to Jamie. And, to Jamie's chagrin, he required him to help with the dividing out. It will be good for your maths, he said. Jamie acknowledged this but felt that there was a time and a place for maths and this was not it. All the same, it kept him busy and this was probably a good thing.

After they had helped Nicholas Effendi to check supplies, Mohammed and his boy joined the driver and the guard when they sat in the shade behind the Royal Carriage. And Jamie, from time to time, joined them too. It was shady there and they had the benefit of whatever air there was. Late in the afternoon a gentle breeze crept up and began to sift the sand around the carriages. It didn't make much difference but Jamie noticed the sand gradually build up around the wheels of the train. If it went on like this they would eventually be covered. Jamie envisaged the whole train being subsumed but the Mamur Zapt said that might take ages and that Jamie would probably die of old age long before then.

From time to time, when the conversation beneath the carriage stilled, Jamie went for a little walk up and down the train. He was the only one doing that now. Everyone else was lying low inside the train.

As he reached the end of the train and prepared to turn round he thought he saw something move in the desert. He stopped to look, thinking it might be a mirage. Mirages, he knew, were deceptive but they were an image of something. It might be far away and would come and go with the shifting light, but all the same it was a sign that there was something out there, a sign that they were not entirely alone in the desert.

He went on peering. Something out there was definitely moving. It might be simply that the contours of the mirage were changing or perhaps that the growing breeze was blowing swirls over the sand. But he thought that something out there was gradually coming into sight.

He wondered if he should go and tell someone – the Mamur Zapt, perhaps – but decided he wouldn't yet. Instead, he crouched down on the sand and watched.

The sun was now burning his knees and he wished he had brought his hat. The English in the Sudan usually wore sun helmets, or *topees* as they called them in India, but they didn't always carry them around with them, much less actually put them on their heads. All the same he would have been glad of the protection now. He could feel the back of his neck burning.

He considered moving. But then the swirls of light and sand seemed to lurch and he saw that there definitely was something coming across the sand towards the train. And it wasn't a mirage. It was definitely a rider on a camel. He was a tribesman, with a short spear and a short skirt, drawn back to show black knees pressed into the camel's neck.

By this time others beside Jamie had seen him and he could hear windows and doors opening.

The rider rode right up to the train and then stopped, looking at it.

Jamie became conscious that the Mamur Zapt was standing beside him. He called something out to the man, in Arabic, and then walked across the sand towards him.

They stood talking for a moment and then Owen walked back to where Nicholson Effendi was now standing beside Jamie.

'Can you try him?' he said to Jamie's father. 'My Arabic is Egyptian Arabic and he doesn't understand me.'

'He's a Hadendoa, from the Red Sea Hills,' said Jamie's father. He went across and talked to the man.

He was what the British Army called a Fuzzy-Wuzzy, with a great mane of wiry black hair which stood straight up in a kind of dense halo. When, not many years before, the British had reoccupied the Sudan, the Fuzzy-Wuzzy had been a significant part of the Mahdi's army. The spear was not just for show.

Jamie's father came back.

'He says it was just a *haboob*,' he said. 'They get them at this time of the year.'

'He's a long way from home,' said Owen. 'What's he doing here?'

'He's come to meet someone.'

'Here?' said Owen, surprised.

'By the line. Not far from the water tower. But which water tower I cannot make out and he can't tell me. He can say only that it was by a water tower. There are water towers all along the line and we are between two of them. He can't say which.'

'He was going to meet someone?'

'That's what he says.'

'Does he say whom he was supposed to be meeting?'

'Abdul Dahab.'

'Who's he?'

'Can't say. He thought the name was enough. It probably is out here.'

'Does he say what he was meeting him about?'

'He's rather vague on that point.'

'Out here? Miles from anywhere?'

'It's not miles from anywhere as far as he is concerned. It's by the railway line. In the desert that's a good reference point.'

'Does he know about trains?'

'This may be the first he's actually seen.'

It certainly seemed so. The man sat there on his camel studying the train as if he had never seen one close up before.

'He is not able to tell us about rescue trains, then?'

'No. He probably cut straight across the desert.'

'From?'

Jamie's father shrugged. 'Who knows? Possibly the Red Sea Hills from the look of him.'

'But that's miles!'

'People travel long distances here.'

'For a meeting? With a friend? It seems odd.'

For the first time the rider volunteered something.

'What is he saying?'

'He wants some water.'

'Shall we give him some? We've got enough, haven't we?'

'Provided the trains get here soon. Which they will do. I'll ask Mohammed to let him have some.'

Mohammed came out with a bowl. The rider shook his head and said something.

'He doesn't want it for himself. He wants it for his camel.'

'A camel can drink a lot!'

Jamie's father talked to the man.

'I've told him about the rescue trains. I said he can have more when they get here.'

The man slipped off his camel in one easy movement and sat down on the ground.

'He'll wait,' said Jamie's father.

'For the water? Or for his friend?'

'Both. I would have thought he's more likely to get the water.'

The Pasha climbed down out of his carriage and came across to them.

'Who is that man?'

Owen told him as much as he could.

'Can he say where he comes from?'

'Only vaguely. The Red Sea Hills, we think.'

'But they're miles away!'

'It is strange, I agree.'

'More than strange: suspicious!'

'Strange. I'll only go as far as that.'

'I think you need to go much further, Mamur Zapt. A man arriving like this out of the desert! Coming from nowhere and saying he's going to a meeting. Here in the middle of the desert! Intercepting the train like this!'

'I don't think his intention was to intercept the train, Pasha. More the railway line.'

'He was coming to intercept the train. Because he knew that I was on board!'

'How could he have known that, Pasha?'

'In exactly the same way as they knew that I was on board coming down here. Intelligence, Mamur Zapt. Intelligence! Have you not heard of that?'

'I think the attack on you might well have been a casual attempt at robbery.'

'Well, I don't! I don't think there was anything casual about it. They were after my briefcase!'

'If they were, their intelligence cannot have been good, because the briefcase was empty.'

'They were on the right lines. The attack was just a little premature, that's all. They are waiting now for the return journey. And then they'll strike again!'

'If they do, Pasha, we shall be ready for them.'

'Were you ready for this man riding across the desert? Hah! Tell me that! Were you ready for him?'

'I doubt if he is anything to do with the attack on you, Pasha.'

'We shall see. We shall see. I think it is all carefully planned, Captain Owen, and I wonder if you are prepared for *that*!'

'I don't think it is possible to plan for a *haboob*, Pasha. Not a particular one.'

'*Haboobs* happen all the time in this dreadful country, Captain Owen. You should be prepared for them.'

'We are, Pasha. Rescue trains will already be on the way.'

'And so will be my adversaries, Captain Owen. They will have assessed the likelihood of a *haboob* on our journey and taken steps. Taken steps, Captain Owen! Have you?'

'You will soon be safely back in Cairo, Pasha.'

'I hope so, Captain Owen. I only hope so. For your sake as well as mine.'

FOUR

Towards evening, Owen went for another patrol along the train. The swirls of sand around the train had died down but from time to time there was a little scurrying in the sand as if unseen rodents were surreptitiously stirring it. Imperceptibly the sand about the wheels of the carriages had grown deeper. Yet above the surface of the sand the air was still. There was nothing to disturb the layer of heat that stretched across it. Even the increasing shadow seemed to have no effect. In the darkness it was as warm as it had been in the middle of the afternoon.

The tribesman was still sitting beside his camel. He had made it kneel and now it had put its head down and seemed to be sleeping. The tribesman, sitting with his head against the camel, seemed to be sleeping, too, but when Owen came back from his patrol he was talking to someone. Owen saw it was Aisha's father, Yasin al-Jawad. They were deep in conversation but looked up when Owen approached and drew apart. Yasin stood up and came towards Owen.

'We have found a friend,' he said. 'Or at any rate, someone who is as lost as we are.'

'I see you speak Red Sea Hills Arabic,' said Owen. 'How does that come about? I rather gathered the impression that you spent your life around the court?'

'I do. Or too much of it. But when I was a young man I spent some time in the Red Sea Hills. It's a place where they send young men.'

'Even if they're from Egypt?'

'The Parquet seconded me. There was a complex case, too complex for the local people to handle, and I volunteered. It's the kind of mistake you make when you're young.'

'Well, at any rate you returned!'

'I did. And, actually, it didn't turn out too badly for me. It brought me to people's attention. I suspect that otherwise they might never have noticed me.'

He laughed. 'You're too bright for that!'

'Cairo is obviously the place to be if you want to get on. The trouble is that it is full of bright young men trying to get on! But, of course, you know that. You're a Cairo man yourself.'

'It's nice of you to say that to an Englishman,' said Owen, laughing.

'Oh, but you are! You've been in Cairo almost as long as I have. And done much better for yourself, I have to say.'

'Luck!'

'Not just luck. Although luck is, I agree, important in a career. Take our friend Mahmoud, for instance. He is very able. He should have done better for himself. He has just not had luck, that's all.'

'His time may come.'

'Oh, I'm sure it will.' He hesitated. 'He's very highly thought of, you know. But . . . He's shown his hand too obviously, I'm afraid.'

'He's made it too clear he's a nationalist, you mean?'

'That is what I mean.'

Yasin al-Jawad hesitated and then said tentatively: 'You know, it has always been a surprise to us that you and he should so obviously get on so well.'

'We were young men starting off together. There was so much in common.'

'Even so, he an Egyptian from the radical side in politics, and you . . .'

'Not from the radical side. An Englishman, in this situation, can't be.'

'Why, then – excuse me – did you choose it?'

'I needed the money. And I was young and romantic. And I had just been in India.'

'India?'

'I was in the Indian army. And I found it – not the army particularly, but the life, the English life, out there – not to my taste.'

Yasin shook his head in bewilderment. 'But then why come out here?'

'The English are not so apparent. And the Egyptians are more apparent. And Cairo appeals to me.'

'But the English still rule!' said Yasin bitterly.

Owen shook his head. 'No, no. The Khedive rules. We only help.'

'Yes, you say that, but . . .'

'It is just, for you, I think, a question of waiting.'

'How long do we have to wait?'

'That remains to be seen. I can understand you feeling impatient.'

'It is not just the British. It is the Khedive.'

'I think every generation feels like that. Impatient. But the time will come.'

'I shall be old,' said Yasin bitterly. 'Too old. We'll all be too old. You, my friend, will be too old.'

'I'll be waiting,' said Owen, 'to hand over. To Aisha.'

'Aisha!' said Yasin, startled. Then he shook his head and laughed. 'No, no, my friend, you're wrong there. That time will never come. It is a step too far.'

Owen had met many young Egyptians like him. Mahmoud was another. Impatient to take over and put things right. Enact all the reforms the country was crying out for. The British wouldn't do that. They were interested only in sorting out the finances, in securing a return for their shareholders. The Khedive, even more certainly, would not do that. He liked things the way they were, thank you. The Pashas even more so. But would Yasin's generation be any better? Owen rather doubted it. If anyone, it would be the generation after that. It might be up to Aisha after all.

Jamie heard something suspiciously like a squeal from inside the Royal Carriage. She must be in there again! Why couldn't she just own up to it? He kicked irritably at a heap of sand and turned round the end of the carriage, ducking under the coupling connecting the Khedive's carriage to the next one, which happened to be the Nicholsons' carriage.

And ran straight into Aisha.

'But . . . how can you be here? I've just heard you in there!'

'It wasn't me, stupid! It was someone else. Some woman the Pasha's got in there.'

'I thought it was you!'

'Well, thank you very much. I'm obviously just the sort of girl to be found lurking in rich men's apartments!'

'I'm sorry! I thought it was you. When I heard a woman's voice. And when I saw a woman standing behind the Pasha. But it can't have been.'

'No, it can't!'

'I didn't know there was a woman there. I thought it was just the Pasha.'

'As a matter of fact,' said Aisha, 'so did I.'

'What is she doing there?'

Aisha gave him a long, level look. 'You can't guess?'

'No. At least—'

'Well, you are a ninny, then!'

Jamie flushed. 'I was just taken by surprise, that's all!'

'Young,' said Aisha. 'Very young.'

Jamie began to get cross. She always rubbed him up the wrong way. Talking to him as if he were a little boy when she can't have been much older than he was.

The trouble was that in some ways he did feel like a little boy beside her. She seemed to know much more than he did, to be familiar with a world that he knew about only in hints and guesses. So far he had not had much to do with that world. He had come across it mainly through stray remarks overheard at grown-ups' parties and never quite understood. But he knew enough about it to recognize the terrain or to know that Aisha knew a lot more about it than he did.

All the same he did not want to yield her the advantage without putting up some sort of fight.

'Is she his mistress, do you think?' he said, hazarding a shot completely in the dark.

'One of them, I dare say,' responded Aisha airily.

Mr Nicholson, who did not take responsibility lightly, now assumed it on behalf of the entire railway system. In the saloons the little lamps were beginning to come on but before it became dark entirely he went along the train speaking to everybody, checking that there was nothing seriously wrong with anybody and finding encouraging words for most. The trouble with that was that words came back in perhaps greater abundance than he had anticipated. They were not on the whole words of abuse nor even, mostly, words of complaint. Most of the passengers resignedly accepted that although the British had responsibility for most things in Egypt and the Sudan and were therefore to be blamed for most of them when things went wrong, their control did not extend to the elements. There had always been *haboobs* and it was likely that there would go on being *haboobs*. They covered their heads against the sand, which seemed to sift in even though the wind had died to the occasional flutter across the desert. Mostly they concentrated on scratching up some sort of an evening meal. Here they showed themselves at their most resourceful, finding food in the most unexpected of places and readily sharing it round.

Mohammed, no less resourceful, had scoured up from nowhere what smelled like a splendid dinner. However, Jamie was not allowed to start on it until his father got back. This was, perhaps, fair enough but as time went by and the lamps came on and outside the train it grew pitch dark, Jamie became ravenous.

The Mamur Zapt, who had been making his own patrols, joined him at the table and even found a small loaf, which he broke in two, handing one half to Jamie.

He asked Jamie about the school he was going to go to in England. He didn't know it himself, he said; he was out of date on such things. The school he had attended, a minor public school, all his family could afford, in the west of England, had perhaps long since closed. The Mamur Zapt said he hoped Jamie would enjoy himself but that he personally was glad that he had long since put school behind him. Jamie asked him about the North West Frontier and the Mamur Zapt said it was all right, provided you didn't mind being shot at, but that he himself preferred Egypt.

He kept looking out of the window as if he was expecting something and after a while apologised and said he just wanted to go out and check something.

Jamie hoped he was checking about dinner but maybe adults didn't feel the need for dinner as much as boys did. In fact, both Jamie's father and Owen arrived mostly together so they could get on with eating more or less straightaway.

Dinner began, as it usually did in Atbara, with *ful Sudani*, peanut soup, which Jamie particularly liked. After that there was no fish straight from the Nile but instead lamb cutlets. They went in for lamb cutlets rather than pork cutlets in Egypt.

While they were eating, his father asked Owen if the man on the camel was still there. Owen said he was. He had gone over to check that particularly.

Jamie's father asked him if he thought it meant something.

'Probably not. It's just that it's a long way to come to meet a friend.'

'And so you're checking?'

'I'm checking, yes. But not necessarily expecting.'

Jamie's father was silent for a while. Then he said: 'The Sudan is different from other countries. Different, even, from Egypt. The distances are immense. The Sudan is as big as India. Most of it is desert. And yet people can find their way across it as easily as you can find your way across Cairo.'

He said that about two years before, the Sudan railways had been worried by a series of audacious and rather large thefts. They had occurred while the train was crossing the desert, miles from anywhere. How did people get into the train when it was moving between places? And, even more puzzling, how did they get the stolen goods out of the train?

The answer was accomplices. They boarded the trains in the usual way, as ordinary passengers, and then at night when the train was in motion, they worked their way along the train until they reached the goods vehicles that they wanted. Then they threw the goods out.

'On to the sand?'

'On to the sand. The train moved on, and the stolen items were picked up by accomplices on camels who had ridden their way across the desert, located the agreed spot and the goods, and then made off with them. Easy. Except that the accomplices on camels had had to ride hundreds of miles across the empty desert to find an unmarked spot along the railway line, retrieve the goods, and then ride hundreds of miles back across the desert. Which they began to do regularly.'

'How did you spot it?'

'Trackers. Government trackers. Who were also desert men and knew the desert like the back of their hand. It was easy for them to make out where the goods had been thrown from the train. And even easier, for them, to follow the track of the accomplices who had picked the goods up and track them across hundreds of miles of desert. Eventually they caught them by tracking their foot prints right the way to Port Sudan and then picking out, in a crowded market place, the camels that had made them.'

'Impressive,' said Owen. 'But some of them are.'

'You don't use them in Cairo, of course?'

Owen shook his head. 'We used them when I first came to Egypt and worked along the coast. Smugglers, we were after, then.'

'It might help to explain your solitary camel rider.'

'It might, yes.'

'But what would they be throwing out?'

'A briefcase, perhaps,' said Owen. 'Or possibly a Pasha.'

But how had the camel rider known where to come, wondered Jamie? And how had he known the train would be stopped there? That there would be a *haboob*?

Perhaps he hadn't known. Perhaps he had an accomplice on board who was going to steal the briefcase anyway and throw it out, and the *haboob* had come along by accident?

Ah, but they wouldn't need to have known that the train was going to be stopped there. The accomplice could have thrown it out at any time. Or maybe this was where he was always planning to throw it out, and that was why the camel rider was waiting there. The *haboob* was just a coincidence. The train didn't have to be stopped.

Of course, it wasn't necessarily the briefcase that the man was waiting for. That was just something the Mamur Zapt had given as an example. Except that the Pasha *had* been bothered about losing the briefcase. So it could have been that.

A briefcase was a pretty small thing to pitch out into the desert, though. How could you be sure of finding it again?

Maybe it wasn't a briefcase, after all. Maybe . . .

Phew! That was a thought! Suppose it was to be the Pasha himself? His body? Murdered! That really was a thought! He would like to talk this over with someone, but there was no one.

Aisha?

The Mamur Zapt was talking to the driver of the train. He was a middle-aged man with grey hair and his name was Ismail. He had been driving this line for years, he told Owen, but he had never been in a *haboob* like this one. There are always *haboobs*, he said, and they're not very nice to drive in. Sometimes you have to stop. And sometimes, yes, you have to dig the train out. Usually it was just the engine because that went first and ploughed into a bank of sand if there was one. But it didn't usually amount to much, and if it did, a rescue engine would arrive pretty quickly. This storm, however, had been denser than most and he suspected that it might have affected the line for a long way both ahead and behind. He had known one stretch, the whole way to Wadi Halfa, where they had had to dig the line out first before they could even get the rescue engine started. So by the time the rescue engine had reached him everyone was getting pretty hungry. But it had not been as fierce as this one.

They were sitting under the tender and he was eating his breakfast, which he hospitably offered to share with Owen. Owen didn't take much but he knew better than to refuse the gesture. He took a pickle – the Egyptians were very fond of pickles – and pushed it into a flat pocket of bread and began to eat. Ismail had already fanned up some ashes into a small fire and was boiling a kettle. They drank tea, the bitter, black tea of the *fellahin*.

So early in the morning you could fancy a chill to the air and both of them huddled closer to the fire. Within a very short time the sun would be up – you could see its red rim coming along the horizon already – and not long after that you would be huddling close to the tender not for warmth but for shade.

They were the only ones, it appeared, so far to have risen. Owen always woke early and the driver was used to driving through the night. Night or day, he said, it didn't make much difference to him. His home, he said, was at Atbara. He had gone there years before in search of work. Atbara was the big railway hub of the Sudan and there was work in plenty. There wasn't much work anywhere else. It wasn't like Egypt, where there were factories all over the place. The Sudan had two lifelines, he said: 'the Nile and the railways'. They both ran straight through the desert from north to south and that was about it. There wasn't much in the way of roads, not anywhere in the Sudan. There was just the desert.

Had he ever been tempted to work in the railway workshops, Owen asked him.

He said that he was in a good job and when you had got that, if you had any sense, you stayed in it. Also he didn't like the work-shops. There were too many people and they were always arguing. And there were too many troublemakers. They sucked you in and then very soon if you didn't watch out there was trouble and you were part of it! And after that it was not long before you were out on your ear! He and his wife were too old for that. That's why he preferred to work alone on the train. If you got into trouble then it was your own fault. But in the workshops there were always people talking and the words were a web and if you didn't look out you were very soon caught up in it.

Owen said it sounded as if Ismail spoke from experience.

Too true, said Ismail. He had once nearly been drawn into a workshop dispute through his son-in-law, who was a nice lad but, Ismail thought, a bit simple. He wouldn't dare say this at home because his wife and his daughter would jump on him but you couldn't get away from the fact the lad was always in trouble. It wasn't usually his fault; it was just that he got drawn in. There were always people ready to make trouble and he found it only too easy to listen to them. That's what Ismail meant by saying that he was too simple. 'Listen to them, by all means, if you have to,' said Ismail, 'but you don't have to believe everything they say.'

'Listen to you,' his daughter said, 'and no one would ever get anything done!'

'My engine always gets to Halfa,' Ismail said.

'Yes, but that's not really doing anything,' his daughter said.

'It's getting the train to Halfa,' Ismail explained.

'But who benefits from that?' she said. 'Not you. And not us. Ali says . . .'

'It's always what Ali says with her. And that simpleton, Yussuf, goes along with her. But what Ali says doesn't amount to a bag of warm camel shit in my opinion. I went along to one of his meetings once. It was all hot air. That's what it was. Just hot air! "How's this going to get the trains there on time?" I asked him. "Maybe it would be better if they didn't get there on time!" he says. "What then?" "Well, then you wouldn't have pickles with your bread!" I said. But then they all shouted at me and my daughter says, "You should be ashamed of yourself!" And my wife takes me by the arm and hustles me out!'

'There's always hot-headed talk,' said Owen. 'Always has been and always will be. Is there more of it about than there used to be?'

'There certainly is!' said Ismail. 'And has been ever since that bugger Ali got here!'

'Things are getting a bit lively in the workshops, are they?'

'And in the offices. I don't know what's getting into people these days.'

Even in the Sudan, thought Owen. The one place where you would never have expected industrial unrest. Mainly, of course, because there wasn't any industry in the Sudan. Linseed oil, cotton, gum arabic, durra – the grain much eaten in the Sudan – that was about the sum of it. All agricultural products and not, really, an abundance of those.

Factories? A few. Workshops? By far the biggest was the railway, which employed more workmen in a semi-industrial setting than all the rest put together.

There was, of course, a lot more industry in Egypt. But there was very little industrial unrest. Unrest of other sorts there was in plenty: religious (mainly between Muslims and Copts, who were Christians), ethnic, tribal, national, Egypt was a country of many nationalities – Arabs, Jews, Greeks, Italians, Armenians – you name it, they had it, and all of them at each other's throats. Throw in the English, who, Owen sometimes thought, caused more trouble than anyone, and you had enough violence to keep a Mamur Zapt busy for a lifetime.

But of industrial unrest he had had very little experience. Marx, he had just about heard of, but mullahs were more his line.

So he was intrigued by what Ismail had said about Atbara workshops. This was new. The shape of things to come, perhaps – although he thought it about as likely as women rising in revolt in Cairo! Egyptian suffragettes! There was a thought! Suffragettes themselves were new to him. He had read about them in London newspapers delivered two weeks late in the English clubs in Cairo, but he had been in Egypt for some time now and he hadn't come across the suffragettes when he was in England. He shook his head. Whatever next? A thought came to him.

'Did you know Sayyid?' he asked.

'Sayyid?'

'The one who was drowned the other day. He worked in the workshop, I think. Or was it the offices?'

'The offices,' said Ismail.

'You knew him?'

'A little,' said Ismail guardedly.

'A kinsman of the Pasha's, I believe.'

'If he hadn't been, no one would have taken any notice,' said Ismail.

'I wondered if you had come across him?'

'I came across him, yes,' said Ismail. 'He was a friend of Ali's.'

'The troublemaker?'

'I don't want to bad-mouth anyone,' said Ismail evasively.

'Of course not! But you were worried about the influence he had on your son-in-law, if I remember.'

'Up to a point,' said Ismail hurriedly. 'And who wouldn't be?' he couldn't help adding.

'The thing is,' said Owen, 'once you take a son-in-law into your family, he's with you for life, isn't he? And he brings his friends!'

'Well, that's just it!' said Ismail.

'One affects another: the friends affect your son-in-law, your son-in-law affects your daughter, and the next moment the evil influence is everywhere.'

'Too true!' said Ismail with feeling.

'And Sayyid, too!'

'Sayyid, too. Mind you, he was a different kettle of fish from the other one.'

'From Ali?'

'Yes. Ali was a person . . . well, of no account, really. He'd got the gift of the gab but that was about all. He was never going to get anywhere. Not in the railway!'

'Whereas Sayyid . . .?'

'A man of substance. You could tell that as soon as you saw him. The boss, that's the boss in the offices, used to give him special things to do. Trusted him, you know. And he could do them, that's the thing. So he got on in the office, and would have got further.'

'And being the Pasha's kinsman did him no harm, I'll bet!'

'You wouldn't lose your bet. Never heard of him until one day he lets slip that he knew the Pasha, and then, well, things began to move!'

'You didn't know he was a kinsman of the Pasha, not at first?'

'No, not until he told us. He's not from these parts.'

'Came in from outside? Like Ali?'

'That's it. The pair of them. And after that he seemed to know everybody. Big people. *Really* big people.'

'Oh, yes?'

'That chap who's on the train, for instance.'

'Which train? This one?'

'Yes, this one. I saw him last night talking to that Hadendoa.'

'The one who rode in from the desert?'

'Yes, and that's very funny. How does an ordinary Hadendoa from the back of beyond get to know a person like him? A man who's been at court?'

'You think they knew each other?'

'They were chatting away as if they did.'

'Well, that does surprise me! You're sure they knew each other? I mean, I've talked to him a bit, and so had Nicholson Effendi. But I don't know him, just met him the once. And I suspect it's the same for Nicholson Effendi.'

'There are ways and ways of talking, and they were talking like long-lost friends.'

'I'll take your word for it. But, as I say, it does surprise me.'

'It surprised me, too. Mind you, you get all sorts on the train. The Pasha is not the first. Nor is the bloke who they say is a friend of the Khedive himself!'

'The one who's brought his daughter with him?'

'That's right. The girl who's a friend of the young Effendi.'

Owen laughed.

'You see everything,' he said. 'And all from the back of an engine!'

Jamie was one of those irritating children who wake early and are fully awake as soon as their eyes open. This morning was no different.

The room was full of light. A thick film of sand lay over everything. It was over half an inch thick on the table and the floor. It lay on his pillow and he could see the impression his head had made. There was a gritty taste of sand in his mouth.

He rolled out of bed and started off to the little bathroom to wash it out. His footsteps followed him in a line across the floor.

When he pulled up the blind and looked out of the window he saw that the sand outside was utterly smooth. Only one person had so far walked across it, a European, or, possibly, an Egyptian Effendi, wearing shoes not sandals. The shoe prints went right up to the front of the train and the driver was just coming out from under the tender. He was carrying an oil can and a piece of dirty rag. That

didn't mean anything because drivers were always carrying oil cans
and bits of dirty rag. The driver crawled underneath the engine and
so Jamie couldn't talk to him.

He turned round and went back to his saloon. The Hadendoa
wasn't in the place where Jamie had seen him the night before. Nor
was his camel. Perhaps he had found a place to sleep somewhere
along the train? Jamie went to look for him. He couldn't see the
camel, either.

What he did see was the Mamur Zapt coming round the coaches.

'Salaam Aleikhum!'

'Aleikhum salaam!' returned Jamie automatically. *And to you,
peace.*

'I was looking for the Hadendoa,' said Jamie.

'He's gone.'

'Where has he gone to?' asked Jamie.

'Possibly back where he came from.'

'The Red Sea Hills?'

'Perhaps not quite that far.'

'Perhaps he's gone to look for his friend?'

'Perhaps he has. Although I think he would be safer sticking to
the railway line.'

'Perhaps when he found his friend didn't come, he gave up?'
suggested Jamie.

'Jamie, give the Mamur Zapt a break!' said Jamie's father, who
had just joined them.

'It's all right,' said Owen. 'They're good questions.'

The Mamur Zapt found a carriage with a little workman's ladder
going on to its roof. He climbed up it and stood on the roof looking
out over the desert.

'See anything?'

'Jamie!' said his father warningly.

'No. I was hoping for a train.'

'They won't get here for a while yet,' said Jamie's father.

'What about the Hadendoa?' asked Jamie. 'Can you see him?'

'No. I can't see him either.'

'You'd think that on the desert you could see for miles,' said
Jamie's father. 'But it's never quite as flat as you think it is. You
very quickly get out of sight.'

Owen shielded his eyes against the new rising sun, which wasn't
far above the horizon yet, still at the blood-red orange stage, but

the combination of light and shadow made it tricky to see things at a distance.

'There are wadis, too,' said Jamie's father. 'Little valleys in the sand. Not so little sometimes. You could hide an army.'

'Not as many as that, I hope,' said the Mamur Zapt, climbing down. 'But possibly a few of his friends.'

Further along the train there was some sort of commotion. A door opened and Aisha came out. She dropped down on to the ground.

'Hello!' said Jamie. 'Salaam Aleikhum!'

'Bonjour!' said Aisha. 'I was thinking of calling on the Pasha.'

'No, you're not!' said her father, who had come out behind her.

'To ask him about his wife.'

'She may not be his wife,' said her father.

'That doesn't matter. I was wondering why we hadn't seen her. Do you think she could be ill? Finding the heat too much, perhaps?'

'No,' said Aisha's father.

'It's a question of politeness,' insisted Aisha.

'It's a question of nosiness. Plain nosiness,' said her father.

'We are fellow travellers, after all.'

'No!' said her father firmly.

'How about some breakfast?' said Jamie.

'Is there some?' asked Aisha.

'I think Mohammed could find a little,' said Jamie's father.

'Food is in short supply,' said Aisha's father. 'We couldn't dream of . . .'

'A small one,' said Jamie. 'Maybe just an egg.'

'An ostrich's egg, perhaps,' said Aisha hopefully.

'Aisha!'

'I'll have a word with Mohammed,' said Jamie's father.

'If it's an ostrich's egg, we could share it,' Aisha said to Jamie.

'No eggs!' said her father, returning. 'Bread and marmalade only.'

'What is marmalade?' asked Aisha.

'Orange jam,' said her father. 'But, look . . .'

Aisha and her father joined them for breakfast.

'What about the Mamur Zapt?' asked Jamie.

'Yes,' said Aisha, 'what about the Mamur Zapt?'

'He had breakfast a long time ago,' said Mohammed. 'With the driver.'

'With the driver?'

'Yes. A good, healthy Egyptian breakfast.'

'Pickles?' asked Aisha, wrinkling her nose.

'And good Egyptian bread,' said Mohammed.

'Well, I'm surprised,' said Aisha. 'Why doesn't he eat normally?'

'Aisha!' said her father, Jamie's father and Mohammed in unison.

'I'll bet the Pasha doesn't eat pickles,' said Aisha.

Her father sighed.

'Nor his mistress.'

'We don't know she's his mistress,' said Jamie.

'She is, as a matter of fact,' said Aisha's father. 'But that is no business of yours, Aisha.'

'I was just thinking that if that was what she was going to eat, it would make her worse.'

'I eat them every day and I am the picture of health,' protested Mohammed.

'You are, Mohammed, you are,' said Jamie's father soothingly.

'Daughters are sent to try us!' said Mohammed with dignity.

'They certainly are!' said Aisha's father with feeling.

Owen came into the saloon at this point.

'Do you have a daughter, Mamur Zapt?' asked Aisha.

'Just. She's very new.'

'Really? The ladies of Cairo don't know this yet?'

'Well, they wouldn't—'

'They know most things,' said Aisha. 'Or so my mother tells me.'

'They don't know this.'

'Good!' said Aisha, with satisfaction. 'Let us keep it a secret, shall we?'

'Please!'

'I wonder if the Pasha has a daughter. I wonder if he had a wife?'

'Several.'

'But a daughter?'

'A son, I believe.'

'That will make him happy, I expect. Egyptian men are quite silly about sons. Don't you think so, Mamur Zapt?'

'I think there is a lot to be said for their preference,' said Aisha's father. 'Now, Aisha, we have detained the Mamur Zapt for long enough . . .'

FIVE

The heat built up quickly. By ten o'clock you could feel the sand burning through the soles of your shoes. The metal of the engine was too hot to touch. Even the woodwork seemed to burn. Everyone retreated inside.

Not that this helped much. There was no movement in the air; the fans couldn't be worked. Inside the saloon the heat lay in a thick layer, almost palpable. What it must have been like in the ordinary carriages was hard to imagine.

Aisha, of course, did try to imagine, but her mind strayed off into wondering what it was like in the Khedive's carriage, and in particular what it was like for the nameless Pasha's mistress. Aisha dwelt on this for a long time, more on the mistress than on the heat. What was it like being a woman in such circumstances? Being someone's mistress, for a start?

She thought she could just about imagine being a mistress (when she was older she realized that it was with rather mixed accuracy) but being the Pasha's mistress seemed quite impossible. He was old and fat and grey, nearly white haired. She couldn't stop herself feeling a shudder of repulsion.

But there you are, she told herself toughly. If that was what you went in for, that was what you got. The girl in the saloon must have decided to go in for it. Or perhaps she hadn't – perhaps she had been taken, or bought. A pretty girl from one of the Pasha's estates, or someone the Pasha had seen in a cabaret (Aisha had never been in a cabaret but thought she had no difficulty in imagining *that*). Or maybe one of those women her mother mixed with had known a friend of a friend with a pretty daughter, and someone else in the circle had murmured a name, and then, hey presto, there it was.

If Aisha's mother ever murmured *her* name like that, Aisha would kill her! But Aisha did not think she would. And if she did, her father would put a stop to it.

Or would he? Aisha knew enough about court circles to have a twinge of doubt. But surely not her father! But if the Khedive

commanded, or if, perhaps, her father saw it as a way of getting on
. . . The twinge was still there.

Aisha decided she must make the most of Paris when she got
there. A young French diplomat, for instance. Or perhaps a Russian
one, of whom there seemed to be so many in Paris. Perhaps one
with a title? But Aisha, listening to the talk in her mother's circles,
knew that a title was no guarantee of wealth, and a garret, even
with a title attached, did not on the whole appeal to her. For all her
romantic dreams, Aisha was a realist when it came down to it.

Some people managed it. The Lady Zeinab, for instance, if what
people said was correct. A Pasha's daughter and yet she had married
Owen! *If* she had married him – but as to that, Aisha was a free
thinker and did not mind. Anyway, it was the other things that sent
a delicious frisson down her back – the fact that he was a foreigner,
free from the attitude of Egyptian men, whom she despised. No
being shut up in a harem for her, nor selling your daughters off; no
hang-ups about women doing a job . . .

Or perhaps there were. She would have to ask someone about
that. The Lady Zeinab, for instance. She would know. Who better?
Aisha had long had it in mind to accost her and have a decent
conversation with her. And now, perhaps, through Owen, she could
well have the chance.

Like Owen, Jamie's father was continually prowling round the train.
Mr Nicholson did not have direct operational responsibility for the
running of the trains. Nevertheless, as a senior man in the administration of the railways he felt responsibility for operations. That did not
extend to responsibility for the weather. It did not include responsibility
for *haboobs*. He accepted, however, that he had responsibility for the
recovery of the system after a *haboob* had occurred. And he had actually planned for the contingency. *Haboobs* were not uncommon in the
Sudan. They were less common in Egypt, but since the line ran through
both countries emergency planning covered both areas.

And, in fact, he was sure that the emergency planning was sound.
It would already have kicked in. Rescue trains would converge on
the stranded train from both ends of the line. But it could take time.
It might well be the case that the *haboob* had affected a greater
stretch of the line than had been anticipated. The rescue trains would
still get through; it would just take longer, that was all.

There was not much he could do about that. But what he could do was check the provisions were holding out and make arrangements for rationing if necessary. At the back of his mind was the case a year or two ago when a train had been stranded and people had been reduced to eating raw vegetables and, by the end, not many of those.

He had, of course, already thought this through and had prepared a schedule of measures that would have to be taken if the supplies did look like running out, if the rescue trains were delayed more than could reasonably be anticipated. Still, there was no harm in checking the arrangements once again.

What he was particularly looking for was the extent of leakage. Was some of the food slipping away? The stores diminishing at a faster rate than they should? Because the people preparing the meals were consuming more than they should? Because the cooks or whoever were being dishonest? Or because people were breaking in and helping themselves? He had already set up systems to guard against this but there was no harm in checking how well they were working.

He mentioned this to Owen and the two of them went round together. Or, rather, the three of them went round together, because Jamie, and sometimes Aisha, tagged on behind them. But Jamie and Aisha soon dropped out. Her job was to eat meals, not see how they were prepared. Wasn't that the sort of thing that cooks did? Her mother was never to be seen in the kitchen – nor, of course, her father. The upper classes of Egypt followed their masters, the Pashas, in leaving all that to underlings.

And, certainly, the present Pasha showed no signs of being any different.

To everyone's surprise, though, midway through the morning he stuck his head out of his apartments in the Royal Saloon and enquired if everything was under control.

'I have to get back to Cairo,' he said.

'Me, too,' said Owen, uncomfortably aware of the things piling up on his desk.

Jamie's father was also aware. But his plans had been changed as well as disrupted. They would need to think through the incident, go through again the emergency planning, inquire into the addressing of resources – he knew the answer to his questions already: the reserves were inadequate. This meant protracted discussions, and arguments, with the finance people, and at the top level. That meant that he would have to go on to Cairo rather than leave the train at Wadi Halfa as he had intended.

But what, then, would he do with Jamie? Perhaps he would have to come to Cairo, too. There were plenty of friends who would put him up. Or they could stay in a government rest house, used by the Khedive's servants in passage. They were quite decent.

Jamie had figured that out already; and was not at all unhappy about it.

The driver had spent most of the morning under the engine and now emerged with a worried face. That, too, was not unusual. Anyone who looked under an engine would come up with a worried face. But Ismail looked even more worried than that. He put the oil can down and strode purposefully towards Owen.

'Effendi,' he said, 'there is bad.'

'Damage, when it ran into the sandbank?'

'No,' said Ismail. 'Worse.'

Mr Nicholson joined them.

'I will show you,' said Ismail grimly.

Mr Nicholson, who despite his present desk job knew something about engines, crawled after Ismail. Owen, who definitely didn't, crawled after him.

'It's been filed,' said Mr Nicholson.

Jamie, who had somehow intruded himself, crawled up alongside them. They were looking at what appeared to be a coupling. As with all such couplings, it was stout. It wouldn't fail. At least, not in the ordinary way of things. But this wasn't the ordinary way. He followed Ismail's finger. The coupling had been deliberately filed through.

'When?' said Owen.

'Before we started,' said Jamie's father. 'And it's only been part filed through. So that it would last until we were well on our way.'

'Not wear and tear?'

'Deliberate. And probably done in the workshop. While the saloons were being checked. I had everything gone through when I realized we would have to use the Royal Carriage.'

'But this isn't the carriage. It was the engine,' said Owen.

'I had that checked, too.'

'Someone in the workshop?'

'Must have been. And carefully done, so that you wouldn't see it. Not at once. It might have made it to Wadi Halfa if not for the sandstorm.'

'You mean it wasn't necessarily planned to break down in the middle of the desert?'

'Perhaps not. It would probably have been picked up at Halfa. They would automatically have done a quick check there. Even so, they might have missed it. It's filed through behind the bearing.'

'But it would have broken down at some point?'

'Oh, yes. No doubt about that.'

They crawled back out.

'The question is,' said Owen, 'whether it was merely intended to delay the train, or . . .'

'Worse. It could have led to a fatal accident. Mind you, the train would not have been travelling fast. It goes pretty steadily across the desert. None of our trains are what you might call speedsters. They're reliable workhorses, rather.'

Owen nodded. This wasn't England. Out here you had other needs.

'What I can't get over,' said Nicholson, 'is that it was probably done in the workshops. It had gone in for servicing before it had been hitched on to the carriages. I had that done, too, since, with the Khedive's saloon on board, it amounted to a royal train. And I don't think it was that they missed it. They're good workmen and take a pride in their work. This was deliberate.'

'A deliberate attempt at sabotage?'

'It must have been. I can't understand it. We've never had anything like this before. In Egypt that kind of thing happens occasionally, but in the Sudan . . .!'

'The modern world is catching up with us, Nicholson,' said the Mamur Zapt quietly.

There was nothing they could do about it here. It would have to go into the workshop at Halfa. The rescue trains might be able to patch it up enough for it to get there. Once there they could either mend it or find another engine temporarily. It would not interfere with the journey greatly. Once the rescue train arrived they would resume the journey and get to Cairo fairly quickly, in forty-eight hours at most. But Owen knew that would be only the beginning of his own work.

'What is it, Mamur Zapt?' asked Yasin al-Jawad, coming up to the little knot of men gathered round the engine. Owen saw no reason why he shouldn't tell him.

Yasin al-Jawad didn't seem surprised. 'We were afraid that something like this might happen,' he said.

'But you didn't think fit to mention it,' said Owen.

Yasin shrugged. 'What was there to mention? Vague fears, that was all. And I should think you'd have enough of those.'

'Why should there be such fears?' asked Owen. 'It would help if you told me.'

Yasin hesitated. 'I don't know whether I should.'

'Is it to do with the meeting you and the Pasha attended in Khartoum?'

There was another delay before Yasin responded. 'I'm sorry,' he said. 'I know I'm not being very helpful. The thing is we were enjoined by the Khedive to say absolutely nothing about this to anyone.'

'Especially the British?'

Yasin al-Jawad laughed and nodded. 'Especially the British.'

'There would be papers about this in the Pasha's briefcase.'

'There would. And you are not going to see them.'

'We are,' said Owen firmly, 'when all is said and done, colleagues. We are on the same side.'

'Nevertheless,' said Yasin al-Jawad. He shook his head with what seemed like genuine sadness. 'I am sorry,' he said.

'It doesn't alter anything,' said Owen. 'It's just that it would have made it easier for me to follow the Khedive's instructions and guard the Pasha.'

'I am truly sorry. It is not the way I would have chosen to do things.'

'It doesn't matter.'

'It doesn't, really,' agreed Yasin. 'We shall soon be in Cairo and once we are there, you can forget the whole business.'

Some hope of that, thought Owen.

'Some hope of that, I know,' said Yasin al-Jawad aloud.

Aisha went up to the Khedive's saloon and knocked on the door. It was opened, after some delay, by two men, only one of whom she recognized. He was the Pasha's personal cook, assigned him by the Railways for the duration of the journey, an experienced, trustworthy man, Jamie had said, who could be relied on, his father said, not to poison him. Neither Jamie nor Aisha were completely sure that this was just a joke.

The other had joined the train at Khartoum. He was a squat, thick-set man with scars on his face and arms, and not tribal ones, either. He was, she guessed, an extra man the Pasha had picked up to guard him. He already had Owen, of course, but this one was the traditional personal manservant-bodyguard, who would never move more than a few feet away from his master and would kill if necessary.

'I would like to speak to the Pasha's lady,' said Aisha.

The Pasha's servants were stunned. This was a question they had never anticipated being asked. Firstly, because they thought that no one knew of the existence of the Pasha's companion; and secondly because, well, you would never ask to speak to a female servant. A male one, you might, just, but a female one, no, never. They fell back from the door and conferred urgently.

Eventually the cook returned and poked his head round the door. 'Why?' he asked.

'I thought she might be grateful for some female assistance,' said Aisha. 'In the circumstances.'

The cook withdrew and there was further conferring. After a while, he turned. 'No,' he said.

By this time Aisha had wedged her foot in the door. 'Why not?' she said.

The Pasha's servants were now entering an area of speculation they had never entered before. This time the conferring was prolonged. It was broken by a woman's voice.

'Who is she?' it said.

'Who are you?' the man asked.

'I am the daughter of Counsellor Yasin al-Jawad, Plenipotentiary to the Khedive.'

This was untrue, but Aisha liked the sound of the word and knew that the two men would never have heard it before. She hoped they would be impressed.

'I am travelling on the train,' she said, 'with my father, and he wondered if I might, as another woman, be of assistance to the lady, given the plight we are in.'

She hoped this would never get back to her father.

The door was pushed open and a veiled lady appeared in the doorway. 'What is your name?'

'Aisha.'

'Come in,' said the lady.

She led Aisha into the comfortable sitting quarters of the saloon.

'Would you like some lemonade?'

'Yes, please,' said Aisha.

The cook, who saw all order slipping away from him, went off. The bodyguard, evidently having a difficult intellectual wrestle with all this, fell back from the door and stood bemused in the entrance to the sitting quarter.

'You may go, Abdul,' said the Pasha's companion.

Abdul retired with a jerk, and the cook returned with two glasses of lemonade.

The Pasha's lady lowered her veil and looked at Aisha with undisguised curiosity. 'What do you do?' she asked Aisha.

'Do?'

'On the train.'

'Sit, mostly,' said Aisha.

'Me, too,' said the Pasha's lady. 'But then, I do that anyway. Mostly.'

'It's very boring,' said Aisha.

'It is.'

'When I'm in Cairo, I go to school.'

'School?' said the lady, as if uncertain quite what that was.

'Yes. Where you learn things.'

'I learn things when I'm with the Pasha.'

'These may not be the same things,' said Aisha hastily.

There was a long pause.

'When I get back to Cairo, I am going to Paris. Perhaps.'

'Paris?'

'A big city,' said Aisha. 'With lots of shops.'

'I have been to shops,' said the lady. 'Occasionally.'

'Which ones?'

'Andelaft's?'

'I've been there. Do you like it?'

'Oh, yes. But it is . . . very big. And busy. Lots of people.'

'There are usually. Too many, I think. I usually go to Joseph Cohen's.'

'I have never been there,' said the Pasha's lady. 'In fact, I have hardly been anywhere.'

'I prefer Paris,' said Aisha. 'Or, rather, I think I will when I've been there.'

There was a little silence.

'How I envy you!' the Pasha's lady burst out.

'Me?'

'You can do so many things.'

'Well, up to a point . . .'

'I just stay in the house.'

'I do get around a lot more than that . . .'

'And see things!'

'Well, yes. I suppose. I *do* see things. And when I'm in Paris . . .'

'Do you have a lover?'

'Lover?'

'I don't. The Pasha sees to that. But you – you must have lots. Able to get around as you do.'

'Well, no – not many.'

Not *any*, said the still small voice of truth. Except . . . did Jamie count? On the whole she thought he didn't.

'It would be nice to have a lover,' sighed the Pasha's lady.

'Failing everything else,' said Aisha sternly.

'I thought I might find a lover when I was in Khartoum,' said the Pasha's lady. 'When I was waiting for the Pasha. He put me up in a hotel and I thought this was my chance. But it wasn't. That hateful old sheikh was watching me all the time. He stood that dreadful bodyguard man outside my door and wouldn't let me speak to anybody. And then the Pasha came and it was all over. Khartoum wasn't much of a place, anyway. The Pasha took me out once to the shops, with that awful bodyguard man an inch behind me, but they weren't up to much, really, compared with the ones in Cairo.'

'There's not a lot in Khartoum,' agreed Aisha.

'You have been there?' said the Pasha's lady eagerly.

'I have.'

'What did you think of the shops?'

'Not a lot.'

'Which ones did you go into?'

'Actually, I went to the zoo,' said Aisha, who had still not forgiven her father.

'The zoo is – what?'

'It's a place where they keep animals.'

'Animals? What for? To eat?'

'Just to look at.'

'Just to look at? That is very strange!'

'And dull,' said Aisha.

'What sort of animals?'

'Elephants.'

'Elephants? Those animals with long, wavy noses?'

'Yes – trunks.'

'I have never been to a zoo. I wouldn't mind going there.'

'Once,' said Aisha.

'You have done everything,' said the Pasha's lady bitterly. 'And I have done nothing!'

The door opened and in came the Pasha and Aisha's father. 'Aisha! What are you doing there?'

'I invited her in,' said the Pasha's lady. 'To talk.'

'Talk?'

'It's very boring here,' said the Pasha's lady. 'I wanted someone to talk to.'

'Couldn't you have talked to Abdul?' said the Pasha, glancing at the bodyguard.

'No,' said his lady.

'Why not? I would have thought . . .'

'You've had his tongue cut out.'

'I certainly have not! He is a little silent, that is true, but that is his nature.'

'A woman sometimes wants another woman to talk to,' said Aisha.

'And this is . . .?' said the Pasha, looking at her.

'My daughter,' said Yasin al-Jawad. 'Who is *not* silent by nature!'

'So,' said Aisha, 'I went in.'

'And?'

Aisha shrugged.

'We talked.'

'You and this woman?'

'The Pasha's lady, yes. I never knew her name.'

'What did you talk about?'

'Shops, mainly. And the zoo. And a woman's life.'

'You and the Pasha's mistress?'

'That's right.'

'I am not sure that either of you would have been much qualified to speak on the topic.'

'No?'

'Neither of you would have had much experience to draw on.'

'That is just the point,' said Aisha. 'Actually, I felt rather sorry for her. She seems to have missed out on life altogether. I suppose she was very young.'

'Young?'

'When the Pasha took her. The result is that she knows a lot, probably, about some things – Pasha's sort of things – and nothing about ordinary life and what everyone else knows about. I felt sorry for her. She was so desperate that when she was in Khartoum she tried to find a lover—'

'Aisha!'

'That's what she said. She thought that maybe while she was in the hotel . . . But she was under lock and key the whole time. That dreadful old sheikh was keeping an eye on her.'

'What dreadful old sheikh was this?' asked Owen.

'There seems to have been some old sheikh in the background . . .'

'Do not speak disrespectfully, Aisha!' warned her father. 'That was our host.'

'There was some sort of meeting,' said Aisha, 'and he was in charge. He was in charge of her, too, and it was like being in prison.'

'Aisha, you are exaggerating.'

'That's how it seemed to her. I'm just telling you what she said.'

'You have told us quite enough, Aisha!'

'Well, you did ask . . .'

'I am sorry, Mamur Zapt, to subject you to all this. Aisha, you had better get back to the saloon.'

'And there she was,' said Aisha, 'like some princess shut up in a tower. *La tour abolie* . . .'

'What?' said Jamie.

'It's a quotation from a French poet. The ruined tower. Like in a fairy story. The Pasha is the ogre keeping her locked up. Come to think of it, he *does* look a bit of an ogre . . . Perhaps we might rescue her.'

'Now? Here? In the desert?'

'When we get back to Cairo.'

'I thought you were going to Paris?'

'Perhaps not immediately.'

'Actually, I may not be going to Cairo. It's not definite yet. It's just that my father says it might be simpler to go on to Cairo rather than go back to Khartoum. He says he'll probably have to go to

Cairo anyway for a day or two to sort things out after the sandstorm
and he might take me.'

'Well, then . . .'

'It wouldn't be for very long. Just a day or two.'

'We would have to strike fast.'

Jamie wasn't sure about all this. He had learned to distrust the
wilder flights of Aisha's fancy.

'What would we do with her?' he said practically.

'Oh . . .' Aisha waved an airy hand.

'I'm glad Jamie's getting on well with your daughter,' said Mr
Nicholson. 'I was afraid he would be getting bored shut up out
here.'

'It keeps them out of mischief,' agreed Aisha's father.

The sun scorched on. The roof of the carriage, when Owen went
up there, was too hot to touch. Across the desert little eddies of
light circled constantly. In the carriage the heat became almost
unbearable. People were drinking more. This began to worry Jamie's
father because although he had reckoned that they had enough water
to see them through, the longer this went on, the greater the risk
that their supplies would run out.

He discussed it with Owen.

'There'll be watering points ahead of us and behind,' said Owen.
'Which is the nearer, do you think?'

'The one ahead, I think.'

'Perhaps we should go and take a look? We could also check on
the state of the track.'

They agreed that this might be a good idea. But then another
consideration occurred to them. Was it sensible for both of them to
leave the train?

'Perhaps we ought to make it just one of us. There are plenty of
able-bodied passengers. One of them could go. The girl's father,
for instance. He seems pretty fit. And to have his wits about him.'

'No,' said Owen. 'No, I don't think so.'

Jamie's father was surprised.

'Why not?' he said. 'As I said, he seems pretty fit. Plays squash,
he tells me.'

'I don't want him to go too far out of my sight,' said Owen.

'No?' Mr Nicholson looked puzzled. Then he shrugged. 'Well,

all right. We are sure to be able to find someone else. Would you like me to look along the train and find a likely person?'

'I'll do it,' said Owen. 'I want to take another look at the people, anyway. Could you get under the engine again with the driver and make sure there's just the one thing wrong? If there was another, it might delay us when eventually we do get going, and I'd prefer that not to happen.'

He had, of course, looked at the passengers before but now he was looking in a different light. The longer the train was stuck here, the more uneasy he felt. Word by now would have got around the desert, empty though it seemed, and he didn't want too many people coming to take a look. There would be too much temptation – if only to pilfer.

Nicholson had found a likely man and the two of them set off. It would be evening before they got back. By that time they would be knocked out by the heat. Nicholson, at any rate, was used to it. Besides, Owen wanted him, as an engineer, to assess how, if the days went by, and their supplies of water ran low, water might be brought back from the watering point to the train. It would not be easy, given the heat, and the probable increasing weakness of the passengers.

Jamie didn't feel the heat. At least, he thought he didn't. But when he climbed up on the roof of the carriage for the third time he became conscious of how much hotter everything was. He was wearing shorts and as he was climbing up the ladder he touched the metal of one of the rungs with his bare knee. He pulled it away sharply and looked down to see if it had made a mark. It hadn't but it felt as if he had been burned. After that he went more care-fully. But then he found that the wood was almost as hot as the metal, so he contented himself with standing on the ladder and peering out over the desert.

The Mamur Zapt had asked him to keep an eye open for any signs of activity in the desert. He couldn't see any, except for the swirls of light where the dust devils were playing. The occasional bit of grit rose up and stung his face. He wished he had brought his sunglasses with him. He hardly ever wore the things. It was the same with his sun helmet. When he was at home at Atbara his mother was always making him put his sun helmet on to go out but Jamie didn't like wearing it and often didn't. Today, though, if he had one with him he would have put it on. He put his hand up and felt the top of his head. His hair was almost burning. That was when he decided to go back into the saloon and find his helmet.

Of course, he couldn't find it. He must have put it down somewhere. Mohammed, the cook, clicked his teeth reprovingly and offered to lend him a turban. Jamie quite liked turbans so accepted the offer. Mohammed found a spare one and wound it round Jamie's head. It was, actually, better than a helmet, cooler and softer on the head.

He climbed back up on to the roof. With the turban on it was certainly much better. But now he was wishing even more that he had brought his sunglasses. The glare from the sand made him half-close his eyes and squint.

Somewhere, over to his left, something was flashing. He couldn't think what it could be because in the desert there was neither water nor metal.

Also, the dust devils were dancing more than they had been. The bits of grit were whirling at about knee height, stinging his bare knees.

He wondered how his father and the other chap were doing. If it was beginning to be unpleasant here, what would it be like for them? He decided he had better go and report the change to the Mamur Zapt.

On his way, he met Aisha. She was wearing a huge pair of sunglasses, the fashionable ones which had recently come into the shops and which were quietly envied by her mother. Another pair of glasses, the less fashionable sort, were stuck into her belt. He asked her if he could borrow them. He didn't like these much either. But he could see better. The glare was reduced. The sand didn't get in your eyes. You didn't have to half-shut them.

He thought he would take another look at the flashing. At first he couldn't see it at all but then, there it was again.

This time he did find the Mamur Zapt. He was wearing not a sun helmet but a fez. It was the sort of thing you wore in Cairo. Out here it looked a bit silly, but Owen obviously felt he needed something. The other thing he had done was tie a sort of scarf round his neck, shielding the back of the neck where Mohammed some-times let a fold of his turban dangle down.

He and Jamie stayed up on the ladder for quite some time. And then they thought they could see what was causing the flashing. It was two men on camels. One of them might even be the man they had seen before. Could this be him and the other man his friend?

They couldn't see Jamie's father, though, or the man who had gone with him.

The Mamur Zapt had become very fidgety. He was up on the roof of the saloon every half hour. And after a while it became clearer that the two men riding across the desert towards them were indeed the Hadendoa they had met before but this time he was accompanied. They rode right up to the train and then stopped, as before, hunched up on the camels and standing there surveying the train.

Owen went over to them. 'You have returned, then,' he said to the Hadendoa.

The Hadendoa ventured an 'Iwa' – yes.

'And this is your friend?'

The Hadendoa inclined his head. His friend did not even do that.

Aisha's father came up the train towards them. He began speaking to them. He was, of course, the one who *could* speak to them, having, as he had said, spent some time in the Red Sea Hills. The Arabic was different from that spoken in Cairo and Owen found it difficult to make out. He could, however, make it out well enough to follow roughly the others' conversation – or what there was of it. The Hadendoa was monosyllabic and his friend seemed to find it difficult to manage just the one syllable. After a while, the men slid off their camels and made them kneel down. Then they positioned themselves comfortably against their flanks and lapsed into immobility.

'Get anywhere?' asked Owen.

Aisha's father shrugged. 'He went to meet his friend. As he said. And when he found him he came back with him.'

Owen considered this. 'So meeting his friend was not the prime, or only, object in his being here?'

'It would seem not.'

'It is to do with the train,' said Owen.

'It must be.'

Owen would have liked to probe further, but in a way Yasin had already done that. And got nowhere.

'How long will it be before the rescue train gets here?' asked Yasin.

'I'm hoping it will get here tomorrow. If not, then the next day.'

'There is a limit,' said Yasin, 'to what people can stand.'

'We may be coming to it.'

'Obviously, there is nothing you can do,' said the Egyptian.

'I am more worried at the moment about Nicholson Effendi and his companion.'

Jamie was worried about his father, too. He considered going along the line to look for him, but knew what his father would say if he did. 'The hardest thing is to do nothing,' he would say. 'But if you don't, if you do something, that may merely add to the difficulties. Then we'd be looking for you as well.' So Jamie contented himself with climbing up on to the roof of the carriage yet again.

The shadows were beginning to lengthen now. They fell across the desert grotesquely enlarged.

Yasin came back. 'Should we send out a search party, do you think?'

'I am reluctant to split our party up still more,' said the Mamur Zapt.

'You are expecting an attack?'

'Not expecting; just not ruling it out.'

'I don't think . . . I don't *think* that the Hadendoa is a scout,' said Yasin.

'Perhaps not. But what is he waiting for?'

Mohammed made tea, which they drank in small cups. They didn't want to use too much water.

The shadow now stretched right across the desert. It had become much cooler, at last. But on the roof of the carriage the woodwork was still unpleasantly hot. You wouldn't put your hand on it. Every time Jamie went up there now, he looked back along the line, but he couldn't see his father or the other man.

Aisha had come up.

'How do you think the Pasha is?' asked Jamie.

'Melting!' said Aisha. 'He could do with it!'

They had not had a sign of the Pasha's woman all day.

'She must be melting, too,' said Aisha.

'You would think he could let her out for a little walk. To get some air.'

Precisely at that moment the door of the Royal Saloon opened and the Pasha appeared. He climbed down on to the sand. Surprisingly, a second form followed. It was his lady, heavily veiled against the world's eyes.

'She must be hot,' said Jamie, 'in all that!'

Aisha was considering going up to her and renewing their conversation. Her father could see what she was thinking and shook his head.

The woman stood for a while outside the saloon, then climbed back and went inside again.

The Pasha came over to them. 'Where is Nicholson?' he asked. No one replied.

'It was a mistake,' said the Pasha, 'being out in this heat.'

'He was assessing the water supply,' said Owen.

'We wouldn't want to run out of *that*,' said the Pasha.

It was already dark when Jamie's father finally returned. He was supporting, half-carrying, the other man.

'We had to stop,' he said, 'for a rest. Idris was pretty well done in. Me, too.'

They had waited for it to get cooler. By this time they were dehydrated and labouring. They had, of course, taken water with them and refilled their bottle at the water supply point when they got there. On the return journey they had tried not to drink too much. But the heat by then was taking its toll. They felt that energy had been drained out of them. They *had* to put something back in. And gradually the water level in the bottles had gone down. In the end they were sucking on the empty bottles.

The sun had gone down by this time and the moon not yet come up, but they had been able to tell their way by the railway track, half-covered with sand though it was. Mr Nicholson then became aware of his companion tripping and stumbling, and then he had fallen. They had decided to rest there awhile before continuing.

They had heard calls and thought they might be coming from the train. On the other hand they might not have been.

The moon had come up and at last they had seen something shining. The sand had become deeper and now they were wading through it. Idris had fallen one last time and Mr Nicholson was finding it hard to support him.

They had come upon the train at last almost by accident.

'At least we know now there *is* water back there. We'll be all right for another day or two.'

And if they exhausted that supply, they could go the other way, to the next water point along the track.

Jamie's father and Idris were sponged down and put into their beds.

Jamie didn't know whether to be shocked or relieved. He kept waking up during the night so that he could look at his father. His father seemed all right and by the morning both of them, he and his father, were sleeping normally.

When Jamie woke up he went outside. The wind had got up and the sand was tugging round his ankles. There was no sign of the relief trains. All the passengers were staying in their carriages. When Jamie looked in they were just lying there inertly.

The Hadendoa and his friend had stayed outside all night, their headdresses over their faces, sheltering beside their camels. Owen was now checking on them as well as the desert. Jamie could tell he was waiting for – expecting – something.

Whatever it was, it didn't come. The Hadendoa and his friend went away.

Owen began making arrangements for all the passengers to move into the front carriages. These included the Royal Saloon where the Pasha was staying. He demurred but was overruled by Owen. Anyway it was just, as he said, a possibility. But if he gave the signal they would have to move immediately.

He was constantly going up on the roof of the saloon and looking out. After the first few times Jamie stopped going with him. Even he was feeling a bit wiped out by this time.

Then, at nearly four o'clock, there was a shout. Jamie rushed out. The Mamur Zapt was standing on the roof, waving. And then, from far away across the desert, came an answering toot.

SIX

The passengers piled out of the carriages and cheered. Answering toots came from across the desert, but it was hours before the rescue engine came into view. Then they saw why its progress was so slow. A gang of men was walking in front of it with spades, shovelling the sand out of the way. When they had loosened the heavier drifts the engine came up behind and pushed the remaining sand out of the way. It was slow, laborious work and the engine crawled along. As it came closer they saw that the track was buried under huge drifts of sand. When it was cleared, two banks rose on either side of the railway line. It was like going through a ravine.

The jubilation among the passengers died down and now they stood silently watching the engine's progress. It moved painfully slowly and seemed no nearer when the light began to fade.

A great search light came on at the front of the engine and the work continued. In its light Jamie could see the brawny forms bending into their shovelling. They were mostly huge Nubians.

At some point in the night two men came along the line and talked to Mr Nicholson. Then they went off again and a little later work stopped. The Nubians lay down where they were and fell asleep.

All the time, the Mamur Zapt was fussing around. He was continually going up and down on to the roof of the carriage with a ladder. At one point he came back and lamps were lit all around the train. From across the desert the rescue engine lent its light and the whole of the stranded train was bathed in a strange luminescence.

Jamie had gone to bed in the saloon, but he couldn't sleep and instead sat looking out of the window. In the moonlight the scrub stood out clearly and cast sharp shadows on the sand. Further away to his right he could see the big searchlight of the rescue engine.

The Mamur Zapt couldn't sleep either. He spent the night up and down on the ladder or walking round the train. He seemed to be carrying a gun.

This excited Jamie and he sat and watched him. But then he felt his eyes closing and he must have fallen asleep because he woke up with a jerk and found that his father had put him into bed.

He looked out. The moon was dying away and there was no sign of the sun. But the desert was illuminated by an eerie half-light. Someone went past the window but it was only his father.

He opened the door of the saloon and climbed out. Outside, it was surprisingly chilly. He almost wished he had a jersey to put on. He became aware that there were several figures now moving about the train – his father, yes, and the Mamur Zapt, but Aisha's father, too, and various others. Some of them were carrying sticks.

It was getting lighter, but the sun had not yet risen. The engine's spotlight was still on and so were some of the lamps around the train. One or two of the Nubians had joined the patrollers.

A thought struck Jamie. Where was the Hadendoa and his friend? They had gone. He wondered if he should tell Owen but guessed that he already knew. Perhaps that was why he was patrolling. Jamie decided to patrol, too. The Mamur Zapt spotted him and told him to keep close to their saloon. Jamie's father came in and told him to stay inside.

Jamie tried to go back to sleep and must have dozed off for when he next looked out he saw Aisha. She was wrapped up in a shawl and standing by her saloon. He climbed down to see her.

'What's going on?' he said.

'My father says the Mamur Zapt thinks there might be a raid.'

'On the train?'

'Yes.'

'What for?'

'The Pasha. Or some briefcase of his.'

'Aisha,' called her father, 'go back inside.'

Aisha prepared to obey when suddenly a woman's voice came out of the darkness.

'She can come in here.'

It was the Pasha's lady.

'All right,' said her father. 'But don't stay long.'

'I could have stayed longer,' complained Aisha, sometime later, 'only the Pasha began moving about and Leila thought it would be better if I went.'

'Leila?'

'The Pasha's lady. She asked me to call her Leila.'

Jamie was impressed by the sudden intimacy.

'I asked her if she wanted to be rescued. She said no.'

Jamie couldn't help feeling relieved.

'Of course, I'm not going to take that as her final word.'

'Why not?' said Jamie.

'She doesn't know what's best for her. She's been shut up far too long. I think she's frightened by the world outside.'

'So what are you going to do?'

'I've asked her where she'll be staying in Cairo. She says at the Pasha's house. Which, of course, makes it a bit difficult for us.'

'Us?' said Jamie.

The rescue engine nudged nearer. All the passengers were now outside, cheering it on. It came steadily but painfully slowly towards them. The heaps of sand on either side of the track were growing. Some of the labourers had started to free the wheels, not just of the engine but also of the carriages. An engineer with the rescue team crawled under the engine. The diggers went on past and began to clear the track behind the train.

'There'll be another engine working its way towards us from the other direction,' said Mr Nicholson. 'We may need both engines to push our train on to Wadi Halfa.'

'How long will that take?' asked the Pasha, impatiently.

'We should be at Wadi Halfa tomorrow,' said Mr Nicholson.

'Tomorrow!' said the Pasha, aghast. 'I was hoping we'd get there today!'

'Tomorrow,' said Mr Nicholson firmly.

'Cannot they be hurried?'

'No.'

'A good kick up the backside?' suggested the Pasha.

'They'll be working straight through. It will be a very long, hot day.'

'Cannot they work through the night? It will be cooler then.'

'They'll be doing that, too,' said Jamie's father, and moved away.

Grumbling, the Pasha withdrew to the Royal Saloon.

A moment later there came an anguished shout.

'It's gone!'

'What's gone?'

'My briefcase! It was right beside me!'

Owen rushed up the steps.

'It was right beside me. At my feet!'

'Where were you sitting?'

'Here. I was having breakfast.'

The Mamur Zapt looked under the table. 'Who was serving you?'

'Babikr.'

'Babikr?'

The cook. Owen called him. 'You were serving the Pasha at breakfast.'

'I was, Effendi.'

'Did he have a briefcase with him?'

'Briefcase?'

'You're sure you brought it in with you?' Owen said to the Pasha.

'Yes! I always take it with me wherever I go!'

Owen went to the bedroom and threw the door open. An indignant shout came from inside. It was a woman's voice.

'Just a friend,' the Pasha explained hurriedly.

Owen went in.

The Pasha's lady was sitting up in bed with a single sheet pulled up to her face.

'Really, Owen—' began the Pasha.

Owen went round the room quickly. There was no sign of the briefcase. He turned back to the bed.

'Off with that sheet!'

'Owen—'

'Clothes, too?' asked Leila.

'If necessary. Now, out!'

The Pasha's lady climbed sulkily out. She was fully dressed.

'In bed?' said Owen.

'On the bed!' said Leila.

'*In* the bed. Fully dressed!'

'I had been up half the night,' said the Pasha's lady. 'Those men shovelling. Just outside the window!'

'I will have them spoken to,' said the Pasha.

'Not a wink!' said Leila.

'And so you got back into bed? With your clothes on?'

'I lay down *on* the bed,' said Leila. 'Someone must have covered me with the sheet. Very thoughtfully, I must say. I was very tired, and I lay down for a moment, and the next thing I knew, the Mamur Zapt was stripping me!'

'Disgraceful!' said the Pasha. 'You will hear more of this, Owen.'

'Is that how you come into a lady's bedroom?' asked Leila.

'The briefcase!' said Owen. 'Where is it?'

'Briefcase? What briefcase?'

'The Pasha's briefcase. Where is it?'

'How do I know? I have enough trouble making sure *he* doesn't get lost, never mind a briefcase!'

Owen pulled the sheet back and felt under it.

'This man is very peculiar,' said Leila.

'I think that is enough, Mamur Zapt,' said the Pasha. 'The briefcase is obviously not here. I remember now: I am almost sure I took it into breakfast with me.'

Owen went back into the dining room. The cook was still standing there, open-mouthed.

'Did you see a briefcase when you were clearing away the breakfast things?'

'What briefcase?' said the cook.

'The Pasha's. He says he brought the briefcase in with him to breakfast. Did he?'

'If the Pasha says so, then the Pasha must be right.'

'He *was* right!' said the Pasha.

'But you don't remember seeing it?' asked Owen.

'I don't remember seeing it,' said the cook. 'But I don't remember not seeing it.'

'You don't remember seeing it – or not seeing it – when you cleaned away the breakfast things?'

'No, Effendi.'

'You didn't clear it away *with* the breakfast things?'

'I only do the breakfast things,' said the cook.

'Does anyone go round afterwards, doing a general tidy up?'

'Abdul does,' said the cook. 'Sometimes.'

'Abdul!'

The bodyguard emerged from the kitchen. 'Yes, Effendi?'

'Did you tidy up in here this morning?'

'I'm a bodyguard,' said Abdul, with dignity. 'Not a general servant.'

'But you do help sometimes. Did you help this morning?'

'I may have done,' said the bodyguard unwillingly.

'And did you see a briefcase when you were doing so?'

'As God is my witness—'

'He is your witness, so speak the truth. Did you see the Pasha's briefcase in here this morning?'

'What have briefcases to do with me?'

'Did you see it?'

'I may have seen it,' said Abdul, reluctantly.

'Ah! So where was it when you saw it?'

'On the floor,' said the Pasha. 'Beside me.'

'On the floor. Beside the Pasha,' said Abdul.

'There you are!' said the Pasha triumphantly.

'When was this? When he came into breakfast?'

Abdul looked at the Pasha.

'Of course it was!' said the Pasha impatiently.

'But you weren't here, then,' said Owen. 'You were only here afterwards. When you were tidying up.'

'Enough of this shilly-shallying!' said the Pasha. 'My briefcase was already stolen!'

'Yes, but *when* was it stolen?'

'After breakfast,' said the Pasha firmly.

'I thought you kept it with you? Always?'

'In general, yes,' said the Pasha.

'But perhaps not on that occasion? Possibly you left it behind. In the saloon, where you had breakfast?'

'It is *possible*, I suppose,' said the Pasha. 'But very unlikely.'

'What did you do after breakfast?'

'Something, I expect. Nothing much.'

'You went for a walk,' said Leila.

'Did I? Yes, that was it. I went for a walk.'

'And I went with him,' said Leila.

'And I went with them,' said the bodyguard. 'That is my job. To go with the Pasha. Everywhere.'

'So the saloon was empty at that point?'

'Apart from me,' said the cook. 'I was there.'

'And what were you doing?'

'Sanding up.'

'Sanding up?'

'No water,' explained Babikr. 'So I used sand to scour the dishes.'

'And then?'

'And then? Well, I sat down and rested, I suppose. And then went outside for a little breath of air. It gets hot in that kitchen. It's only a small space and—'

'All right, all right,' said Owen. 'You went out. So the Royal Saloon was empty at that point.'

'Yes. Hey, what are you saying? I didn't go far. I hardly moved away from the saloon! As God is my witness—'

'Yes. Yes. You didn't go far. But that was the point at which someone could have got in . . .'

'I was only a few feet away! I would have seen them.'

'And *did* you see anyone go in?'

'No. At least . . .'

'Yes?'

'There was that girl, of course.'

'But I came out again!' cried Aisha. 'And, anyway, I was there with Leila!'

'Speak respectfully!' her father ordered. 'The Pasha's lady, to you!'

'She said I could call her Leila! All right, the Pasha's lady.'

'But that was earlier,' said Owen. 'You came out because you heard the Pasha moving around.'

'Yes, but then I went back in again. When Leila came back. She and the Pasha came out together and went for a walk. Then Leila – the Pasha's lady – came back alone and went back in to the saloon. And after a bit I went in. Because she had told me I could and should. She said to come in when the saloon was empty and there was no one around, because then the place was like a morgue!'

'So you went in a second time?'

'Yes! But she wasn't there. I thought she might have gone in to the bedroom but I didn't want to go in there because I thought she might want to be by herself. She said she sometimes got headaches. Well, I thought she might have one coming on. Already it was pretty hot. And airless. Lots of people were complaining—'

'So you came out again.'

'Yes. I didn't stay long. Once I had seen she wasn't there . . .'

'So the saloon was, to all intents and purposes, left empty again. But someone could have gone in at *that* point!'

'That's right,' said Aisha. 'No one was there—'

'Wasn't Babikr there? I thought he was there or nearby practically all the time?'

'I was!' said Babikr. 'Only it just happened that at one point I went behind the saloon to have a pee . . .'

'I thought that was where he was going,' said Aisha.

'So, let me get this clear – you came back out of the saloon, and Babikr had gone round the back to have a pee, and the Pasha's lady was somewhere inside, and Abdul was with the Pasha . . . So someone could have got into the saloon unobserved and picked up the briefcase!'

'What,' said Mr Nicholson a few moments later, 'would they have done with it? They wouldn't have gone walking round with it, because you don't walk round with a briefcase in the middle of the desert. Unless you're a Pasha, of course.'

'But I was the one from whom it was stolen!' cried the Pasha.

'Nicholson Effendi's point remains,' said Owen. 'What was done with the briefcase after it was stolen? It can't have been taken away. So it must still be on the train somewhere. In which case, the train must be searched. I'll work from this end and, Nicholson, if you wouldn't mind starting from the other end . . .'

'Want some help?' asked Aisha's father.

'No, I don't think so. Or, rather, yes I do, but a different kind of help. Can you get up on the top of the carriage, from where you'll be able to see most of the train, and watch that nobody moves the case out while we're searching?'

'I can certainly do that. If you will trust me.'

'Of course I will trust you!'

'Well, you see, I was just wondering why you didn't want me to help you with the searching. And, of course, the answer is clear: Aisha.'

'Daddy!' cried Aisha.

'You are under suspicion, my dear. You were in the saloon at or near the time when the briefcase was stolen. And if you are under suspicion then I must be, too.'

'Daddy! That's ridiculous!'

'No, it's not. Not if you think about it. As, of course, the Mamur Zapt has been doing for some time.'

'But—'

'Don't worry, Aisha,' said Owen, 'there are plenty of others under suspicion, too. If you think about it.'

'The Pasha himself,' said Yasin.

'And the Pasha's lady.'

'In bed,' said Leila, still bridling. 'Along with about everyone else on the train!'

'The cook,' said Owen.

'As God is my witness—'

'And Abdul,' said Leila.

'What's this?' said the bodyguard, waking up.

'Well, it could be.'

'I swear to God—'

'There will be others, too,' said Owen. 'So don't worry, Aisha. You're in company.'

Owen began with the engine.

'But . . .' the driver began to protest.

'Just the place,' said Owen. 'No one would think of it.'

Muttering darkly, the driver went round with Owen, even into the most confined of spaces.

'You're a big chap, Owen,' said Mr Nicholson. 'Let Jamie do it.'

'If *he* can do it,' said Aisha, 'then why can't I?'

'It's not a job for a girl,' said Jamie.

'Why not?'

Jamie was taken aback. 'Well, it's just not,' he said.

'I am thinner than you.'

'Yes, but . . .'

'And can wriggle just as well.'

'You would muck up your dress.'

Aisha gave him a look of withering scorn.

'I think not, Aisha,' said her father.

'Is it because I am under suspicion?' demanded Aisha.

'You are not *very* under suspicion, Aisha,' said Owen.

'We are both under suspicion, Aisha. You and I.'

'I don't see why you are under suspicion,' said Aisha, frowning. 'You've not been up in the saloon on your own.'

'It is because I am an Egyptian,' said her father bitterly. The fact that he had not been chosen as one of those to search the train rankled.

Owen sighed. 'Not that, either,' he said. 'Now can we go on and search the rest of the train?'

Mr Nicholson went to the rear of the train and began working his way along. Owen did the same from the other direction. Jamie's father said he was used to searching trains. Anyone who worked on the railway was. There was a lot of petty pilfering and in his early days on the railway he was always being called upon to check carriages and people. Owen, doing his own searching, had an eye on him initially but was soon satisfied that he knew what he was about.

And, of course, that was even truer of Owen himself. Not searching trains specifically, but searching pretty well everything else. Nowadays he had his own people to do the searching. He wished that he had them with him now. Searching was a highly skilled art: with something as big as a briefcase there was no need to search up the rectum, for which small mercy he was grateful.

The thought sent him back to Aisha's father, who had unwillingly accepted the restricted role assigned him and was up on the roof of a carriage keeping the train under scrutiny. Owen hadn't liked to make the distinction he had done but he felt it was necessary. It would have been necessary to get rid of the briefcase to dump it somewhere, and that was perhaps a moment when the search could be narrowed. Owen climbed up and stood beside Yasin.

'I would like, if I might, to make use of Aisha,' he said. 'And Jamie.'

'Despite her being "under suspicion"?'

'This may reassure her,' said Owen. 'It will show her that we think she can be trusted. I would like her and Jamie to walk up and down the train, one on each side, looking to see if the briefcase has been dumped.'

'I see no objection to that,' said Aisha's father.

'The young have sharp eyes, particularly when their sense of responsibility is engaged.'

'Jamie less so,' said Owen, 'but with the example of Kim before him, he will not let us down.'

'I haven't read the book,' said Yasin. 'I see I must.'

'And can you keep an eye on them from up on the roof? I wouldn't want anything to go amiss with them.'

'You fear that?' said Yasin.

'Not very much, or I wouldn't let them do it. But I believe in taking care. Perhaps I have an overdeveloped sense of responsibility myself.'

'I will watch over them,' promised Yasin.

Jamie agreed at once.

Aisha hesitated. 'Whose side am I on?' she said.

'Whose side are you on?'

'The British or the Egyptian?'

'There's no conflict here. Both. It's in the interests of both Britain and Egypt that the briefcase is traced.'

Seeing that she was still doubtful, he said: 'I do work for the Khedive, you know.'

'And the British.'

'Certainly. But it was the Khedive who asked me to look after the Pasha. He spoke to me. Directly. And I am not disloyal.'

'I don't see how you can be loyal to both sides.'

'Nor do my Egyptian friends. Nor I myself, sometimes.'

'On that basis, although I still don't quite understand it, I will go along the train.'

'Look under the wheels especially. But allow for someone having covered it with sand.'

Halfway through the search, Owen went up on the roof to have a word with Yasin. It was very, very hot up there and he knew that he would be wilting. He gave him a spell under the carriage, in the shade, and took over his position himself.

Yasin didn't stay down there for long but soon climbed back up and said he was ready to continue.

'I had a thought,' he said. 'The Hadendoa and his friend. They are no longer here. Could they have gone off with the case?'

'I have wondered that, too,' said Owen. 'And I don't see how that could have happened. The timing doesn't work out. But I agree with you. That's the only time the opportunity could have arisen. I just cannot see the mechanics of it.'

'And if it was them,' said Yasin, 'who were they acting on behalf of? That is what I can't puzzle out.'

The rescue engine had come up to them by now and its engineers were swarming over the engine. McIlroy, the Chief Engineer, was standing just below them.

'What's all this about?' he asked, as Owen descended from the carriage.

Owen told him.

'So you think these two, the Hadendoa and his friend, might have stolen the briefcase and ridden off with it?'

'It's a possibility.'

'Where would they have headed for? It's just desert all round here. It's desert for miles.'

'A man like the Hadendoa, on his camel, can cover miles. His home is in the Red Sea Hills and he would have had to cover miles to get here,' said Mr Nicholson.

'Why would they have used *him*?' said the Chief Engineer. 'Couldn't they have found someone nearer?'

'I don't know,' said Owen. 'And the Hadendoa may have had nothing to do with it. It's just a possibility. But the thing is, you see, it's rather odd that he should be here anyway, miles, as you say, from home. And just at this spot.'

'Where the engine broke down,' said Mr Nicholson.

'They wouldn't have been able to be as precise as that,' said the Chief Engineer. 'All that they could have done was ensure that it would break down somewhere.'

'But somewhere between Atbara and Wadi Halfa,' said Mr Nicholson, 'and roughly halfway.'

'On the railway line,' said the Chief Engineer. 'So they would know where to look.'

'They couldn't have predicted the *haboob*,' said Mr Nicholson, 'but once they had heard about it, they would know roughly where to look.'

'Do you have any idea of where they might be making for?' asked the Chief Engineer. 'Because if you have, I might be able to help. I've got a buggy about to go back to Halfa for spares. If you could tell me who to send it to, I could get a telegraph message sent from Halfa.'

'Try Crockhart-Mackenzie,' said Owen. 'At Atbara.'

Now that the rescue engine had arrived, the mood among the passengers had brightened. The rescue train had brought extra supplies of food and water and almost everyone settled down to a good breakfast. As a precaution, Mr Nicholson had been holding back on the distribution of reserve rations, but now he felt he could reduce them.

Mohammed, the Nicholsons' cook, allowed two eggs for each person at breakfast. That was normal when they went away in the saloon but since the *haboob* he had been holding off. Now everything was back to normal and Jamie, who fancied that he had been conscious of a gap in his stomach, was a man again.

The ache in his stomach had, however, been replaced by another anxiety. What would happen when they got to Wadi Halfa? His father had talked about possibly needing to go on to Cairo to talk to the people there about the effects of the *haboob*. They had *haboobs* all the time in the Sudan but this had been an unusually severe one. It had, Jamie had overheard the Chief Engineer saying, really tested their defences. Some shortcomings had been found and Jamie's father had half-suggested that it might be necessary for him to go on to Cairo to talk about them to the people there.

In which case, what would become of him? Would he be sent off by the next train back to Atbara? Or would he be allowed to go on with his father to Cairo? Jamie had been to Cairo once or twice but never for long enough to really get a look at the place. Aisha had told him there were lots of things to see. Besides, of course, there was what Aisha referred to as 'their project'. Jamie had hoped that she would forget all about that the nearer they got to Cairo. Unfortunately that didn't seem to be happening. Ever since breakfast she had been sitting on the steps of her own saloon waiting for the Pasha to leave the Royal Saloon so that she could go in. She wanted to have another word with Leila. She thought it outrageous to keep an educated woman so closed in – well, perhaps not very educated, but certainly privileged, and privilege, so her head mistress at school insisted, carried with it responsibilities. One of them was to make the most of your opportunities. That was something her mother and father were always telling her, although in her mother's case that seemed mainly to consist of lying on the beach at Alexandria or having a cream cake at Groppi's. Aisha's own ambitions extended much further.

But what about Leila? She was certainly in a privileged position, and what was she doing with it? Sticking around indoors all day? Either in the saloon, or in the hotel at Khartoum, or back in Cairo, in the Pasha's house there. All she was doing was exchanging one prison for another. The modern age had not yet reached either her or the Pasha, it seemed. They were still living in the harem age. But that was past, done with. Aisha felt that she owed it to Leila to prise her out of backwardness and into the great modern world of opportunity and activity. Although, now she came to think of it, there wasn't enough of either for bright sixth-form girls in Egypt just at the moment. However, a start could be made, and start was exactly what Leila was not doing. She needed someone to get behind her and give her a push.

So Aisha sat on the steps of her saloon and waited for the door to open and the Pasha to come out so that she could go in and start pushing.

And then, miraculously, the door opened and the Pasha did come out.

Owen, seeing the engineers at work, was impressed. They got on with it. Getting on with it was not a notable feature of Egyptian life. And this was true not – as was commonly said by visiting Europeans – just of native Egyptians. Egypt was a mixture of Italians, Greeks, Jews and Levantines in general, and although they certainly injected energy into Egyptian society, somehow a lot of that energy ebbed away into the sand. On the whole they didn't get on with it. And this was true of the English also. Or most of them. Not, he thought, of the men who built the dams or the ports or the railways. They were different. They got on with it.

Why weren't there more Egyptian engineers? Egyptians like his friend Mahmoud, or like Aisha's father, Yasin, were certainly bright enough. It was just that their talent did not go with engineering. It went with law or the offices. Into the Parquet or the great bureaucracy which Egypt had inherited from the Ottomans, refined by the French and the British. Owen supposed that young Egyptians saw that this was where the power lay and made their career choices accordingly. Plus, of course, the fact that Arab culture was so heavily a verbal, indeed, literary one. Education was in words. The children you saw with their slates were learning linguistic things. Mostly they were religious things as well. Each child learned to recite the Koran. And when they went to university – to, say, the great University of Al-Azhar – what they were learning was theology.

It did Egypt no good, he thought. But then, he told himself, wasn't that to think in too Western a way? If words and theology were what they wanted, why shouldn't they have them?

The trouble was, they wanted other things as well. Things that the developed world had. Cars and lights and telephone, mechanical things, things not built with words but with engineering.

Which was why Owen was thinking now about the railway and about Atbara, the big railway junction of the Sudan. Atbara, home to the railway workshops and the new men who repaired the trains and maintained the track. And who, perhaps, thought differently from the Egyptians of the past. And among them men whose political understanding and ambition were different from those of Egyptians of the past. Men who thought less in terms of religion and more in terms of the social organisations that went with industrial things – of unions, perhaps, and industrial action as a means of political goals; of, perhaps, filing through a railway engine coupling at a place and a time which corresponded to political and social goals.

The Pasha came across the sand to speak to Owen. He hesitated for a moment before speaking.

'So, this will soon be over,' he said.

'Yes.'

He hesitated again. 'I would never have believed it,' he said. 'That so much unpleasantness could come about from a simple trip into the provinces.'

The Sudan was not, in fact, one of Egypt's provinces, but Owen let it stand. It was what many Egyptians believed, especially among the ruling class. The British had taken the Sudan from them; whereas, actually, the Sudanese had taken themselves some years before, when the self-proclaimed Mahdi, the religious leader, had risen out of nowhere to expel the Egyptians and seize control for the Sudanese themselves. The British had later re-conquered the Sudan and since then the country had been governed jointly, as a condominium, by Britain and Egypt.

That was the formal, legal position. In practice, the Sudan was governed by Britain, who appointed its Governor-General and ran the country through District Commissioners, independently of Egypt. Not, of course, completely independently. Some things were administered in common, necessarily, among them the railways.

Educated Egyptians, however, tended to look down on the Sudan. They regarded it as backward – indeed, often, barbarous. It lacked Cairo's comforts. And it was far too hot. And had unpleasant things like sandstorms.

'I shall not be coming here again,' declared the Pasha. 'I would not have come here in the first place, if the Khedive had not commanded.'

'It was your Sudanese connections that influenced him, I expect,' said Owen.

'Best forgotten about,' said the Pasha. 'And that is what I have always done: forget about them. But the Khedive thought they would be useful.'

'And have they turned out to be?' asked Owen.

'No. Decidedly the reverse. They dragged me in. That unfortunate man who was eaten by a crocodile!'

'Well, I don't know, Pasha. Wasn't it fortunate that there was someone like yourself who could give him some dignity at the end?'

'Of course, there *is* that. But did he deserve it? Wasn't he, as all those railway people are, a trouble-maker? He certainly made trouble for me!'

'Really? How was that?'

'The Khedive had entrusted me with some important business and this man was proving difficult. A trouble-maker, as I said. But then, all these railwaymen are!'

'This was to do with the railways, was it?'

'It was. But, Mamur Zapt, you will not trick me into saying more!'

'Pasha, I wouldn't dream of it! Not,' he laughed, 'with such a wily and experienced man as yourself.'

'Two wily men together,' said the Pasha. 'Let us leave it at that!'

Unfortunately, of course, he couldn't. 'I have never understood railways,' he complained. 'These great, mechanical things! Engineers! The bewildering modern world thrusting its snout in! The Khedive should have sent someone else!'

'But there were your connections . . .'

'A fat lot of good they turned out to be! It sounded so simple in Cairo! But on the ground, let me tell you, it is nothing like so simple. And that is what I shall tell the Khedive.'

He reconsidered. 'Perhaps.'

'I wonder, Pasha, if I can be of some help here. I shall be seeing the Khedive myself. I can underline, if you wish, the point about things not being so simple on the ground. Sandstorms, theft, that sort of thing . . .'

'That would be most kind!' said the Pasha, plainly relieved.

'Difficulties are not always appreciated.'

'They are not!' said the Pasha fervently.

SEVEN

Owen knew that the Pasha was feeling uneasy. That was why he had come to talk with him. And Owen was feeling not uneasy but dissatisfied with himself. He had done all that he was supposed to do. He had protected the Pasha, so far, but there was still the matter of the missing briefcase. That had not been part of his mission. But he knew what was expected of him. Besides, the briefcase had been stolen from under his very nose. As far as he was concerned, there was unfinished business.

And there was also unfinished business in another sense. Something was going on in the workshops at Atbara, something to do with the railways. And it was important enough for a man to be killed over it. *If* he had been killed over it. Certainly it seemed that a Pasha had been attacked over it. That was no light matter. Pashas were still important people in Egypt and this one particularly. He had connections with the Royal Court. He had been sent on a mission by the Khedive himself. It was easy for English people to belittle the Khedive, but those in the know, those who really held sway in

Egypt, knew that preserving the delicate balance of power in Egypt's government was very important, and part of this was preserving the Khedive's self-respect. There were fictions that had to be guarded.

One of these was that the Khedive and his interests were paramount, and Owen, like the other senior British officials in Egypt, went out of his way to always give the impression that this was so. The Khedive had appointed him. The Mamur Zapt was the Khedive's man. (He was also, of course, the Consul-General's man, but that was beside the point; he resolved these difficulties by being, or so he liked to tell himself, his own man.) An attack on a Royal Pasha was an attack on the Khedive and had to be dealt with accordingly. More broadly, an attack on the Khedive was an attack on the government and had to be put down.

Owen was clear where his duty lay. But, as generally in Egypt, things were not quite so clear. The Khedive was up to something. The attack on the Pasha was part of that. And whatever was going on, it was happening independently of the British. The Consul-General didn't like that. And nor did Owen, who prided himself that nothing went on in Egypt without his knowing about it.

The contents of the briefcase would, perhaps, reveal what was going on, if they could be recovered. They might be yet. But it looked as if it was something to do with the railways. The railways, British-financed and British-run, were a significant British interest in Egypt. He would have to look into it.

But how could he look into it when he was in Cairo and the briefcase and its contents were somewhere in the Sudan?

It was a pity that he was going back to Cairo. The roots of this business seemed to lie in the Sudan, either in Atbara or in Khartoum where that important meeting had taken place. That was where the investigation had to start. If he couldn't do it himself, he would have to send somebody. But who?

Georgiades was the obvious man. In some respects but not in others. He was a city man, not a desert man; a Cairo man through and through. Had he ever been out of Cairo? Owen doubted it. And he would hate it. The Sudan was not his kind of country. He lived for the crowded little back streets of Cairo, the gatherings round the street trays that served as restaurants for the humbler people of Cairo, the back-chat, the rumour, the story-telling (Georgiades was a master storyteller himself), the dark-veiled women carrying baskets of vegetables on their heads, the donkey-boys competing with them for space. The camel-men leading their camels heaped with great piles of berseem clover, forage for the donkeys and the camels that swayed through the narrow streets blocking up the traffic of all. The underworld of Cairo, that was where Georgiades thrived. Would he thrive as well in the workshops of Atbara?

Possibly not. But with his gift for wheedling his way into the confidence of every passer-by he would soon tap his way into the exchanges of the workers in the Atbara workshops. And the fact that he was a Greek wouldn't tell against him. The Sudan, like Egypt, was full of Greeks. They ran most of the stores, and Georgiades would soon make himself at home there. The stores were where the railway workers went after the day's work was done, and where their wives had been earlier to shop for food. Yes, Georgiades it would have to be.

The main engine was now being coupled up to the rescue engine. The last workman crawled out from underneath. He thought it would last until they got to Wadi Halfa.

The passengers were climbing back into their carriages. Aisha appeared beside Jamie.

'Find out where you will be staying in Cairo,' she whispered. 'You can tell me at Halfa.'

Then she was gone. In fact, Jamie wondered if he would ever see her again. He thought that Mr Nicholson would probably go back to Atbara after they had arrived at Halfa and take Jamie with him. All the same, he ought to try.

Mr Nicholson was standing talking to the Mamur Zapt beside the engine. 'How's it going, Dad?'

'We should be off in a couple of minutes.'

'That rescue engine will take us all the way?'

'I hope so.'

'Backwards?'

'If need be. These rescue engines are very powerful. But there are bypasses between here and Wadi Halfa and they may be able to switch round.'

'Dad, when we get to Halfa . . .'

'Yes?'

'Are you going on to Cairo?'

'Probably.'

'And will you take me with you?'

'Why not? It would only be for a couple of days.'

'I would like to see Cairo.'

'You should, perhaps, while you've got the chance.'

Because after that Jamie would be going to school. In England. And Aisha? Perhaps in France. Although Jamie was beginning to have doubts now about some of the things she said. She seemed to have difficulty in distinguishing between what she would like to do and what she was *likely* to do. Maybe Paris was another of her speculative fantasies. Perhaps she wasn't going to Paris at all. Perhaps she would stay in Cairo. In which case there was a chance that he might see her again.

The truth was that she would be older and probably wearing a veil. In which case, even if he saw her, how would he know that it was her?

He had a sneaking suspicion that if they did meet – at Groppi's, perhaps, or Andalaft's – she would find some way of declaring her identity.

The rescue engine blew its whistle and then took the strain. The last passengers hurried back on board, including the Mamur Zapt and Jamie. Mr Nicholson remained by the engine looking down at the coupling. The link tightened again and the carriages began to respond. The driver raised his hand and let it fall and gradually the train began to gather momentum. Mr Nicholson swung himself up and through the door but remained standing in the doorway. The train hiccoughed at first but then started to run smoothly. Only then did Jamie's father come right inside.

He sat down opposite Jamie and he and the Mamur Zapt began talking. After a chat the Mamur Zapt got up and went off. Jamie's father began to make notes.

Jamie remained by the window watching the desert slip by. Mostly it was sand and scrub, but from time to time they passed a group of *tukuls*, little conical huts thatched with straw, often clustered around a *sakia* or water wheel, pulled by an ox. Once they came upon thorn trees and as the train passed a flock of weaver birds flew up. There was a weaver bird in Jamie's garden at Atbara. It had made its nest in the archway leading down to the river and sometimes you saw the weaver bird going in and out.

Once, he had seen a crocodile on the other side of the river, looking like a log but surprisingly yellow. Its jaws were open and a little bird, not a weaver, was picking at its teeth. Jamie watched for some time to see if the crocodile would close its jaws, but it didn't.

There were no birds now, as he looked out, and no *tukuls* either. There was just sand. But from time to time, wavering on the sand, there was a clear, vivid mirage. Jamie watched them come and go. But then the light began to change, it grew darker and he could no longer see outside the carriage.

At some point early in the morning, the train pulled into Wadi Halfa. Although it was still only half-light, workmen began to cluster round the engine. They uncoupled the damaged engine from the rest of the train and the rescue engine pulled it away. Shortly afterwards, a new engine backed along the track towards them. In an amazingly short time, before the sun was properly up, the train was ready to continue its journey.

Yasin al-Jawad had gone into the Royal Saloon to talk to the Pasha, and a little later came out and walked along the platform. There was a sort of platform at Halfa.

Aisha seized the opportunity to go in to see Leila. The bodyguard had got used to her now and made no difficulty. He was in any case walking along the platform behind the Pasha. The Pasha's cook, too, had got out of the saloon and gone along to the stores in search of the right delicacies.

Mr Nicholson was talking to the station staff about not removing his saloon. He wanted it to go on to Cairo.

Jamie was at a loose end. He didn't want to move too far from his father in case he changed his mind and decided to send him back to Atbara; and he didn't want to miss possibly his last chance of seeing Aisha.

Eventually she climbed down the steps of the Royal Saloon and came towards him.

'I've found out where the Pasha's home is,' she said. 'It's near the Bab-es-Zuweyla. You know where that is?'

'No,' said Jamie.

'It's by the Bazaar of the Tentmakers. You will see the minarets.'

'How will I know it's that gate?'

'You will see the weapons of the Afrit giant high up on its sides. And you will see the rags stuck to its door nails by those with sick children. Why they put them there I don't know. But you can't miss them, it's such a mess. You turn right there and the Pasha's house is on the left. She says I can call on her.'

'I don't think that means me, too,' said Jamie hesitantly.

'I want to get her out of the house,' said Aisha confidently. 'I'll suggest we go for a walk or something.'

'What about that bodyguard?'

'When he's off with the Pasha somewhere.'

Her father reappeared with the Pasha.

'I'd better get back. See you tomorrow.'

'It cannot be tomorrow. We won't get to Cairo till tomorrow evening.'

'The day after, then. I'll send you a message. Where will you be staying?'

'At the Railway Rest House. It's not very glamorous but it's where officials usually stay.'

'We stay at a place near the Palace. Off Abdin Square. It's very poky but it's handy for the Palace if he's needed. Which is hardly ever. But he's got to be there in case he is needed. Anyway, it gives him a chance to talk to his friends. They all hang around there. Usually in one of the coffee shops. My father says he's gone off coffee. But he has to be there or he'll miss out on what's being said. My mother hates it. That's why she's away so much. She would prefer to live in Alexandria. But I think that's merely exchanging one lot of gossiping for another. She wants me to move down there with her. But I think I prefer my father's gossiping to hers. At least it's about something. But he doesn't let me in on it much.'

Jamie was astounded. It didn't sound at all like what went on in Atbara. He didn't think he would like it much.

Aisha said she didn't like it much either. She said she rather envied Jamie going away to school.

Jamie wasn't so sure. Especially now that his move to school in England was coming closer. He wouldn't admit it but he felt nervous at the prospect. He had spent all his life up to now in the Sudan. The schools at Atbara and Khartoum were not that good but at least you knew where you were. What would a school in England be like? His father said he would enjoy it. But Pollock said that the great thing about school was that it didn't go on forever. You knew that it would end sometime.

Aisha said that it was all very well for boys because when it ended they would go on to a job. But girls had to marry. Their parents would fix it up. And the prospect of being married to some fat Pasha years older than herself didn't please her at all. She would run away, she said.

And that's what she was trying to get Leila to do. In her own interest. Which was a phrase she had picked up from her mother and didn't like the sound of.

The station at Cairo, the Gare Pont Limoun, was huge, much bigger even than the one at Khartoum. And all the signs were in French. This was a blow to Jamie, who had never taken his French lessons seriously. You would have thought that at least some of the signs would be in English but they were either in French or in Arabic. But Jamie had difficulties with Arabic writing. Spoken Arabic he could manage, up to a point. But these bizarre squiggles, he struggled with.

And the language being spoken, at least around the station, was also French. His father said that was because an earlier Khedive had been very keen on France, especially after the British had moved in, and that the posh hotels were all French. And in the office they went to they spoke French. What was the point of winning, thought Jamie, if then you gave it all away and used the other side's language instead of your own?

He wondered if Aisha spoke French. She probably did, and that was why she wanted to go to Paris. Already she seemed to have moved further away from him.

Fortunately at the Railway Rest House they spoke English. Jamie had no difficulty there.

Owen went straight to his office at the Bab el Khalk. His desk was piled high with papers and the official clerk smiled at him maliciously. Nikos was a Copt and heir to two thousand years of bureaucratic tradition. Conquerors – the Pharaohs, the Romans, the Arabs, the French, the British – came and went but the man in the office went on forever. The Copts were the real rulers of Egypt. Nikos, Owen's official clerk, ran his office and, probably, Egypt as well. He didn't approve of Owen's going away and showed his disapproval by erecting paper mountains. Owen pushed the piles aside.

'Get me Georgiades,' he said.

If Nikos was the pulsing (or perhaps not-so-pulsing) brain of the Mamur Zapt's office, Georgiades was its fat, podgy feet. He was a Greek. The Greeks had been in Egypt nearly as long as the Copts. They ran all the shops and quite a few of the businesses. The British might think they did, but the Greeks and the Copts knew better. Between them they controlled the economy. Always as Number Two, of course. They didn't believe in putting their heads up over the parapet and were content for the unsophisticated English to do that. That way they were the ones who got hit, when brickbats were flying.

Owen looked at the papers before him. They were arranged in neat piles awaiting his perusal. He turned over the pile which had been furthest from him and looked at the paper that had been on the bottom.

Nikos was pained. 'The ones on the top, too, are important.'

'But not as important as the ones on the bottom,' said Owen, who had learned a lot about the wiles of bureaucracy in his time in Egypt.

While he was looking at them, Georgiades padded into the room. Georgiades, as his wife frequently pointed out to him, was carrying too much weight. It slowed him down as he made his way through the Cairo streets: but this, he pointed back, was actually an asset. As he wandered around he heard things. His sympathetic brown eyes invited confidences, and the confidences frequently found their way into Nikos's piles of paper. Georgiades gathered intelligence; Nikos used it. Or so he claimed. And Owen? Owen merely eavesdropped, they both claimed.

'I was thinking of a move for you,' he told Georgiades.

'No, thanks,' said Georgiades, who did not like movement, especially when it was hot.

'I need something done in the Sudan.'

Beginning to be seriously alarmed, Georgiades said, 'Isn't it all desert?'

'Not all,' said Owen. 'The bit where you'll be isn't.'

'It doesn't sound like it's for me,' said Georgiades.

'It's just the thing for you,' countered Owen. 'You could go as a Greek.'

'I have children,' said Georgiades.

'You wouldn't be away for long.'

Georgiades shuddered. 'Heat? Sand? The emptiness?'

'The peace,' said Owen. 'The great still stillness.'

'No thanks. It really doesn't sound like me.'

'You can catch the train this evening.'

'My wife! My children—'

'Rosa will be glad to get rid of you. And you can buy things for the children.'

'Rosa buys all the things for the children. I haven't any money, since you pay me so badly.'

'Actually,' said Owen, 'I pay all the money to your wife, since you are so bad with it. And there will be an allowance for living away from home.'

'What would be the point? It's a seriously Muslim country and they don't approve of alcohol.'

'But the British are there too. And they do approve of alcohol. Besides, I was thinking of you as spending a lot of your time in the Greek shops. Where you could give everybody your advice. You'd like that, wouldn't you?'

Owen explained what was needed, which did not make Georgiades any happier.

As Jamie was walking along someone took him confidently by the hand and when he looked down he was very surprised to see that it was a monkey. Behind him stood a grinning Arab.

'He very good monkey,' said the Arab. 'He want to say goodbye to you.'

Jamie took this to mean hallo and shook the monkey's hand warmly. It was wearing red flannel trousers.

'American lady give,' said the master. 'No like see no trousers.'

'Give him ten milliemes,' directed Jamie's father. 'No more, or there'll be hundreds round us.'

Jamie did as he was told; the monkey seized the money and went off. Not very far, because its master grabbed it, took the money and gave it a cuff. Then he pulled it back to its position, which was beside a small Sardinian donkey, also dressed in fine robes but with the addition of various small drums and other accoutrements. The monkey, a large dog-faced baboon, leapt back up on the donkey's shoulders and rode off.

Another one took its place. Jamie's father waved it away.

'The only interesting thing about them,' he said, 'is that you see pictures of them in the tombs.'

They were passing a hotel. Along its front was a large veranda on which people were sitting. Some of them were drinking coffee and one was smoking from a large bubble pipe. One end of it consisted of a gourd containing water, from which a tube led up to the smoker's mouth. The gourd held water and you could hear it bubbling. There was a railing along the front of the verandah and tied to it were some donkeys, which his father said were for hire, 'like taxis'.

Jamie contemplated taking a taxi.

'Another time,' said his father, looking at his watch.

Right next to the donkeys were some snake-charmers. The snakes were cobras about seven feet long and they stayed in baskets mostly, which was as well, because when they were charmed out of their baskets they took up most of the pavement. From time to time a policeman came and moved them on. However they didn't seem to be bothered when a man drove four or five turkeys along the pavement on the way to the hotel's kitchen.

There were also lots of people selling things – beads and scarab beetles made of glazed earthenware, and little blue or green statues of the gods. One had an ape's head just like the baboon that had held his hand.

There were so many things to look at that Jamie found it hard to take them all in. It wasn't like this in Atbara or Khartoum. And then he saw the acrobats in their skin-coloured tights, turning cart-wheels. Jamie could do a cartwheel, but not like this. He could have watched them for ages.

His father, however, took him into the shop with things hanging from the ceiling and which smelled overpoweringly of leather. He bought him a little pocket diary. That was very nice but Jamie already had one. This one, though, had a map of Cairo on its inside cover.

'Handy if you get lost,' said his father. 'This is where we are, and this is where our rest house is. You can go off on your own, provided you stick to the main streets. Meet here for lunch at two o'clock.'

Late in the morning Owen was sitting in his office, the great fan turning above him. On the desk in front of him was an earthenware jug covered in a damp towel. The jug contained drinking water, kept cool by the wet towel placed over it. At intervals a boy came round the offices carrying a bucket of water with ice in it. The boy dipped the towel in the bucket, squeezed it out, and replaced it over the earthenware vase. As it dried it had a cooling effect on the water. You needed that because as the morning wore on the heat in the offices built up. There were shutters on the windows, which helped to keep the office dark and cool, and there was the huge fan overhead, but that served more to move the heat around rather than disperse it.

Where Owen rested his forearm on the desk while he was reading his papers a pool of sweat soon gathered, but it dried again before his eyes. He kept the top of his tunic unbuttoned and from time to time dried around his neck with a handkerchief. That soon was sodden. When the boy came round with the bucket, Owen dipped his handkerchief in. The iced water refreshed him, but only for a moment.

Nikos came in with a message from Crockhart-Mackenzie. It had been telegraphed from Atbara that morning. It read:

Two Hadendoa picked up at six o'clock this morning. I am holding both of them, plus a briefcase I think you maybe are interested in. Shall I send it on?

'Send this message back,' said Owen: 'Well done. Yes, please.'

He sat there thinking for a moment and then put on his fez and went out.

He might have taken one of the new trams but preferred to walk. It gave him more time to think. Besides, he relished being back in Cairo. Although it was hot, it was nothing like as hot as in the Sudan. If he had been still in Atbara he might have considered wearing a sun helmet. Here, a fez was enough and cooler round his head. The fez showed people he was not a tourist and perhaps persuaded them not to try it on with him.

Ahead of him he could see the mighty form of the Bab-es-Zuweyla, with the weapons of the Afrit giant high on its sides, and the crowd of beggars in the shade beneath. When he got to it he turned right down a little alley, which gave him access to a different world. Instead of the press of people there was just a forage donkey and a bread-seller coming towards him. The forage donkey was heaped high with clover, mostly for the street animals, and the bread-seller had a huge tray on his head equally high with flat loaves. In front of him was a beautiful old fountain house, with carved stonework, lattice-like in its delicacy. On either side were traditional old Arab houses with meshrebiya windows which let the air in and kept viewers out. Presumably they were harem windows.

One of the houses was the one he was looking for. It had a heavy wooden door. He hammered on it and asked for the Pasha.

The Pasha was not looking his best. Owen at first put this down to Leila. It occurred to him for the first time that the Pasha was much older than she was. However, when they started talking he realized that the Pasha had other things on his mind.

They talked in the Pasha's *mandarah*, or reception room, which was about thirty feet long and had a sunken fountain. Around its sides was a long bench for the broad-cushioned seats of the women of the harem. Overhead, letting in the light and air, were fine meshrebiya oriels. Scattered around the room were large, soft, bright-coloured cushions and some fine brass tables.

At one end was a long, low couch, to which the Pasha led him.

'You will be pleased to know, Pasha, that I bring some good news.'

'You do?' said the Pasha, the creases of his brow beginning to smooth out.

'Your briefcase has been recovered.'

'Recovered? But that is splendid news, Captain Owen, and . . . and a tribute to your fine work!'

'More a tribute to modern technology, I'm afraid.'

He told the Pasha about the use they had made of the telegraph system.

'And the rascals were seized?'

'They were indeed.'

'I hope you will punish them severely.'

'Well, no.'

'No?'

'Or, rather, not at once. I want to speak to them myself first. And find out what and who lies behind this.'

'Very wise, no doubt, Mamur Zapt. But their transgression must not be lost sight of just because of foolish liberal considerations.'

'It won't be, Pasha, I assure you.'

'Good. Good. And when it happens, I want to see it.'

'Meanwhile, Pasha, there is just another consideration. Have you spoken to the Khedive yet about the theft?'

'Well, well, as a matter of fact, not yet. A little fatigued after the journey, you know. Tomorrow, perhaps. Yes, tomorrow.'

His eyes had never seemed so pouchy.

'I was wondering,' said Owen. 'Need it be at all?'

'You . . . you mean . . .?'

'It is a small part of a mission which, I am sure the Khedive will agree, had been completed most satisfactorily.'

'But . . .'

'If you don't tell him, I won't tell him.'

The pouches below the Pasha's eyes fell away miraculously. 'You're – you're quite sure?'

'We are old friends, are we not?'

'Oh, we certainly are!' said the Pasha, looking younger by the minute.

As Owen left the house, he found himself accosted.

'Why, it's Aisha, isn't it?'

You could never quite tell under those veils.

'It certainly is!' said Aisha crossly. Her mother had insisted that she return to respectability.

'What brings you here? Are you going to call in on Leila?'

'No, no. Not just now. Later, perhaps.'

'Give her my regards.'

'Gladly. But, actually she is not the one I wished to see.'

'Oh?'

'I wished to see you. You should really keep a servant, Captain Owen. When I inquired at your house, there was no one there who could tell me where you were.'

'Sometimes that is an advantage.'

'I do see that. Especially if you are Mamur Zapt. But is it efficient?'

'Well . . .'

'I suppose it depends on what you're after,' said Aisha, relenting. 'One thing you don't want is crowds of supplicants outside your gate. Which was the situation, my father tells me, with the previous Mamur Zapt.'

'Different Mamur Zapts do things in different ways.'

'Quite so. And you like to do things undercover. Or, as my father says, underhand.'

'Well, I'm not sure I would put it quite like—'

'I can see it is much more efficient. But is it *transparent*, Captain Owen? And oughtn't government to be transparent? I can see that if you are the British ruling illegally in Egypt, you might not wish for that. My father's newspapers might make much of that but, on the whole, I am in favour of effectiveness.'

'That is, actually, what I strive for.'

'Me, too,' said Aisha. 'I believe in going straight to the person who has power. That is why I have come to you. I need your help, Mamur Zapt.'

'If I can help you, I will do so willingly. But you should realize, Aisha, that I may have rather less power than you think.'

'All I want is an introduction to your wife.'

'My wife?'

'The Lady Zeinab. Is she not your wife? Well, never mind, Captain Owen. I am broadminded about such things. I just wanted to speak to her, that's all.'

'Cannot you go to her directly yourself?'

'No. Women don't do that sort of thing in Cairo. And schoolgirls even less so. My father says I am too pushy. Do you think I am too pushy, Captain Owen?'

'Well . . .'

'Possibly I am,' Aisha admitted. 'But it is hard to get anywhere in Egypt if you're a schoolgirl and you're not pushy. People don't take any notice of you.'

'I am sure they'll take notice of *you*, Aisha!'

'There you are: you *do* think I'm too pushy!'

'I will speak to Zeinab with pleasure. I am sure she will be willing to talk to you. Why don't you drop in one afternoon? Afternoon is a good time because she is more likely to be in. She usually likes to have a rest then.'

'Oh, yes. The baby.'

'The baby? Look . . .'

'You can hardly expect to keep it a secret. The whole of Cairo is waiting eagerly. When I say the whole of Cairo, I mean the women of Cairo. You won't believe how much interest they take in such things, Captain Owen. Well, I suppose they don't have much else to think about. Me, I can take babies or leave them. Although, of course,' she added hurriedly, 'in the Lady Zeinab's case . . .'

Owen laughed. 'She will be glad to see you, I'm sure.'

'And I'll try not to be too pushy. But, you see, the Lady Zeinab is a person we greatly admire. All the sixth form, that is. She is someone who has made an independent life for herself. Not only that, she has placed herself in a position of power. Right in the heart of power, you might say. It's the only way if you're a woman, believe me, Captain Owen. We've talked about it a lot at school, and we've agreed that the only way a woman can get anywhere in Egypt is to marry a rich man. Of course, that's not the only consideration: some men you wouldn't marry no matter how rich they were. But we all agree that this is the right strategy.'

'I've met men like you!'

'It's not just men who think like that, it's women, too.'

'Isn't there a snag here? You'd have to get your parents to agree.'

'Oh, they'd agree, all right!'

'And do you have anyone particularly in mind for yourself?'

'Not yet. But I will. Unless I decide not to go down that route. I mean, it's a bit pathetic hitching yourself to a man's wagon to get on, isn't it? I would prefer to get there by myself. Actually, that is one of the things I want to talk to the Lady Zeinab about.'

Owen talked to his wife about Aisha later that evening. 'She scares the wits out of me,' he said to Zeinab.

Zeinab laughed. 'I look forward to meeting her,' she said.

The train from the south had just come in.

'Package for the Mamur Zapt!' someone shouted.

Owen went across.

A burly man was carrying a large package. Another man, equally burly, was standing beside him. Crockhart-Mackenzie was taking no chances.

'For me, I think,' said Owen.

The train was in fact the one which would shortly take Georgiades down to Atbara and the Greek was already waiting on the platform.

Owen appeared beside him. 'A few words before you go,' he said.

The Pont Limoun terminus was not far from the Bab-es-Zuweyla and even closer was the Bab-al-Khalk, where Owen's office was. He called in there before going on to the Bab-es-Zuweyla, where he had arranged to meet the Pasha.

The Pasha was already standing anxiously by the massive mina-
reted towers.

'Is everything . . . all right, Mamur Zapt?' he said worriedly.

'Everything is perfect, Pasha,' said Owen reassuringly.

He gave him the package. The Pasha clutched it to his heart.

'You should have no difficulty with the Khedive now, Pasha.'

'I hope not!' said the Pasha fervently.

'If you like I will walk with you to the Palace,' Owen offered.

'That would be most kind!' said the Pasha. 'We wouldn't want
anything to go wrong at this late stage.'

'Indeed not!'

'It *is* a responsibility, you know. The Khedive should have given
an escort from the start. Then I wouldn't have been so dreadfully
assaulted. When I took it on, I didn't realize there was a possibility
of being actually assaulted!'

'I am sure the Khedive didn't think that either. But he knew he
could rely on you whatever the circumstances.'

'You think so?'

'Certainly!'

'Well, perhaps you are right,' said the Pasha, a little pleased and
very relieved.

EIGHT

Georgiades had hardly ever been on a long train journey
before, and the journey from Cairo to Atbara, way down
in the Sudan, was certainly a long one. He sat in his
corner, next to the tinted window protecting his eyes against the
glare, and watched the Egyptian countryside go by. Georgiades
was an entirely urban man. The longest journey that he had ever
made in his life was down to Alexandria. Looking now through
his window at Egypt unfolding beside him he thought that outside
Cairo there was a lot of nothing. At first they travelled beside the
Nile. Well, there was the Nile in Cairo, too, so he did not feel
initially that the world's frame had suddenly been wrenched out
of joint. Feluccas crept by on the water; fellahin working by the
fields straightened their backs and looked at him. No doubt

somewhere in the background a sageeyah was creaking peacefully. For a time he felt at home.

But then the palm trees alongside the river disappeared and the train ran inland for a spell and he was plunged into the great open space of the desert. Georgiades was not used to desert. Even looking at it made him uncomfortable. Where were the people, the houses, the bustle of life? Was it all like this – empty? Did the world go on forever, empty? Georgiades began to miss his home. At home now Rosa would be getting Andreas ready for school, picking up Daphnis to put her in the buggy. Georgiades suddenly had an achingly hollow feeling.

Sometimes when Rosa left the house late, and for some reason Georgiades was late too – all right, there was a reason, he just didn't like to take leave of his children – they met the family of Owen's Parquet friend, Mahmoud. Rosa and Aisha – Mahmoud's Aisha – got along very well and had been known to combine the families on the way to the infant schools while one of them dashed off to make a purchase somewhere. On one occasion they had both dashed off, leaving Georgiades to marshal the troops all by himself. It had made him apprehensive but also proud. Having married late in life Georgiades had taken to it like a duck to water and now saw himself very much a family man.

And now he was going away and wouldn't see them for a long time – well, a couple of weeks, perhaps – and he felt bereft. And what was all this Atbara stuff about? Trains, Owen had told him. It wasn't that Georgiades didn't believe in trains, they were a fact of life, in the way that camels were. But there was a difference between trains and camels: trains were part of the modern life in a way that camels weren't. They were part of that big life out beyond the desert, bigger even than Athens and Thessalonica, a world which everyone told him was his homeland but which Georgiades didn't know.

There were Greeks, though, everywhere. There were Greeks in Atbara – not many but they were prominent. The Greeks did well for themselves. They made money. Not Georgiades, of course, but the big ones, whose names were on the lips of the Greek world community. He did not deceive himself; he was never going to be one of them. But Rosa might be. Always she was showing signs of a disquieting talent for business and for finance. The business, Georgiades could understand; the finance terrified him. And yet Rosa seemed quite at home with it.

Well, that was one consolation anyway. If anything should happen to him while he was away in the Sudan, that cauldron of unholy lusts, she would take over and the children would be all right.

The train took a dart towards the river and now they were running alongside it again, and the feluccas were still moving gracefully towards the palm trees and Georgiades began to think about lunch.

Owen, as it happened, was also thinking about lunch. The meeting had already been going on for more than two hours, which was long by the Old Man's standards. They had had coffee before they started, they had had coffee about halfway through when the meeting had got sticky, and now the *suffragi* was bringing in a new pot. But what Owen felt he needed was something to eat. What with the train and the sandstorm and missing out on a few nights' sleep and now this meeting going on and on forever, his routines were badly disrupted.

The Consul-General was waiting for the Legal Secretary to appear. He felt that it was necessary to establish where they stood legally. This was not a straightforward matter because Egypt had several competing legal systems. There was the French-based ordinary system derived from the Napoleonic Code; there was the English-based system of commercial law; and, of course, there was the Muslim system of religious law to which the Khedive habitually turned when necessary. Another, and more important, complication was that international issues could be referred to a quite separate system of mixed tribunals where specialist judges weaved a way through the system known as the Capitulations, a set of treaties imposed on Egypt by foreign powers and now worked by all and sundry to the advantage of its different international claimants. Wily criminals, of whom there were legions in Cairo, flitted from one tribunal to another, invoking the different laws of different countries, changing their nationality all the time. The system was a nightmare for the British Consul-General, who was trying to make it work; and, of course, a gold-mine for the lawyers, who were trying to do just the opposite.

And now here was a case which fell squarely into the hotly disputed territory of the *tribunaux mixtes* (the cases were all conducted in French). Except that this fact was disputed by the British, who argued that it didn't. They had been listening to legal arguments all morning and now the Legal Secretary was coming in to decide the matter.

Owen knew what would happen. He would decide and everybody else would challenge the ruling and appeal the issue back to their own individual countries.

This was, naturally, the beginning, not the end, of the matter. In fact, there would be no end to the matter; it would rumble on into the never-never, which was where the lawyers, and the different countries, and the various criminals wanted it to be. Meanwhile, of course, the British would get on with it, leaving legalities and scruples aside but claiming that the issue required a temporary but practical solution. The potato, hot, would then be passed to the Mamur Zapt to sort out, a decision accepted by no one, least of all the Khedive, in whose name, allegedly, the decision was made.

Owen was happy with all this – he just wanted his lunch, and by now he was getting desperate.

The issue before them was the stolen briefcase, now recovered and restored to the Khedive, but the contents of which had been thoroughly examined by the Mamur Zapt on the way. A list of the contents lay before them.

The Khedive, it appeared, had been secretly negotiating with a foreign government to purchase rolling stock for the Egyptian (and Sudan) railway – a process greatly facilitated by the fact that it was being financed by the foreign power and no immediate exchange of money was required, except to the Khedive, who would receive a handsome backhander.

'Disgraceful!' said the Consul-General, referring not to the backhander but to the fact that it was all due to take place in an area which the British regarded as their backyard. 'We must put a stop to it.'

'We can't,' said the Legal Secretary, who had now joined them. 'There is nothing wrong with it in law. The Khedive is quite free to purchase goods from another country.'

'We'll see about that!' said the Consul-General.

'We can't. It's explicitly in the Treaties.'

'Can't we get round that?'

'That,' said the Legal Secretary, 'is the issue before us.'

'So what do you suggest?'

'In principle,' said the Legal Secretary, 'our hands are tied.'

'But in practice . . . ?' murmured Paul, the Consul-General's ADC, and a particular – and strategically well-placed – friend of Owen's.

'There would be insurmountable practical difficulties, we would say. I have been talking to Nicholson this morning. He says that there would be major problems of compatibility. The stock would be of a different gauge from the one that we currently work to.'

'Good one!' said the Consul-General.

'If you've got a system, you can't have parts of it working to a different system. The result would be chaos. There would be no interchangeability for a start. If a part broke down you couldn't count on its replacement. Take that train this week, caught in the sandstorm: we were able to switch engines. If the gauges were different, we wouldn't be able to.'

'Stuck there for ever!' the Consul-General exclaimed.

'That sort of thing could happen all the time everywhere.'

'Ridiculous!' said the Consul-General.

'Unless . . .' said the Legal Secretary.

'Unless?'

'Unless we changed the whole system to the new gauge.'

'The cost!' wailed the Consul-General.

'And, of course, it would mean letting other countries into the market. At the moment Britain supplies all the track, all the rolling stock, all parts, back-up, virtually everything. If we threw all that away, business wouldn't like it.'

'Nor would Whitehall! They'd go crazy!'

'And what about the press?'

The Consul-General shuddered. 'We'll have to put a stop to it,' he said.

'That's easy,' said the Legal Secretary. 'We simply require permits for all imports of essential railway goods; then don't issue them.'

'That's straightforward,' said the Consul-General. 'But how are we going to dress it up?'

'Grounds of practicality?' suggested Paul. 'We're committed to a system and can't change horses in midstream? Incidentally, what are the horses doing in midstream? Lost, I suspect.'

'Can't change the system halfway,' said the Consul-General. 'Everyone will understand that.'

'All practical people will,' said the Legal Secretary. 'But will politicians?'

'English ones will,' said the Consul-General. 'And stuff the rest!'

'What about the Khedive's backhander?' asked the Legal Secretary.

'We won't tell anyone about that,' said the Consul-General.

'Oh, but we will!' said Paul. 'It reinforces our case. Corruption, and all that. See what would happen if we let it out of English hands! That's what we'll say.'

'Exactly!' said the Consul-General. 'And no one can dispute that! Mamur-Zapt, were you going to say something?'

'Not directly on this, sir,' said Owen. 'But on related matters.'

'Well?'

'Who is the other player?'

'Other player?'

'The Khedive is one player. But who is the other player? The one who ordered the attack on the Pasha? The Khedive's agent?'

'Does it matter?'

'Yes. Obviously, he didn't know how things stood, and that's why he wanted to get hold of the briefcase. And wasn't unwilling to resort to violence to do that. But he didn't succeed. And so he'll try again.'

'It will be too late now.'

'But who is he? And what's he after? Because, you see, he might not be after the contracts himself; he might be trying to stop the contracts altogether.'

'I think I see what you mean,' said Paul. 'It's a third party who is opposed to the Khedive. And anti-us. He doesn't want the contracts to go through at all.'

Jamie's father had people to see and things to do, so he parked Jamie for the morning in the Cairo Zoo. The first thing he saw was a crocodile. It was young, only about seven feet long and waddled around in its pen. In front of it an Egyptian was standing shaking his fist at it.

'You ate my brother!' he was saying. 'And pretended he got drowned!'

'Did he really?' asked Jamie.

'No,' said his father, 'but perhaps a crocodile did.'

Jamie thought of the man who had been drowned stepping off – or falling off – the river's ledge back in Atbara. Did a crocodile get him, he wondered? Obviously not, for otherwise the people would have said. But it could have happened. The people had been worried about the possibility. He could imagine it – the crocodile sneaking along close to the bank, the Sudani splashing in the water, and suddenly, snap! And it would have him by the leg and the next moment be pulling him down and making off into the river, and that would be it for the poor chap.

The Egyptian moved away and Jamie went up to the railings and looked down on the young crocodile. It seemed really too small to do much damage. Jamie had imagined bigger crocodiles, huge ones. He knew they existed but mostly down south. They usually didn't come as high up as Atbara. But suppose there had been one when the man pushed him? It wasn't a nice thing to do.

He turned away. Close beside him, just standing there, was a secretary bird. It had a long horny bill and very long horny legs. It was a protected bird, which meant you couldn't kill it, or else you would be heavily fined. Secretary birds spent their time tracking down snakes and eating them. But it was hard for the zoo to find enough snakes so they had to give them something else to eat as well.

Jamie thought the bird did not look very much like a secretary. He knew what a secretary was because his father had one. But he didn't have a bill and horny legs. You couldn't really see them, it was true, because he usually wore trousers. And he was very tall, much taller than Jamie's father, even. That was because he was a Dinka. They were very tall and came from the south and weren't Arabs, unlike the people around here. They herded cows, so Mr Nicholson's secretary was an exception. Nor, as far as Jamie could tell, did he stand on one leg. That's what Dinkas did. They stood on one leg for ages. Jamie had tried it but it wasn't easy. You fell over after a bit.

Did the secretary bird stand on one leg? Jamie went back to have a look.

'Psstt,' said somebody right beside him. It was Aisha.

'What are you doing here?' he said, astonished. He had rather gathered that a zoo was the last place where you would find her.

'I'm casing the joint,' said Aisha.

'What?'

'It's an American expression my father uses sometimes. He picked it up from some book or other. It means sizing the place up.'

'Why would you be sizing up the zoo?'

'Because I want to bring Leila here,' said Aisha impatiently. 'Then we can get her away from the Pasha and set her free.'

'Couldn't you set her free somewhere else?'

'No. They only let her out with that loopy bodyguard. But in a place like this you could get away from him.'

'Isn't it a bit . . . out of the way? Why would she come here?'

'Because she wants to. She's said so. She wanted to go to the

zoo in Khartoum. She's a bit . . . limited in the things she wants to
do. Going to the big shops is the other. I have thought about luring
her away in Andalaft's but that wouldn't be easy. They have all
these shop assistants watching anything you do. I suppose it's in
case you steal something. But no one here thinks you're likely to
steal anything. I mean, if you stole a bird, a macaw, say, or something like that, it would squawk and people would wonder what
you were doing.'

'If you stole Leila away, wouldn't she squawk?'

'No, silly! She'd be doing it because she wanted to.'

'*Would* she want to?'

'I'm working on it. Actually, it's not proving as easy as I thought.
But we'll get there!'

Jamie's father had paid for him to get in so he had some piastres
left. He asked Aisha if she would like an ice cream and she said
she would. They bought two at a little kiosk and went into one of
the zoo's pavilions to eat them. The pavilions were all covered with
hibiscus flowers and bougainvillaea so you could sit inside in the
shade and not be seen. But you could see out.

Mostly you could see birds: dhurra birds, which normally lived
among the corn, and fire finches with their brilliant patches of red,
and lots of sand grouse almost pushing themselves through the floor
of their cage in their anxiety to become invisible in the rather scanty
sand. There were enormous macaws and toucans and hornbills of
metallic blues and reds, chained to perches – not, Jamie supposed,
because someone might want to steal them but because they might
fly away.

Perhaps the Pasha ought to have chained Leila to a perch! But
in a way, he had done.

Actually, it worked the other way, because a lot of wild birds,
huge Egyptian kites and a variety of water fowl, from storks down-
wards, spotted the enclosures and rather fancied them and flew down
and settled in them.

There was a purple heron in a little enclosure with a pond. It
stood on one leg, like the Dinka (perhaps that was where they
got the idea from?), peering down into the water looking for fish.
But the pond was only a few inches deep and there didn't seem
to be any fish in it.

Aisha, however, was getting bored and suggested they leave the
zoo and go out into the Gizeh; but Jamie had promised his father

that he would stay in the zoo until his father got back. 'You could go out and come back,' suggested Aisha, but Jamie felt that was cheating. He stayed where he was but Aisha said that she was going to go home. She had achieved her object, which was to 'case the joint' and assess its suitability for what she had in mind. She thought it would do very well. They could slip away and lose themselves in one or more of the little pavilions. Once inside they would be safe from discovery. And then they could choose their moment and when the time came slip out of the zoo altogether.

'If Leila agrees,' said Jamie.

'Oh, she'll agree,' said Aisha airily.

Jamie wasn't so sure.

'Ever since I was a boy,' said Georgiades, 'I've loved trains. The railway used to run past our house. I would look out of the window and see the trains going past. And do you know what I liked best? It was the engines. When I was small I thought they were Afrit giants. You know, like the ones who put their weapons on the Bab-es-Zuweyla. You know the Bab-es-Zuweyla? No? Well, it's one of the big gates of Cairo. It goes up and up for ever. That's because it has the minarets of the Al-Muayyad mosque on its towers. Very tall and thin little columns near the top, just below the minarets. And right up on the tower you see their weapons. They're supposed to have been put there by the Afrits when they were visiting. Well, I don't know about that, but how else could they have got up there? Don't tell me someone climbed up and put them there. It would be no ordinary climb, I can tell you. You'd have to be an Afrit giant to do it.'

None of his listeners had ever been to Cairo and they were enthralled.

'I didn't know they had Afrits in Cairo!' said one of them.

'Well, they do. Not many. And I don't know whether they are there now. Maybe they just came and left their weapons, to show they'd been there, and then went home again.'

'Where *is* their home?' asked someone.

'I was hoping you were going to tell me! Because it's somewhere down here, in the south. That's where the magic is, or so they tell me. That's where it is these days. It's sort of faded away from the towns in the north. But the evidence is still there.'

'Well, that's amazing!'

'And shall I tell you what I think? I think they have such big mosques – I mean, they really are big – because it takes a lot of mosque to keep the magic under control. You can laugh at me if you like, but that's what I think.'

They didn't seem disposed to laugh at him. They didn't believe in magic or, really, in Afrit giants, but they didn't disbelieve enough to be quite sure.

'And when those big engines used to thunder past, I thought *they* were the giants my mother used to tell me about! Laugh at me if you like, but I was very small.'

'I'm not laughing,' said one of the men around him. 'I thought that, too. When I was small,' he added hastily.

'Of course, you get used to them,' said someone else.

'Sometimes,' said Georgiades, 'at night, when I couldn't sleep, my mother would take me out of the house for a little walk, so that my father *could* get to sleep, and she would take me down to the railway, and I would see one of the monsters right up close, coming towards me with its great green eyes – they were the lamps, of course – and I would think it was out to get me!'

The men laughed.

'I'll bet you cuddled up to your mother!' one of them said.

'I did. And there are times even now, when things go wrong, when I wish I could cuddle up to her again!'

'It's like that with all of us.'

'Although on the whole we prefer to cuddle someone else these days!'

They all laughed.

'You here for long?' someone asked.

'A few days. Really I'm just having a look around to see if it's worth putting more of an effort here.'

'Well, if it's paper you're selling' – which was the story Georgiades had told them – 'there's plenty of need for that!'

'They'll have other suppliers,' said Georgiades. 'What I'm really here for is to get the general picture. As you say, though, the way Atbara is growing it's getting to be big enough to interest us.'

'Growing all the time,' one of the men said.

'It looks to me to be a nice place,' said Georgiades.

'But nothing like Cairo.'

'Not like Cairo, no. And that's what my wife would have against it. But if you were a young chap starting off . . .'

They agreed it might be a tempting proposition.

'Provided you can stand the mosquitoes.'

'There are mosquitoes in Cairo,' said Georgiades. 'But what there is here and there isn't in Cairo is a lot of space. I went for a walk along the river early this morning, and there were a few people washing themselves but otherwise no one. Of course, you do have crocodiles as well as mosquitoes.'

'No, we don't, not these days.'

'Oh, I had heard you did. Someone told me a man was snatched only the other day.'

'No, no, no. That was just – well, you know the sort of thing people say. It wasn't a crocodile that got him, it was just that he went in too deep and couldn't swim. There's a ledge on this side of the river and it's easy to step over it. And that's what happened.'

'Well, I am relieved to hear it,' said Georgiades. 'Crocodiles I don't want when I'm having a little stroll beside the river.'

'There are not many. You don't see them.'

'I don't find that altogether reassuring. I'd prefer to see them than just be walking along and thinking they're a piece of driftwood and then, bang! Suddenly, they've snapped their jaws and you're inside, and it's goodbye to you!'

The man laughed. 'Don't worry,' he said. 'It hardly ever happens. You'll be all right.'

'As a matter of fact,' said Georgiades. 'I've got a message to deliver to the family. You know, the man who was drowned. Someone in our office knows the family and when he heard I was going down to Atbara, he asked me if I would take a message for him. You know, condolences and that sort of thing. These things are important at a time of bereavement. The family gathers round, if you know what I mean. So I'd like to do it if I can. I suppose you don't know how I might get in touch with them?'

'I do,' said someone. 'They live in my street. They'll be glad to hear from someone in the family.'

'Well, I'm not exactly in the family. The friend of a friend, if you know what I mean. It's someone in my office. The name of the place comes up, Atbara, or whatever, and they think it will be just round the corner. Mention my name when you see him, that sort of thing. And, of course, you never do see him. Still, I'd like to do something if I can.'

'They live just up the street from me. I'll take you there.'

He introduced him as 'a friend of Suleiman's' and so the job was done.

The widow was living with her parents. It was a very small, very ordinary house, and Georgiades was surprised. Wasn't Sayyid supposed to be 'a man of substance'? That, according to Owen, was the expression the engine driver had used. Owen had been rather surprised by the expression. What was a man of substance doing washing in the river? Now, having seen the house, he could understand it. There was no separate bathroom, no running water. Everyone appeared to use the pump in the street outside. And that included the whole street. It was commonplace for women to go to a pump for the household's needs of water. But washing? At times there must have been quite a queue. He could see that people might well have preferred to use the river. All the same . . . A man of substance? The engine driver must have got it wrong.

'He was a good man,' said the father, 'and we shall miss him.'

'We would have missed him more,' said the mother tartly, 'if he had left a bit more behind him.'

There were undercurrents here.

'The money went on the funeral, I expect,' said Georgiades. It was usual for families to spend more on a funeral than they could afford.

'It was a good funeral,' agreed the father. 'I will say that.'

'So it should have been,' said Georgiades. 'Was he not the Pasha's kinsman?'

'So he claimed,' said the mother. 'But it didn't do us much good.'

'Didn't he do us honour?' said the daughter. 'Didn't he come to the funeral?'

'If it was an honour,' said her mother, 'it was one that didn't cost him anything!'

'Shame on you, woman!' said the father. 'He showed us respect.'

'Respect comes cheap,' said his wife doggedly. 'When it's not accompanied by money.'

'And didn't the Pasha give any?'

'No,' said the mother. 'Not a millieme!'

'So you had to pay for everything yourselves?'

'No. No,' said the father. 'We didn't pay. But others did.'

'The employers . . .' said Georgiades.

'Don't make me laugh!' said the mother.

'The men in the office,' said the daughter. 'They all paid something.'

'They at least must have respected him,' said Georgiades.

'I'm not saying that they didn't,' said the mother.

'They all gave something,' said the daughter. 'And that is not always the case!'

'It was because he had done so much for them,' said the father.

'What had he done?' asked the mother contemptuously.

'He had put their case,' said the father.

'Well, that was nice of him!' said the mother. 'And who asked him to do that?'

'Until he got here, nobody did anything,' said the daughter. 'It was left to fools like that Ali.'

'And where did it get us?' demanded the mother.

'It got us a pay rise!' said the father.

'A few milliemes!' said the mother contemptuously. 'Which didn't make up for the money they lost when they came out on strike.'

'You've got to do something,' said the father.

'Why not try working?' said the mother. 'For a change.'

'I *do* work!' said the father hotly. 'I work hard. And where does it get me?'

'Work harder!' said his wife.

The husband spat and turned away.

'You've got me puzzled,' said Georgiades. 'Didn't you say he was kinsman to the Pasha? What is a kinsman of the Pasha doing, telling people to come out on strike?'

'It was another thing that didn't cost him anything,' said the mother. 'It's all talk with people like that!'

'With Sayyid it wasn't,' said the daughter. 'He helped people, and got them to help themselves.'

'He came in and stirred up trouble. And then he would have moved on, leaving us with the trouble.'

'He wouldn't have moved on!' said the daughter. 'He was married to me, remember?'

'He would have moved on. Men like that always do.'

'Sayyid wasn't like that!'

'He might have taken you with him,' her mother accepted grudgingly.

'But he didn't move on,' said the father. 'He died. And that's another thing that needs explaining.'

Less than a mile from Owen's office at the Place Bab-al-Khalk, along the Sharia Bab-al-Khalk, was the Khedivial School of Justice where all the young lawyers started to learn their trade. They learned other things as well and more than a few of Owen's British colleagues felt that was where they picked up their seditious ideas. The school was at the corner of the Midan Abdin, Abdin Square, and running down the side of the square was the Abdin Palace where the Khedive resided.

The Midan was, therefore, handy for both the law school and the Palace, and at any hour of the day the tables outside the little cafes were occupied by people with business at either or both. It was where Aisha's father, Yasin, spent a lot of his time: a sort of lawyers' Commons.

Sometimes they were waiting for a brief and every so often a *suffragi* would dash out of the Law School in search of a particular lawyer. At other times, a bell would tinkle and people sitting at the tables would get to their feet and dash inside to whatever committee they were supposed to be supporting. But for a lot of the time bells didn't tinkle and *suffragis* didn't come dashing.

It was where political and legal hangers-on mixed. There was, of course, no dividing line between the two and young lawyers on the make waited there hopefully.

It was a good place for picking up political gossip and Owen often went there for a cup of coffee, although the coffee was not much more reliable than the gossip. Still, he had his contacts.

One of these was an elderly writer named Yacub, who sat at the same table every day and did copying work for the lawyers. Most copying was still done by hand although, as in other parts of Egyptian life, modern technology was beginning to thrust its way in – in this case in the form of the typewriter. Yacub was one of the old sort and disdained such modern aids, sticking to the old, beautiful and extremely slow Arabic handwriting. Nikos despised such men. Owen quite liked it and from time to time would give Yacub something of his to copy. As a favourite customer Yacub would do it while Owen was waiting, which gave Owen an excuse to linger and pick up gossip.

Yacub had been sitting there for a long time and there was little about the lawyers that he didn't know.

'Effendi!'

'Greetings, Yacub!'

He laid a piece of paper before him. 'Two piastres, two hours!' said Yacub.

Which was not cheap but a fair price as these things went, especially if you were picking up other things at the same time.

'I have just made an acquaintance,' said Owen.

'Oh, yes?'

'Yasin al-Jawad.'

'Do I know him?'

'He has a daughter.'

'Oh, yes. I know him.'

Owen laughed. 'I'll bet you do,' he said.

'He is a lawyer,' said Yacub. 'But not much at the Parquet.'

Owen nodded. 'At the Palace, rather.'

'A political lawyer,' said Yacub.

'Who probably doesn't bring you much work. Which is why it may be worth your while talking to me a little.'

'It is always a pleasure to talk to you.'

'He is very much a Cairo man,' said Owen. 'Yet it was not always thus. At one time he was over in the Red Sea Hills.'

'Yes,' said Yacub. 'I remember.'

'How did that come about?'

'He was too interested in politics.'

'So he thought it was prudent to disappear for a while?'

'He didn't think it was prudent. His father did.'

'And his father was able to work it so that he would be transferred?'

'To some less conspicuous place.'

'Where better, from that point of view, than the Red Sea Hills?'

'His father, and his friends, thought that it would be better to get right out of Egypt.'

'Even as far as the Sudan? Was there any other reason for him to go to the Sudan?'

'I don't know. One of his father's friends had a relative there, perhaps.'

'Was this relative a politician too?'

'I cannot remember. It was a long time ago. But I think, yes, perhaps.'

'Because, you see, I wonder how he came to come back? The Red Sea Hills is not a place you come back from. You usually stay there.'

'He did stay there. For several years. And then the friends were able to work a transfer.'

'Powerful friends.'

'So-so.'

'But at any rate, what had sent him there was now forgotten about.'

'That is so, yes.'

'Can you give me any names?'

Yacub considered. 'I do not think so,' he said at last.

'This was a long time ago,' said Owen. 'Are they still so powerful?'

Yacub considered again. 'They are not as powerful as they were.'

'They were powerful enough to get him out of the way then. But not powerful enough to raise him further?'

'Some men's concerns are disappointing.'

'He is a gifted man,' said Owen. 'Surely he looked for a promising career?'

'I am sure he did.'

'But was it not so promising?'

Yacub spread his hands. 'It happens to us all,' he said. 'I have seen so many.'

'So many Mamur Zapts, too, perhaps?'

'I have seen many Mamur Zapts,' said Yacub. 'Some of them remain promising.'

'Deceptively so.'

'Oh, I don't know,' said Yacub.

'So you won't give me names?'

'Alas, no.'

'Even if it was rewarded?'

Yacub shook his head. 'I am afraid not,' he said, and passed Owen the sheets of paper. Owen took them and passed him some money.

'This is more than I asked.'

'It is an expression of hope.'

Yacub sighed. 'Hope deserves a reward,' he said. 'But it is only a little reward. So it will be only a little information. Names, I will not give.'

'You spoke of interests,' said Owen. 'Can you tell me the nature of the interests? In general. Sudan interests, for example, or Egypt interests?'

'Egypt interests. The Sudan was just a place to get away to.'

'Does the interest persist?'

'That I do not know.' He hesitated. 'All I can say is that his father's interests, like his father, may have become old. They may not be the same as the son's.'

Owen added a piastre. 'Thank you,' he said.

As he moved away, Yacub said, 'I hope no harm comes to the girl.'

'That is my hope, too.'

'Let it be so.'

Although whether this was said as an entreaty or as a warning, Owen was not quite sure.

NINE

Nikos put the list on Owen's desk. Owen read it through carefully and called the clerk in.

'It's a complete list, is it?'

Nikos nodded. 'Yes,' he said, 'everyone who was at the meeting is there.'

'What about the wife?'

'Wife?'

'The Pasha's wife. Or perhaps she is not his wife. Anyway, she was staying there in the hotel, throughout the conference.'

'She may have been in the hotel, but she wasn't at the meeting.'

'Were there any other people who were staying in the hotel but not at the meeting? I am talking only of interested parties. Wives, girlfriends, boyfriends, people attached to the ones who were at the meeting?'

'Oh, yes. I have a list of them, too.' Nikos was thorough, and it was hard to catch him out. He produced the second list. 'As you say, girlfriends, boyfriends, relatives.'

Owen looked at the list again. 'It was a sort of Pasha's jamboree, was it?'

'Jamboree?' said Nikos, for the moment at a loss. His English was perfect, perhaps too perfect, for words like 'jamboree' were not included.

'Treat, party, celebration,' explained Owen. 'What did they do when the masters were at the meeting?'

'What women usually do. They shopped. I think they found it disappointing after Cairo.'

'And the boys?'

'There was only one of them and he shopped, too.'

'Pliable?'

'Oh, yes. Venal, I would say.'

Sometimes Nikos's English was right on the mark.

'I think we'll have him in. Is there anyone else worth talking to? Preferably someone who was actually at the meeting.'

Nikos considered. 'Mahir Bey?' he offered.

'Who is he?'

'A friend of the boy. They have a curious relationship. It is not, I think, sexual. A kind of dependence. Mahir takes him everywhere with him and Abd-al-Halim runs errands for him.'

'That could be useful. Get him in. The boy first.'

The boy was young and slender and gazelle-like. His large, dark eyes roamed curiously round the office. The Bab-al-Khalk often had that effect on people. It was large and featureless, a typical Western-style office with nothing personal to take a defensive hold of, completely alien to the more intimate Arab style of building.

'There is nothing to be nervous about, Abd-al-Halim,' said Owen kindly. The boy was very young. 'Just some things I want to know. But I am sure you won't mind telling me them.'

'I will stay true to the Pasha,' the boy declared.

'I am sure you will! And why shouldn't you? For there is nothing I shall say that is aimed at the Pasha.'

The boy looked surprised. 'It is a long way to go for a meeting. Why was that, I wonder?'

'The Khedive would have it so.'

'Ah, the Khedive would have it so? Was that because he didn't want people to know about the meeting?'

'I don't know. It may be so.'

'And what did you do while your master was at the meeting? Go to the shops?'

'My master said it was not worth going to the shops. They are nothing like Cairo's. No, I went to the zoo. And that was very good. A boy, an English boy, was feeding peanuts to one of the elephants and he kept snatching his hand away before the elephant could get them. And the elephant filled his trunk with water and squirted it right over him. That was very good.'

'The people laughed, I expect.'

'They did. And Sharif, who was with me, said: "That will teach him!"'

'And what did you do when your master came out of the meeting?'

'It was late and I went to bed. And the bed was large and soft.'

'Did your master seem pleased with the way the meeting had gone?'

'He said it was a long meeting. But, yes, he seemed pleased.'

Owen waited.

'He said it would show the English that things could be done without them. It would put them in their place. It was a coup,' he said.

Like many Cairenes the boy spoke French as well as English.

'Ah! A coup! And the Khedive was pleased, I expect?'

'They said he would be. But, do you know, the Pasha Hilmi nearly had a case stolen when he was on the train. He fought the men off bravely. But it didn't matter, anyway, for the case was empty.'

'Why carry an empty case?'

'Oh, it wouldn't be empty on the way back. There would be papers to go in it. The papers were handed over at the meeting. I saw the man who brought them. I was still standing at the door, for the Pasha had just gone in and, lo, a man came up, a foreigner, and said to the *suffragi* on the door: "I have papers for the Pashas." And he was carrying a bag. And when he came out again he was no longer carrying the bag.'

'And then?'

'Then? Why, he went to his room.'

'He was staying in the hotel, too?'

'Yes. He had come the night before. Late. He was staying on the floor above ours and I heard him come in.'

'Thank you, Abd-al-Halim. There, you see, you have done no ill to your master.'

'The Pasha, Mahir Bey.'

'Ah, Pasha! Thank you for making time to come and see us!'

'It is nothing. Glad to help. If I can. It concerns the briefcase, yes?'

'Yes.'

'I gather it has been recovered?'

'It has. In Atbara.'

'How did it get there? Oh, I remember. Did not my old friend, Mustapha Hilmi, go on to Atbara after our meeting in Khartoum? He was attending a funeral, I think.'

'He was.'

'Well, it is easy to lose things on such occasions. One's mind is on other things.'

'Indeed. Now, perhaps you can help me, Pasha. The meeting you attended in Khartoum, at which papers were handed over: that was the first time you had seen them, I presume?'

'That is so,' Mahir Bey agreed.

'You had no idea previously of their nature?'

'Well, I had in general terms . . .'

'But not particular. That was the point of the meeting, I expect. To allow you to familiarize yourselves with the details?'

'That is so, yes.'

'Of the contracts?'

'Well, of course, they would need further perusal by experts . . .'

'This was just to allow you to understand, in general terms, what was at stake?'

'Well, yes.'

'Why was that? Was there any doubt about it?'

'We knew, at that stage, so little about it . . .'

'It was an early stage in the process?'

'An initial step, yes.'

'The first time you had seen what exactly was proposed?'

'Yes.'

'Was this because the draft had been drawn up by people outside the country?'

'Yes.'

'And who did the initiative come from? Them or you?'

'Them. That was why we were having this early meeting. It was a first step in the process.'

'To see that it was worth proceeding?'

'Well . . .'

'But there was really no doubt about that, because you knew the Khedive wanted it to proceed.'

'We are the Khedive's servants.'

'Quite so. As am I.'

'There is a difference, though, Mamur Zapt, between us . . .'

'On some things. Not on others.'

'This would be one of the things on which there is a difference!'

'No doubt. But it was bound to come out at some time, wasn't it? Contracts on this scale?'

'At some point, yes.'

'But the Khedive wanted to delay that point as long as possible.'

'Perhaps, yes.'

'So that it would be very difficult to repudiate or amend them?'

'The Khedive knows what he is doing, Mamur Zapt.'

'So I have always found.'

'The important thing is not to let other bodies interfere in what is legitimately an Egyptian concern.'

'That is, naturally, far from England's intention.'

'Oh, yes?' said Mahir Bey sceptically.

Owen had asked Jamie's father if he could drop in that morning if he had a spare moment. Jamie's father had said he would be delighted to, and could he bring Jamie, who would like to see the Bab-al-Khalk, where Owen worked, and was at a loose end that morning?

'I don't want him wandering around Cairo by himself,' he explained. 'He won't be a nuisance. He can sit in a corner and draw. He likes drawing.'

So Jamie was installed at a table in the Mamur Zapt's office. Nikos brought him some pencils and a supply of paper and he settled down.

'What are you going to draw?' asked Owen.

'Engines.'

'You'd be pretty good at those, I expect.'

'It's the details,' said Jamie. 'These ones haven't properly come into service yet, and I haven't really seen them, so I don't quite know everything about them.'

'I haven't seen them, either,' said Owen.

'Oh, you won't have. They're coming into use on British railways first.'

'Well, you'd be much more up to date than I am.'

It was some years now since Owen had been in England; but in truth he wasn't too good on the engines of Egypt, either.

Mr Nicholson took out some papers from the worn leather satchel that he was carrying. He had had it since he came out to Egypt years before and preferred it to the shiny new briefcases that everyone seemed to be using in Cairo.

'These are our suppliers. We've had them for some time. They're standard British stock, mostly carriages, in fact, not engines, and we've adapted them for Sudan conditions. That's important, particularly for engines. Otherwise the sand gets into everything.'

'Supplied how long ago?'

'Oh, crikey, years! We haven't had anything new on the line for nearly ten years now.'

'Time for some new ones?'

'Not a chance in the present financial climate! We put in for some every year but get nowhere.'

'Perhaps that is what the Khedive has in mind about going abroad?'

'He needs to make sure what he is getting. The Czech engines wouldn't do at all, and I wouldn't be confident about the French.'

'Finance?'

'Oh, no problem there, either for the French or the Czechs. That's why we're worried.'

'I haven't yet found out the identity of the people who are trying to muscle in, but I will.'

'It would be nice to know. Although I don't think they'll get anywhere. We've got it pretty sewn up.'

'I think that may be what the Khedive doesn't like.'

Mr Nicholson shrugged. 'I leave the politics to others.'

Owen tapped the papers in front of him. 'Does that include these chaps?'

'The suppliers? Well, obviously a certain amount of politics goes on, both here and in England.'

'But not to the lengths of sabotage?'

'Sabotage?'

'Our train was sabotaged.'

'I can't understand that. But it wouldn't be people in the business. What would be the point, for foreign suppliers or us? No, it would be some crazy nationalists who want to bugger things up generally. But whatever it's like in Egypt, we don't get much of that in the Sudan.'

'Somebody attacked me,' said Jamie.

Owen turned and looked at him. 'Yes, you mentioned that before.'

'It was probably nothing,' said Jamie's father. 'A lot of people on the bank at that time, people pushing and shoving, bumping into each other—'

'I was pushed,' said Jamie doggedly. 'Deliberately.'

'You don't know that.'

'Yes, I do. It felt different. This was a definite push. They wanted me to fall into the river.'

'How close were you to the water?'

'About a yard.'

'Just playing, I expect,' said his father.

Jamie shook his head. 'It wasn't like playing.'

'Did you see who did it?'

'No. I looked round and said: "What do you think you're doing?" But I think whoever it was had gone, and everybody looked at me blankly.'

'Just an accident, I expect,' said his father. 'Upsetting for you, but no harm intended.'

'A push,' insisted Jamie. 'A deliberate push!'

'I doubt it. Anyway, you would just have fallen into the water.'

'And got snaffled by a crocodile? Like that other bloke,' said Jamie.

'There *aren't* any crocodiles there,' said Jamie's father.

'They think there is. The men on the bank.'

'Well, they're not right, are they?'

'Anyway, I might have drowned. Like that other man.'

'You wouldn't have drowned, Jamie.'

'Because I can swim. That other man couldn't. Not many Sudanese can. That's why they pushed me. They thought they'd get me.'

'Now, Jamie, you're over dramatizing.'

'I know what I know,' insisted Jamie stubbornly. 'Not many Sudanese can swim – and not many Sudanese boys!'

'You're saying he picked you out?'

'That's what I'm saying, yes.'

'Why would anyone pick you out, Jamie?'

'I don't know. I just know that they did.'

'But when we talked about this before, you said you didn't see who did it. So how do you know he pushed you?'

'Because I felt him push me! Hard! And when I said I didn't

see him, that was afterwards. At the time I was stumbling. I nearly fell over. That's how hard!'

'I really think you're embroidering a bit, Jamie.'

'But I *did* see someone just before! I noticed him because he had been looking at me in a funny way.'

'Jamie . . .'

'I did see him, and I didn't like it. So I moved away. And . . .'

'And?'

'He came after me.'

'Jamie, you're making this up!'

'No. I'm not. I really did see him!'

'What sort of man was he?'

'Black. From the south. Not like the ones around here. They're brown. Arabs. And he had red eyes.'

'Oh, come on, Jamie.'

'Wait a moment,' said Owen.

A lot of people in Egypt had infected eyes. Usually it was bilharzia, a disease you picked up from water, and very common in the flooded areas affected by the annual inundation. That was where the snails bred which were hosts to the bilharzia germ.

'Tell us more about the eyes, Jamie.'

'They were not very nice. They were sort of running. Right over his face. You don't usually see them as bad as that.'

'Very bad, then.'

'Almost blind, I would think,' said Jamie.

'Perhaps that was why he bumped into you,' said Mr Nicholson.

'He *didn't* bump into me. He pushed me.'

'Had you pushed him first, Jamie?' asked his father.

'No, I hadn't. He came up behind me and gave me a deliberate push. Hard! He *wanted* to push me!'

'Perhaps he just wanted you to get out of his way.'

'It wasn't that kind of push. I might have fallen in. He *wanted* me to fall in.'

'Jamie, I think you're going a bit far!'

'I wasn't far from the edge. You know, where it cuts down suddenly. He wanted me to step over it. He thought that would do for me. Because he didn't know that I can swim. Most boys, most Sudanese boys, can't.'

'We've got the point, Jamie!' said his father.

'Yes, well, I didn't like it!' said Jamie.

'Jamie,' said the Mamur Zapt, 'when you turned round and saw the man – that was just *before* he pushed you – correct?'

'Correct!' said Jamie.

'There were a lot of people jostling and pushing?'

'Yes!'

'So it could have been an accident,' said his father.

'It could have been. But it wasn't!' said Jamie.

'But this man stood out,' said the Mamur Zapt.

'Yes.'

'Because of his eyes?'

'They were horrid,' said Jamie.

'Was there anything else you noticed about him. About his face? Were there any scars, for example?'

'Yes. Big ones, on the cheeks.'

'Tribal scars?'

'Yes.

'And on the forehead, too?'

'Like a row of beads. Little bumps.'

'Dinka?'

'Shilluk,' said Jamie.

'You know your marks,' said Owen.

'I do. Most of them.'

'They're both from further south than Atbara.'

'They come up,' said Jamie. 'They work in the gangs. The railway gangs.'

'Mending the line, that sort of thing?'

'Yes. Good workmen, my dad says.'

'They are,' said Mr Nicholson.

'So you've seen the marks before?'

'They're quite interesting,' said Jamie. 'When I was smaller, I wanted to have some. But that was when I was smaller.'

'I think you did see someone,' said Owen.

'I did. And he pushed me.'

'Maybe he did,' said Owen. 'And if he did, from what you have told us, we stand a good chance of finding him.'

'Gareth,' said Mr Nicholson warningly, 'there are quite a few Shilluk working on the line these days.'

'And most of them don't suffer from bilharzia.'

'Some do.'

'And some of them suffer so badly that they're almost blind.

But if they do they may well have sought medical treatment. Especially if they have worked on the railways. Where it would certainly have been spotted.'

Owen had arranged for Aisha to call on Zeinab. Despite herself, when it came to it, Aisha was more than a little daunted. To start with, Zeinab was a Pasha's daughter. Aisha didn't altogether approve of Pashas. And Pasha's daughters had not so far come within her horizon at all. How did you address them, for a start. My Lady? Sitt? Princess? Considering it beforehand, Aisha had settled for modern, emancipated equality, woman-to-woman sort of stuff. But as she was about to go into the house she had an uneasy feeling that wasn't quite right. For a dreadful moment, confidence wobbled. Zeinab was, after all, a grand lady. Certainly grander than a school-girl, even one nearly a sixth-former. Suppose she didn't accept the terms of equality that Aisha offered? The servants would laugh at her.

Fortunately, the door was opened by a warm, smiling lady, who turned out to be Zeinab herself. The smiling lady explained that the Mamur Zapt didn't have servants for security reasons, and it was too much of a fuss anyway. Aisha, whose family did have servants – they came very cheap in Egypt – was momentarily taken aback. What did Zeinab do with the washing? she wondered. Send it out, said Zeinab. For Zeinab, this meant sending it round to her father's palatial mansion where there were servants in plenty, but this, too, seemed unacceptable to the Mamur Zapt. Surely he didn't do the washing himself? Zeinab seemed delightfully hazy about what he did do, but she said his clothes always looked clean to her. Perhaps he bought new ones? This seemed unlikely to Aisha and she resolved to ask Owen the next time they met – although on second thoughts, she wouldn't ask him that immediately.

Anyway, she hadn't come to talk about washing. What would Zeinab think of her? For a moment she almost froze and it was a relief when Zeinab piloted her into their mandarah, or sitting room, and even more of a relief when she found that it was rather like their own mandarah: larger, perhaps, and with a fountain, and a sunken floor around it. The floor was a cool marble and there were no carpets. Or rather there were but they were on the walls, but that was fairly normal. What was not normal was the quality of the carpets. Later, she discovered that they were all borrowed from Zeinab's father, whose taste was impeccable, although not matched by the revenue to go with it. But it added to his overdraft, not hers, so that was all right. Aisha began to think that Zeinab's style was perhaps a little unconventional. Well that was all right. Aisha was unconventional herself, although not one to go to extremes.

There were low tables and low divans around the room, on one of which Zeinab lay down. She said that with the baby so recent, her doctor had told her to put her feet up as much as possible. Aisha asked her about the baby and was slightly shaken when Zeinab asked her if she would like to hold it. Zeinab went into another room and returned with the baby in her arms. She gave it to Aisha and Aisha took it gingerly but resolutely.

'There! Put your hand there! You have to support their neck at first because sometimes they're weak.'

Aisha would have laid down her life in the neck's support but that didn't prove to be necessary. What struck her after a moment was how small it was and how like a little animal, which, she supposed, was what it was. It settled itself comfortably in Aisha's arms and, once she had got used to it, Aisha found that rather nice. She still couldn't see why people made such a fuss about babies, although the longer she held this one, the more reluctant she was to let it go.

'It seems rather nice,' she said, and then was cross with herself at calling the baby 'it'. Zeinab didn't seem to mind, however. Doubtless it would become clearer as the morning went on.

Now that she was getting into it, Aisha had a lot of questions to put to Zeinab on being pregnant and having a baby, but pulled herself up. This, she told herself sternly, was not what she had in mind when she had asked Owen to set up a visit. What she had in mind, and she had worked it out carefully beforehand, was how you combined being a woman in Egypt and having a career. And she didn't include babies as a career.

'Not easily,' said Zeinab.

She understood the question, however, which was rather more than Aisha's mother would probably have done.

'And still less having a career with being a mother,' said Zeinab. 'Although I have a friend – whose name, curiously, is also Aisha – who says it gets better all the time. Although the pace hots up.'

'What is her career?' asked Aisha.

'She was a lawyer. But not, she says, a real one. She can't prac-
tise, not in the way her husband can – he's in the Parquet.'

'Like my father,' said Aisha.

'But she can do legal work. Things like contracts. Which she
finds very boring.'

'I would too,' said Aisha.

'But at least you can use your brain.'

Zeinab had put her finger on it. Aisha was aware – perhaps over-
aware – that she had a brain, but as far as she could see if you were
a woman you had precious little chance of using it.

'So what do I do?' she asked. 'When I leave school?'

Zeinab had studied in France. That was easy for her, her father
being a Pasha. Actually, not all Pashas were like her father on this.
Nuri Pasha had been a celebrated politician, a junior minister, no
less. But he had made the mistake of opting for the wrong side,
that of the British, on a notorious case and after that his political
career had come to an end.

He had consoled himself by taking a long holiday in France. Like
many Egyptians of the upper class, he was a francophile and as at
home in French culture as he was in English (he didn't much care
for Egyptian culture). Back in Egypt he had made various attempts
to reignite his political career but without success. He had been very
successful, however, in wooing a prominent Cairo courtesan, up to
the point of actually proposing to her. To the world's surprise she had
turned him down. There was greater freedom in being a prominent
courtesan than there was in being a wife, she said – even the wife of
a Pasha. It was this last part that scandalized Cairo society most.

The relationship had, however, proved to be a long-lasting and
stable one and had produced two children – Zeinab and a brother.
The brother had followed his father into seeking a political career.
Like his father's had done, however, it had ended in disaster. He'd
had to leave Egypt in a hurry and had led a happy life ever after
on the French Riviera.

Nuri had been inconsolable when the children's mother died and
when his son disappointed him too he had transferred not just his
love but his ambition to his daughter. Zeinab had been given an
excellent education and allowed to live a very different life from
that of most Egyptian women, even women of her class. And then
she had ruined it all by hitching up with the Mamur Zapt!

Aisha was entranced as all this came pouring out. Zeinab had led a very full life, although, perhaps, a slightly unconventional one. Was that what you had to do to be a free woman in Egypt? Follow Zeinab's mother's example and become a courtesan? Aisha considered this and was tempted, but in the end shied away.

Where was she getting on the great question of her career? In truth, more confused than when she had started.

'I think there's a difference between where you start and where you aim to finish,' said Zeinab. 'You have to work your way up. You can't *start* at the top.'

Aisha had to admit the justice of this, disappointing though it was. She asked Zeinab how she had started.

Zeinab said she had been lucky. When she was casting around, just as Aisha was at the moment, she had met a remarkable Egyptian lady and an equally remarkable British man. The man was a pathologist of international fame (and therefore even the English didn't dare to muck him about). In administrative matters, as in medical, what he said went. The lady had worked as a matron in one of the hospitals under his aegis, where she had built up a reputation that daunted even the most reactionary Pashas. Again, what she said went.

Zeinab herself worked part-time in the administration, dealing, she said, with paper, not people. She didn't fancy blood and guts, she told Aisha.

Aisha didn't fancy them, either. That, in fact, was one of the things that was holding her up in her pursuit of a career. She had ruled out becoming a brilliant surgeon. And now, having watched her father at work, Aisha had decided that she didn't fancy becoming a lawyer, either. In fact, most jobs put her off.

'Then there is nothing else for it,' declared Zeinab. 'You'll have to become a Pasha!'

Aisha left, cheered up but not sure if she had made much progress.

'Hello!' said Dr Shawfik when Georgiades walked into the little waiting room. 'What can I do for you?'

He had nearly added 'Effendi' to his greeting, for he was the most courteous of men. But was Georgiades an effendi? The title was normally given to people employed in government service, originally those of exalted rank, but then extended to almost anyone, any clerk who wore a fez and a dark suit and brandished a walking cane and fancied himself. A useful working rule was to apply it to any foreigner. But did Greeks count as foreigners? There were so many of them about these days. And they were rather betwixt and between: shopkeepers, often, and did a shopkeeper count as an effendi? Besides, effendis normally wore suits. Well, this one did, but it was so crumpled and faded that you might easily have missed it. This chap looked like a down-and-out. Dr Shawfik decided to reserve his judgement.

'I am looking for a needle,' said the incomer.

'A . . . a needle?' said Dr Shawfik.

'In a haystack.'

'There aren't any haystacks here,' said Dr Shawfik carefully. 'Not in the Sudan.'

'Like looking for a needle in a haystack,' explained Georgiades.

'Yes. Yes. I see.' He didn't. An idea struck him. 'I am not . . . not an alienist, Mr . . .' He glanced at the name he had been given. 'Mr Georgiades, I am afraid.'

'Nor an ophthalmologist.'

'Nor an ophthalmologist, no,' agreed Dr Shawfik. 'Do you have a problem with your eyes?'

Georgiades tapped his head. 'A problem here,' he said.

That clinched it. When the Atbara Chief of Police had rung the surgery and asked him to give what help he could to a Mr Georgiades, Dr Shawfik had not known what kind of help he was being asked to supply. Now it was, perhaps, clearer.

'A touch of the sun?'

'I am a policeman from Cairo, Doctor Shawfik, and I am trying to find someone who may, I fear, be as difficult to locate as a needle in a haystack.'

'Ah!'

'I fear there may be thousands of people like this. We don't know his name, or much about him, except that he lives in Atbara, and possibly works on the railway – oh, and suffers from the effects of bilharzia.'

'Ah! The eyes?'

'Very badly, a witness says.'

'You have a witness?'

'A child.'

'Sometimes children are very good witnesses. They notice things.'

'This one did. The eyes especially. Red, inflamed and weeping badly.'

'It could be bilharzia, yes. He is an Egyptian?'

'We think he may have worked there. But, no, he comes from the Sudan. He is dark, and, we think, from the south. He may well be Shilluk.'

'He would certainly come from the south, then.'

'He has Shilluk face markings, I am told. I wouldn't know.'

'The witness?'

Georgiades nodded. 'Apparently he was sure.'

'The markings are distinctive. Strokes on the cheeks, a row of beads above the brow. The sort of thing a child would notice.'

'And threatening behaviour. Or so it seemed to the child.'

Dr Shawfik went across to a small filing cabinet and began to go through the cards. 'Any other distinguishing marks?'

'Not that I know of. But a strong positive identification.'

'He made a strong impression on the child?'

'Apparently.'

Dr Shawfik sighed. 'Sometime a person's appearance works against them.'

'You know the man?'

'I think so. And I would urge caution. If he is the man I am thinking of, his manner is off-putting. Especially, perhaps, to a child. He comes, as you say, from the south and is finding it hard to fit in here. He is unsure of himself, as well as sick, of course. Not an easy man to handle.'

'He has come to your attention?'

'I see everyone when we take them on. Mainly to make sure they have no infectious illness which they could pass on. I saw him.'

'And?'

'Nearly turned him down. I don't like doing that. Some of these men have come a long way hoping to get a job on the railways. They probably have a family at home that depends on them. It seems hard to turn them down just at an interview, even a medical one. And yet you have to.'

'But you didn't in this case?'

'No. No. I didn't.'

'May I ask why?'

Dr Shawfik did not reply at once. He seemed to be turning it over in his mind. 'I did, at last, reject him. But then someone asked me to think again.'

'Someone who knew him?'

'Yes.'

'From his days in the south?'

'No. He had, as you surmised, spent some time in Egypt. They had encountered him there and thought there was something to him. They thought he had difficulty settling in precisely because he was Sudanese. Well, of course, that attracted my sympathy. I agreed to give him a second chance.'

'A *second* chance?'

'He had been employed in the Egyptian railways. And had been dismissed.'

'On what grounds?'

Dr Shawfik hesitated. 'I don't think it would be right for me to say. There seemed to me to be a prejudice in the matter. Anyway, he was dismissed and came down here to Atbara asking for a job. And perhaps I was over-sympathetic to a fellow Sudanese.'

'Even so,' said Georgiades softly, 'you turned him down?'

Dr Shawfik sighed. 'I did.'

'And then agreed to reconsider. Because someone asked you to?'

'Yes.'

'May I ask about the person who asked you to reconsider?'

'You may ask,' said Dr Shawfik, 'but I shall not reply.'

'Would you be prepared to tell me the name of the man I am interested in? The Shilluk?'

Again Dr Shawfik hesitated. He hesitated for a long time. Then he said: 'There is a child in the case?'

'Yes.'

'Who was the subject of an attack?'

'So the child believed. But that is precisely what I am investigating.'

'And . . . was there anybody else?'

'As a matter of fact,' said Georgiades, 'there was. But that, too, is a matter for investigation only.'

'May I ask you . . .?'

'No,' said Georgiades. 'You may not.'

Dr Shawfik sighed. 'That is only fair, I suppose. But it leaves me unhappy. And worried.'

'I am sorry.'

Dr Shawfik took a card out of his filing cabinet. 'The name of the person with aggressive bilharzia,' he said, 'is Lukudu. Benjamin Lukudu. I tell you only because of the child.'

TEN

'**N**o!' said Georgiades. 'No, no, no, no!'
He put the receiver down and came back into the shop.
'The boss?' asked Tsakatellis sympathetically.

'In a manner of speaking,' said Georgiades. 'My wife.'

'You tell her!' said Tsakatellis supportively.

'I frequently do,' said Georgiades. 'But she never listens.'

'Be firm!' encouraged Tsakatellis. 'There can only be one boss in a household.'

'That's what she tells me,' said Georgiades. 'The trouble is it's her!'

'Another glass?' suggested Tsakatellis. 'You've had a shock.'

'Please!'

The shopkeeper poured him another glass of ouzo. Georgiades watched it cream over.

'It's always like this,' he complained. 'Why isn't she content to just stop at home and mind the baby?'

'There is a baby?'

'Two. You would think that was enough to keep her busy. It's more than enough to keep *me* busy when she leaves them with me!'

'Always gadding around, is she?' said the shopkeeper sympathetically.

'It's the Bourse,' said Georgiades. 'She's always down there!'

'The Bourse?'

'Stock Exchange. Where you buy stocks and shares.'

'She doesn't buy stocks and shares?'

'Mostly she just watches. And then she pounces!'

'With money?'

'Yes.'

'Yours?'

'No longer,' said Georgiades gloomily. 'She's taken over that side entirely.'

'With your money?'

'It's her money now.'

'Look, my friend, you can't let this go on. She'll fritter it away.'

'She doesn't do that exactly. She just doubles her stake.'

'Doubles . . .? My God!'

'Of course, she pulls it out after a time. But then she invests it in something else.'

'But one day . . .'

'That's what I say.'

'She'll lose everything!'

'So far she's doubled everything!'

'It can't go on!'

'That's what I say.'

'Be firm!'

'But it does. Does go on. Each time, she makes a profit! But the sums are getting bigger and bigger.'

'It's got to stop.'

'That's what I keep telling her. "Pull out now," I say, "while you're ahead of the market!" She says no, the market is still going up. She'll pull out before it turns.'

'That's what she thinks!'

'So far that's exactly what she's done. Every time.'

'It can't go on!'

'Two years ago,' said Georgiades, 'we lived in a small house, and I went out to work, and she stayed at home and minded the children, and cooked my dinner. And we were happy. At least, I was. But she wasn't satisfied. "Suppose we have more children?" she said. "The house will be too small." I said: "When it does, we'll move." "But Demosthenes's house has just come on the market!" she told me. "It's been on the market for years!" I said. "But now he's reduced it. He needs the money for his daughter's wedding. So I've made him an offer," she told me. "Jesus!" I said. "You can't do that!" "I have done it," she said. "What are you using for money?" I ask. "I've sold our house." "You've what?" I said. "Sold our house," she repeated. "It will just do for old Mme Pasco. She'll want a smaller house, now that her husband's died." "But . . ." was all I could say. "We've got a much bigger house. For no more money." Still I just said, "But . . ." And then she said, "Actually, we haven't. Because I've sold Demosthenes's house, too, and we've made two million piastras on the deal, and bought Alexander's house." "But that's vast!" I exclaimed. "It will do," she says, "for the time being. And meanwhile I've put part of the proceeds down on the Bourse . . ."'

'My friend, you have to stop this. Put your foot down!'

'She just gets richer all the time!'

'One day it will end in disaster.'

'That's what I tell her. But she just gets richer.'

'I don't like the sound of this!'

'Now she's into commodities.'

'What?'

'Grain. Dates. Cotton. That sort of thing.'

'This will end badly. Take my advice and put a stop to it.'

'I cannot!'

'You must be strong, my friend!'

The telephone rang. Tsakatellis picked it up and then handed it to Georgiades. 'You must be firm!' he said.

Georgiades handed it back to him. 'She wants to talk to you,' he said.

'To me?'

Sometime later he came sheepishly back into the room. 'Figs,' he said.

'Figs?'

'She's sold me some. Twenty sacks, in fact. She says there's been a strike at the docks and the price of figs is rising fast. Take some sacks for myself, she said, and sell the others on next week, when prices are beginning to move.'

'And you've done it?'

'Well . . .'

It was always like this, reflected Georgiades. One day it would end in disaster. But it never did. She had even advanced money – although she had sworn him to secrecy on this – to Zeinab's father. What were things coming to? It was never like this in the old days.

He had taken a room at Tsakatellis's, just behind the shop. Tsakatellis's wife cooked him an evening meal. It was nice to be able to count on a good breakfast. He had been afraid he would have to eat durra, or whatever the benighted Sudanese ate. And the shop was refrigerated. It felt pleasant too – no small thing after you had been out all day in the Sudanese heat. And then, of course, there was the telephone. Not many houses in Atbara had one. But Tsakatellis did. He used it, he said, for his business. But as so few other people in Atbara had one, Georgiades suspected it was more for show. It meant that Georgiades could keep in touch with Rosa and the children – although now he was beginning to wonder whether that was not such a good thing.

It also meant that Owen could keep in touch with him, and Georgiades was even less sure about that.

However, he used the phone to report back to Owen, and in a moment wheels were in motion. Nikos was set loose. This was the kind of work at which the Copt excelled: tracking through files, the ringing up of colleagues, usually Copts, in back offices; the seemingly innocuous but lethal enquiry. Never mind the British, Egypt was in practice run by a Coptic bureaucracy. They never emerged above the parapets – that, in their view, was what bosses were for – but kept their hands firmly on the reins of the Administration. Nikos never went out of his office – it was widely believed that he slept there, probably in one of the drawers of the filing cabinets – but the outside world in some uncanny way seemed to come to him.

In no time at all the Personnel Department of the Railways, also mainly Copts – built, to a man, in Nikos's image, although to a lesser stature – was rummaging through the files. Once you had been filed, and everyone who worked for the Railways was, you were never unfiled. In some cabinet, somewhere, you were on the books. Eventually you could be tracked down. But we are talking Ottoman time here, and it could be a long eventually. But there was also a British time for top executives only. This was the time that Nikos was now moving on, and it was not long before he located Benjamin Lukudu.

Lukudu had joined the Egyptian Railways three years before. Prior to that he had worked for the Delta barrage scheme north of Cairo. Like many Shilluk he was powerfully built and, the note on his file read, excellent for manual labour. He had worked upstream of the barrage where the water was collected in large basins. It was while he was doing this job that he had been infected by the bilharzia germ, as were many others. He had been particularly badly infected and had had to give up work in the flood basins. He had been a good worker, and there was no difficulty about him transferring to the railway, where he would no longer be working in water or in infected areas.

For a time the transfer had proved satisfactory. But then for some reason his work fell off. There was a cryptic note in the files which referred to 'bad associates'. There began to be disciplinary problems.

They worsened and there were instances of violence, as a result of which he was dismissed.

Nikos ferreted around to discover the nature of the disciplinary problems. There wasn't much in the files here but there were a few names and he was able to ask questions. Lukudu had not got on with a particular foreman and a fight had broken out. Both were cautioned and for a while things calmed down. But then Lukudu started drinking and there were other instances of fighting. There was some railway unrest at the time which he became involved in. There was more fighting and more violence, and eventually Lukudu was dismissed.

There was nothing further in the files and Nikos was told that Lukudu had become very bitter. 'Unbalanced,' was the word used. 'He seemed to go off his head.' So much so that there had been no alternative but to dismiss him. After that he had returned to the Sudan and all contact had been lost.

Mr Nicholson had had to extend his stay in Egypt and Jamie had had his stay extended too. He had got used to the busyness of the Cairo streets and could find his way around now. At first he had enjoyed the differences between Cairo and Atbara – the sheer bustle of Cairo. The little streets were always crowded. Things and people were always coming and going: a bread-seller with loaves looped round his arms; a woman with a jar of water on her head and her legs clinking because of all the rings of gold and brass she had around her ankles. Jamie guessed that they were brass but someone told him they were often gold. It was the safest place to keep your money, apparently. Your wife was a sort of portable bank. But didn't it tempt bad men to knock her down and grab them off her feet? It seemed not.

There were lots of things like this to be seen in the Cairo streets. In the early morning the water carts were always out, sprinkling water on the dust. Or there were forage camels blocking up the street with their heavy loads and green dribble forever trickling out of their mouths. Or, when the streets were wide enough, the native buses pulled by two asses, with no sides, just a platform and wooden seats, always filled with passengers, usually by native women in long black burkas, carrying baskets. Of course, in the broader streets there were the new electric trams clanging their bells and occupied by smart young effendis with their fezzes and canes. They all had polished boots and as you walked along little boys would rush out and before you could say anything they were staining them with a sort of spray and then rubbing them hard.

People were always coming up and trying to sell you something, little tartlets or sticky pastries, on which the flies and insects gathered, mostly a sort of Turkish delight, tempting but sickly, or quite useless things like walking sticks and umbrellas and cheap spectacles and belts. And all the time there was this bustle of people coming and going. And sometimes, believe it or not, among the camels and the oxen there were sheep, the ones with fat tails. They wandered around getting in everybody's way. Yet people liked them and tied bright ribbons around their necks. 'Passover sheep,' his father said, but Jamie hadn't really seen how they could be.

Among all this, however, Jamie did not see Aisha until one morning when he ran into her by the Bab-es-Zuweyla, the Bab where the giants hung their things. She seemed very downcast, not her usual self at all. She had just been to see Leila but without getting very far. That was not, however, what was depressing her. She said her mother had started being 'silly'. From what she had said previously her mother had been pretty silly all along, but now things were coming to a head.

'She's always on to me about getting married.'

'But you're only . . .'

'Fifteen. Just. And I haven't even finished school! Some men are disgusting!'

A man had approached her mother only the other day. And her mother had taken it seriously! He had been the son of a Pasha and that had been enough. 'A good match!' her mother kept saying. 'But he was about fifty! And fat and genuinely slobbish,' said Aisha. He had seen Aisha and admired her 'trim' figure. This incensed Aisha. 'Who does he think he is, making personal remarks? And, for God's sake, I am still at school! I've got my exams coming up. And what about my career?'

Jamie knew she had been talking to Zeinab about this, and had been impressed. He wondered whether he ought to be talking about his career to his father. He had, in fact, tried to, but his father had said: 'Finish your schooling first. And then, perhaps, university. And after that it will be time to think about a career.'

'How sensible!' Aisha said.

Jamie was taken aback. It was the first time anyone had said his father was sensible. He had never thought of him in that kind of way. But, thinking about it, he was quite sensible at times.

'Why don't you try your father?' he asked Aisha.

'That is another problem,' said Aisha darkly. 'He seems to be very preoccupied these days and you can get no sense out of him at all. I went to him when my mother had first raised the issue and he hadn't been interested at all! "Oh, your mother will see to that." But she's *not* seeing to it! She just goes along with what other people say. All those silly women lying on the beach. And now this dirty old man!'

'Aisha, he's the son of Pasha Farouk. You mustn't speak of him like that! And he's not an old man. He's hardly thirty.'

'But that's it!' Aisha had cried. 'Thirty! Is that what you want? Me marrying someone who's senile?'

The conversation had broken down at that point.

'They can't be serious!' said Jamie.

'But they are! They are! Both of them.'

'Speak to your father again,' counselled Jamie.

'He won't listen. There seems to be something on his mind. He's always going off with people, talking.'

'My father does a lot of that, too,' commiserated Jamie.

'But I'll bet he doesn't talk to a lot of lunatics!'

'Well, I don't know,' said Jamie. 'From what he says, these meetings can be pretty bad sometimes.'

'They're all cracked,' said Aisha.

Owen, still working his way round the members of the meeting that had taken place in Khartoum, turned next to his old friend, the Pasha, who had started it all with the attempt on him and then the actual loss of his briefcase.

The Pasha was still in a state of deep relief. 'How can I thank you, Owen!' he said. 'I don't mind telling you I had some nasty moments.'

'It goes with responsibility,' said Owen.

'I freely confess I feel quite differently now that the responsibility has been lifted from my shoulders!'

'Not all responsibility, Pasha. Decisions were taken and you shared in the discussions.'

'True,' said the Pasha. 'True. But somehow it's different.'

'I find it a great comfort when others share in the decisions.'

'You do?'

'I do. That's one of the good things about a meeting. When a decision is taken at the meeting, everyone shares in the responsibility.'

'True. Yes, true.'

'Of course, some people contribute more to the decisions than others. Yourself, for instance. The Khedive must have been pleased to have you there. He knew he could rely on you.'

'I hope so, I hope so.'

'It helps, of course, if the meeting is a strong one. Would you say that the membership of that meeting was strong? Apart from you.'

'Well, of course, not everyone . . .'

'Plenty of experience there. But some inexperience, yes?'

'A little, yes.'

'Looking at the membership from outside one can't help being struck by the differences. Not just in experience, but in ability.'

'Well, yes, that is true.'

'Some, I suspect, did not quite pull their weight.'

'That old fool, Rabat, was asleep half the time!'

'Too old, perhaps?'

'Oh, definitely.'

'And some too young?'

'We're all pretty mature. Except, of course, that fellow al-Jawad. I don't know what he was doing there.'

'He does seem to stand out.'

'A last-minute addition to the party. Someone's friend, no doubt.'

'I must say I was surprised when I saw his name there among so many Pashas! And he took his daughter, I believe.'

'Not to the meeting.'

'No, but she was on the train with him.'

'There for a treat, I expect!' Pasha Hilmi sniffed.

'Quite inappropriate!'

'What was her father doing at the meeting?'

'No idea.'

'Someone's friend, I think you said. I wonder whose?'

'You'd have to ask Hussein.'

'Hussein?'

'Hussein al-Tawil. He was acting as our secretary. He wasn't there for all our meetings. He just got things started.'

'So he was the Khedive's man?'

'A very junior man. Merely a secretary.'

'But appointed by the Khedive?'

'I think so. Yes, of course, he would have been.'

'Ya Hussein,' said Owen, linking his arm confidently, in the Arab way, 'may I borrow a moment of your time?'

'Of course, Mamur Zapt!'

'It is on the Khedive's business. It concerns the briefcase that was stolen from the Pasha Hilmi.'

'Stolen, but now restored!'

'Praise be to God!'

'Praise also be to the Mamur Zapt, so I understand.'

'A little. But to a great many people who also had a hand in it. Not least the Pasha Hilmi himself.'

'Who fought valiantly to protect it,' said the young secretary, with no more than the briefest hint of irony.

'I am going over the circumstances in my mind,' said Owen, 'to see that it doesn't happen again.'

'Quite so. Although Pasha Hilmi is not often entrusted with such duties!'

'A younger man next time, perhaps?'

'It would be wiser.'

'Although, of course, all those who gathered in Khartoum that day were men of experience. Necessarily so, since judgements had to be made.'

'Exactly so, Mamur Zapt.'

'Tell me, then – I am asking this about all the people who attended, no matter their eminence – how did it come about that Yasin al-Jawad was there? Among so many eminent people?'

'I – I am not quite sure.'

'Obviously he had been recommended. And for his qualities, presumably, not his youth.'

'He is a man of great ability.'

'And I see nothing wrong with youth. When important decisions are to be made, youth should be represented.'

'I do think that, Mamur Zapt.'

'So who was the wise man who put forward the name of Yasin al-Jawad?'

'I – I do not quite recall.'

'I am asking on behalf of the Khedive.'

The secretary wriggled uncomfortably. 'His name came up, I think, just in the mix.'

'But it was added to the mix in the first place. No, let me correct myself: not in the first place. It was added later, wasn't it?'

'I – I believe so, yes.'

'And you must have added it. Why was that, Hussein? There must have been a reason for it.'

'As you said, Mamur Zapt, to make the meeting more representative.'

'A decision was taken to that effect, was it?'

'I think so, yes.'

'Who by? I have looked through the relevant minutes and I can find no reference to it.'

'I am not sure there was a minuted discussion.'

'Was there a discussion?'

'Well, naturally . . .'

'Between whom? These names do not turn up out of the blue.'

Hussein was silent.

'Or perhaps this one did. Did you by any chance add the name yourself, Hussein?'

Again there was a pause.

'And did the Khedive know? I must ask him.'

And then, as Hussein said nothing, Owen pressed again. 'I shall ask him, Hussein. And see if he remembers.'

'There is no need,' muttered Hussein. 'I added the name.'

'On your own responsibility?'

'Yes.'

'Why?'

'I have said: to make the meeting more representative.'

'And you did that on your own responsibility. Is this usual?'

'I don't know.'

'Obviously you have been the secretary to many committees. Does this often happen?'

'Well . . .'

'Does this ever happen?'

'Why are you pressing me like this?'

'Because you are not replying. This was your own idea, was it? Or was it someone else's?

'Someone else's.'

'Whose?'

'You have no right to ask me in such a way, Mamur Zapt! I object to it very strongly—'

'The Khedive does not know about this, does he? It was all your own idea. As I shall report to him.'

'It – it was someone else's idea.'

'Whose? Tell me, Hussein. You will have to tell me in the end.'

'It was not one person.'

'A group?'

Hussein nodded. 'Yes, a group.'

'Their names?'

'I shall not tell you their names.'

'Were they at the meeting themselves? Probably not. Which was why they wanted someone there. Whose name you added to the list.'

'Did I ever tell you about . . .' Crockhart-Mackenzie continued.

There was an apparently endless stream of things that he had not told Georgiades about, and he related them as they walked along the river bank. Although by the time they reached Mr Nicholson's house, Georgiades was beginning to feel that the flow of reminiscence must surely be about to dry up.

It was early in the morning and Crockhart-Mackenzie had promised to show Georgiades just where it had happened. They had gone early because Georgiades was anxious to capture as much as he could of what it had been like that morning, the morning when Sayyid had drowned. Crockhart-Mackenzie had been more than ready to help. He did not often get the chance to unload the considerable store of anecdotes that he had accumulated over the years in the Sudan, most of them spent at Atbara, and the Greek was an interested and sympathetic listener.

'Take crocodiles, for example: in the old days you would see them sunning themselves on the banks of both sides of the river. Like logs, they were, green and yellow and with their skin corrugated like bark. You had to watch it when you were walking along the banks. One snap and they'd have you! And then they'd take you down to a sort of store they kept beneath the river bank. A crocodile's larder, so to speak.'

Georgiades gave a sympathetic chuckle.

'Never seen one myself,' said Crockhart-Mackenzie. 'But I met a chap who had. He'd been diving for the company that put up the bridge. And down there, tucked in under the bank, were two or three of them. Bodies. I tell you, he got out of there pretty fast! I think they dropped a stick of dynamite there! Had to, before any of the divers would go back.

'Of course, that was some time ago. There haven't been crocodiles on this side for years. The occasional one, perhaps, and that's the trouble. There are reports of one every now and then, whether true or not. The Sudanis believe they're true, that's the point. That's why they wouldn't go down to look for him. Sayyid. In the end, his brother had to go down. It's a question of inheritance, you see. You've got to produce the body. Otherwise they would be claiming all the time. You've no idea of the tricks they get up to.'

'So his brother went down?'

'Had to. Didn't like it much, but had to. Particularly because he wasn't his brother really but his brother-in-law. Sayyid came from Port Sudan; he wasn't a native of Atbara. Married a girl from Atbara soon after he got here. He was quite well off and they thought they'd made their fortune. And then he went and drowned! The family wouldn't have got anything if they had not been able to produce the body. Of course, there was his own family to consider as well, not the Atbara one, the one he'd married into, but his own, back in Port Sudan. They would have wanted a share and would have been prepared to argue about it, so they had to bury him quick, which they couldn't do without the body, so . . .' He stopped for a moment to watch a felucca skim close into the bank before wheeling away again.

'Left that a bit late!' said Crockhart-Mackenzie, with the air of an expert.

'Were was I? Oh, crocodiles. Not many left now. But still the odd one, I dare say. Oh, yes, and Sayyid—'

'You knew Sayyid?'

'Only too well.'

'Only too well?'

'I'd had my eye on him for some time. Ever since he came to Atbara, in fact. What is a man like him – intelligent, educated – doing coming into a place like this and looking for a job as a lowly clerk?'

'That's what he did?'

'He did! Mind you, it was a good job he went into at the office. I was surprised, because I didn't know they were looking for

someone. And the next moment, there he was, straight into a plum
job. Must have known someone, I reckon. Anyway, there he was.
And the next moment, he was causing trouble.'

'Causing trouble?'

'Not just in the office but among the workers generally. They
were all right until he came. The occasional spot of bother, perhaps.
But nothing out of the ordinary. Then along comes this bloke and
the next minute, you've got trouble all over the place!'

'Nasty!' murmured Georgiades.

'It was. And shall I tell you what I think?'

'Please!'

'I think it was not an accident. That's what he'd come here
to do.'

'Come here to . . .?'

'Stir up trouble. Someone was targeting Atbara. That's my
belief.'

'But who . . .?'

'Foreigners.'

'Foreigners?'

'That's right. Because who else could it be? Everyone else here
has got an interest in the railway working. Now, you might not think
it but the trains are pretty important in a place like the Sudan. The
Sudan is a big place. As big as India. And the trains are what hold
it together. So why should anyone inside the country want to smash
them up?'

'Smash them up?'

'Sabotage. There had been instances of sabotage. There was one
only the other day – that train that was caught in the sandstorm.'

'Sabotage?'

'That's right. One example among many.'

'I didn't know that.'

'It happens all the time. Well, not all the time. But more often
than you'd like to think. And stirring up trouble. That's as good as
sabotage. And that's what that Sayyid was doing!'

'Just as well he was drowned, then!'

'My thought exactly!'

The bank beneath the Nicholsons' house was crowding up
when they arrived. Why this particular part of the bank should be
like that was not clear, but it had been the practice for years for

Sudanis to come down early in the morning to wash themselves. Perhaps there lay the answer: the practice had grown up over time and now it was an established tradition. The river bed had dried up at this point and the banks receded, which left plenty of room. Goats grazed, dogs walked and people washed. They never swam. Sometimes they walked out into the river and splashed water over themselves, but they never walked in far, especially now, when the memory of the drowned Sayyid was so fresh in their minds. There was usually, said Crockhart-Mackenzie, more larking about, too. Georgiades could quite see how young Jamie might have been pushed.

'That's the Nicholsons' house,' said Crockhart-Mackenzie. 'Just there where the flight of steps comes down. It leads up to their garden. A very nice garden, too. The boy takes the dog for a walk every morning. Down the steps and along the bank. Usually he keeps away from the people. Not that the dog would do anything. It's a lovely dog. An Alsatian. Big, and I suppose that keeps anything bad from happening. Not that it's likely to.'

'And Sayyid?'

'Just about here. The edge is just a little bit further out. It goes down very steeply. How Sayyid came to fall over it, I don't know. But I suppose that's the answer. He was near here and didn't know about the edge. And then you can quite see how, with all the people here milling about, someone might not have noticed that he was floundering.'

Georgiades could quite see that. 'Did you ask around?' he asked.

'Of course. But no one had seen anything.'

Georgiades knew how it came about that crowds did not see anything. A man stabbed in Cairo and the next moment the street was empty. He thought he would ask around himself. But not when Crockhart-Mackenzie was here.

A dog came down the steps with a lady behind it.

'Hello, Jean!' said Crockhart-Mackenzie.

'Hello! With Jamie away, I'm doing the duties, as you can see.'

'Mind you don't get pushed in!'

'I won't be pushed in,' said Mrs Nicholson. 'They always treat me very respectfully. They usually treat Jamie respectfully too. That's why I cannot understand—'

'It might still have been an accident.'

'Of course. But Jamie doesn't usually make a fuss about things. And if there was pushing being done, he's usually doing it!'

'Times are a bit troubled at the moment.'

'In the works. So I gather.'

The Alsatian walked off along the bank. It passed right by some goats, but did not disturb them. They continued tugging at the knots of grass.

'Did I ever tell you about Old Crocodile?' said Crockhart-Mackenzie as they walked back.

Yes, several times.

'No, I don't think so,' said Georgiades politely. 'The ones on the bank?'

'No, no, the *Old* Crocodile. One of the characters of Atbara. About a hundred years old, old enough to have fought at Omdurman. When Kitchener smashed the Mahdi.'

'Oh, yes. Gun-boats, machine guns . . .'

'And proper artillery. The Mahdi didn't have a chance. Well, after the trouble, some of them got away and followed the Khalifa – that's the Mahdi's Number Two, and successor. But Wingate tracked him down and smashed him, too. And after that there was no more trouble. And never has been since. Ever since then the Sudan has been peaceful. That was the way to do it, you know. Smash them first time and, after that, it's easy. That's what I tell the Consul-General. "Don't pussyfoot around," I say. "Go in hard! And then you won't have to do it again!"

'But he doesn't listen to me, and nor does anyone. They say it's different these days. The times are different and the people are different. That Mamur Zapt: too soft. Useless! Lets people get away with anything! Not like the old days.

'Anyway, I was telling you about the Old Croc: he got away after the battle. Fled with the Khalifa and fought on. Until Wingate rounded them all up and shot them. Did I ever tell you about that? No? Well, when they could see it was all up, the Khalifa ordered all the amirs to dismount. They rolled out their *furwas* on the ground, sat down and faced Mecca. They knew what was coming. Brave men, I'm not saying they weren't. They sat there and let Wingate shoot them.

'But not the Old Croc! Well, he was a young croc then, I suppose. Just a boy. But a plucky one. When the shooting started, he lay down and went on lying until it was all over. By this time it was dark and he crawled away and escaped.

'Well, that was a long time ago and now he lives in Atbara. Been living here for fifty years. I often see him, go over and have a chat with him. Talk about the old days. He's a good sort, the Old Croc. Still spits fire! Well, I don't mind that. I give it back to him, too. He still won't give in, and I respect that.

'He's got a grandson who works on the railways. Well, times change, and change isn't always bad. I often see him, the grandson, that is, when I go past the depot.

'He's fascinated by trains, sits watching them for hours. Works in the sheds. Keeps the trains running. That's the difference, these days. Putting his back into making the Sudan work. Funny, isn't it, that it should work out like that?'

ELEVEN

The Consul-General had blocked the purchase of rolling stock from abroad. The Khedive, in high dudgeon, had retired, sulking, to the Abdin Palace. The elderly Pashas who had formed what might be called the Khedive's Group, the ones who had met in Khartoum to look over the proposed railway contracts, had retired to their homes with, it must be said, not a little relief. And yet Yasin al-Jawad, Aisha's father, seemed to have suddenly become very busy. It was not just Aisha who had noticed it; so had the men Owen had put on to studying the activities of Aisha's father.

There was now talk of Yasin paying a fleeting visit to Atbara. The talk came from the young lawyers who sat around in Abdin Square, conveniently placed between the Palace and the School of Law. Owen knew about the talk because he had been sitting in the Square, too, giving his old friend Yacub, the writer of letters, some copying to do.

'I do not believe for one moment,' said Yacub, 'that you are giving me this just out of regard for me.'

'You might be wrong there,' said Owen. 'I have a very high regard for you.'

'That is not quite the same thing.'

'And I was hoping that through you I could tap into the talk of the Midan.'

'That is more like it,' said Yacub. 'What would you like to know?'

'I hear that Yasin al-Jawad is about to leave us again.'

'I have heard that, too.'

'And not bound this time for Khartoum but for Atbara.'

'That, too, I have heard. It is the talk of the Midan.'

'Is that because things are beginning to stir?'

'There is usually no action without a reason.'

'When we talked before, I asked you if you could give me a name. You said you couldn't. But if I put a name to you, would you be prepared to tell me if that might have been among the names that you would have given me if you had been so willing?'

'Try it.'

'Hussein. He is a secretary in the Palace.'

'That might have been among the names, yes. But at the bottom.'

'Used, but not using?'

'That sounds about right.'

'And Yasin al-Jawad?'

Yacub shook a finger at Owen. 'Now, now,' he said, 'we did not agree that we should go that far!'

Owen laughed. 'You are a wily old bird, Yacub.'

'And so are you, Mamur Zapt! But I will give you a straight answer to that: he is not at the bottom, like Hussein; but nor is he at the top.'

'Like?'

Yacub shook his head severely.

Owen laughed again. 'He is very busy,' he said. 'Could you give me an idea of what he is busy with?'

Yacub reflected on this. 'The copying you have just given me is welcome. For I am not busy.'

'This would be a good moment, then, to give you some more?'

'Well, yes,' said Yacub, as if the idea had just occurred to him.

'Some will be with you an hour after I go.'

'Hussein is a man who makes things happen. He pushes things along.'

'When they have got stuck?'

'Yes.'

'You know,' said Owen, 'I am surprised at the concentration on the Sudan. The Sudan has never been of much interest to the Khedive. Why is it now?'

'That is not the question you should be asking.'

'What is the question I should be asking?'

'Why should others suddenly be taking an interest in the Sudan?'

'Why are they?'

'I am not going to do *all* the work,' said Yacub. 'At the moment I have a lot of copying to do.'

Yasin left for Atbara the following morning. This time he did not take Aisha with him. Aisha was in high dudgeon, too. She had not forgiven her parents for this talk of marriage. Her mother attempted to discuss it 'reasonably' with her daughter but was spurned. Aisha made it clear that she was not ever prepared to listen to talk of a fat Pasha. 'They are not all fat,' said her mother. But this was part of the reasonable unreasonableness that Aisha so strongly objected to. Nor was her father, before he went away, any more use. Normally she could count on him in any battle with her mother to take a different kind of 'reasonable' view – Aisha's – but now he turned a deaf ear. He was preoccupied all the time. All the time. She couldn't get him to set aside even a moment for sensible discussion with her. She even sat on his lap, which she normally did only in the case of emergencies; but this time the magic did not work.

'I am sorry, Aisha, but you are old enough to realize that some-times we have to take a considered view.'

'I *have* taken a considered view!'

'One taking in *all* the factors in a rapidly changing situation. You could yet be useful to me.'

'I was hoping you were going to be useful to *me*.'

But her father was too busy with last-minute conversations before his departure to spend time in talks with her. With him not taking an interest Aisha could see it all rested in the hands of her mother and she was worried that, left to her own devices, her mother might have committed herself too far to be able to withdraw when the time finally came to resolve matters.

There was no one, she complained bitterly to Jamie, to whom she could turn.

'What about that lady who you talked to before?'

'The Lady Zeinab? I have been thinking about her. The trouble is . . .' Aisha hesitated. 'I think she is too worldly wise. I have been thinking of going directly to the Mamur Zapt.'

'Isn't he . . . worldly wise?'

'Not in the same way. I don't think men are.'

Jamie was out of his depth. 'He has always seemed pretty wise to me.'

'It's not the same thing. He is shrewd about some things, politics, and that sort of thing. But on things like this . . .'

'My father says he's a wily bastard.'

'My father says that, too. But don't you see, it's not the same thing. He doesn't know about young girls.'

Jamie also did not know about young girls. Girls like Aisha, for example.

'The trouble is,' said Aisha, 'that he lacks experience. Now that they've had a baby, he'll probably be all right in about ten years. But I can't wait that long!'

To make matters worse, things seemed suddenly to have started to move with Leila, the Pasha's friend. She smuggled a message to Aisha suggesting that they meet.

'At the zoo again,' said Aisha. 'I fear the worst.'

What the worst might be, Jamie was not sure. Anyway, Aisha could not be bothered with Leila just at the moment. She had too much on her mind.

'Although,' she said to Jamie, 'what it may come to in the end is both of us, Leila and me, running away together.'

Georgiades's way in the mornings usually took him through the marshalling yards. There were always engines being prepared to go out and workmen crawling over them and under them, no matter, it seemed to Georgiades, at what hour. There was also, nearly always, a young man doing nothing but sitting on the foot plate of one of the engines, and there he was again that morning, sitting on one of the engine foot plates.

'All right for some!' said Georgiades.

Crockhart-Mackenzie gave the man a wave. The man waved back.

'Young Croc,' said Crockhart-Mackenzie.

'Young Croc?'

'You remember me telling you about Old Croc?'

'I do indeed.'

'That's his grandson.'

'The one you were telling me about? The one keen on trains?'

'That's the one. Selim. Worked here ever since he was a nipper. Younger than that, in fact. Even since he was a toddler. His mother used to bring him up to watch the trains. She said it kept him quiet. And then when he could walk, he used to come up on his own. They would find him sitting under the engines. Of course, he shouldn't have been doing that. It would be dangerous for children, with the engines coming and going. But he was always all right. The men used to look after him, knowing who his grandfather was.

'And then, of course, he reached the stage when he was big enough to work here. He came the first day he could and got down to it in the works. But when he's got a moment off, or before things have started for the day, he still likes to sit and watch. I asked him about it once, and he said he liked to watch them moving, the engines, you know. Big and powerful. And I suppose to him when he was small it looked like magic. And I think it's still like that for him.'

'Just watches?'

'Of course, not when he's got a job to do. They say he's a good worker. Works hard and not the first man off at night. Don't know what his grandfather thinks of it!'

'Amazing, isn't it, how things change? There was his grandfather, fighting against the British, and now there's the grandson, head down under an engine, making sure it works! It's good to see.'

'It certainly is. But that's progress for you.'

They walked on past. There were a number of workmen around at this point, just coming on shift. Several of them exchanged words with the Young Croc, and Selim eventually got up and joined them.

Almost at the last moment, when the shift was about to start, a man came running up. He pushed his way through the works, rather unceremoniously. Several of them looked at him angrily. The latecomer ignored them.

Something about the latecomer struck Georgiades. Then he realized what it was. The man didn't seem to be able to see too well.

Georgiades quickened his pace and caught up with the man. The man's eyes were red and streaming. Some flies came up and settled in the moisture. The man brushed them away.

One of the men in front of him turned back and said something to him, and then they went on into the workshop together.

The man who had turned back was Selim, the Young Croc, and the man he was speaking to, the man with the afflicted eyes, was the Shilluk, Lukudu.

Without Aisha, as he mostly was that week, and in Cairo, a big, unfamiliar city, Jamie was a little bit at a loss. By rights, they should have returned to Atbara before now, but Mr Nicholson was detained in Cairo by train business and now had to stay on for a few more days. Jamie did not mind. He was getting used to Cairo now, the helter-skelter of the trains, the continual clanging of their bells, the press of the people – there were people everywhere, sometimes in the most unlikely places, lying along the top of walls, propped up in doorways, breakfasting in the middle of the streets, the bread looped round their arms, pushing along the street in their dark burkas, great wicker baskets in their hands and huge pots of water on their heads. And, of course, there were the animals: the camels nodding past carrying bundles of forage so great as to span the street, requiring him to dodge into doorways, which were nearly always crowded with people seeking the shade; fat-tailed Passover lambs, painted all the hues of the rainbow by loving owners; donkeys, oxen, geese.

The dog-faced baboon in the posh red trousers – made for it in the interests of decency by the American lady missionary – which had clutched his hand on the first day, still clutched at him when he went past, but with an increasing air of familiarity, and other performing animals, such as the lemurs sitting confidently on the back of donkeys, continued to look at him hopefully.

But the excitement of newness had worn off and Jamie was the tiniest bit bored. He rather missed Aisha but knew that she was preoccupied with momentous things, like avoiding getting married.

So he was quite pleased when one morning he found his arm clutched by a small, burkaed figure which even he soon realized was the Pasha's lady friend, Leila.

'Dzhamie!' she said, and then burst into a torrent of words. Unfortunately, they were in French. Arabic, Jamie could have managed better. The flow of words dwindled, and the screened face of the burkaed figure looked at him doubtfully.

Or so Jamie guessed.

'Fain el Aisha? Where's Aisha?'

'She's very busy. Trouble at home.'

'I wish,' said Leila, 'to speak with her.'

'She's unpredictable,' said Jamie, which was putting it mildly. 'Sometimes we meet at the Bab-es-Zuweyla.'

'Let us go there.'

Today, however, there was no sign of Aisha at the great gate.

'We could try waiting,' said Jamie.

'I cannot stay long,' said Leila. 'They will be looking for me.'

'It's not far to your house,' said Jamie.

Leila stood by uncertainly. Even under the loose, enveloping burka and the long face veil, people could see that she was actually a young girl, which just about made it acceptable for her to talk to a man. Even an Englishman. Or perhaps that, too, made it easier, for Englishmen, especially English boys, could not be expected to know any better. But it wouldn't have done, sixth sense told Jamie, to stand there talking for too long.

Fortunately, Aisha dashed up. 'Oh! You!' she said, seeing Leila and coming to a halt.

'The master is going away!' she said. 'He is going this afternoon. He will be taking Abdul with him, as he is going down to Atbara. It is in the Sudan, and he is frightened. So they will all be away and I thought we could go to the zoo.'

'The zoo!' said Aisha, who clearly thought there were better things to do with freedom.

'And we could hide in one of the little houses, where no one could see us, and watch the birds.'

'The birds?'

'Yes. The parrots. And parakeets. All pretty colours.'

'Well, yes. That would be nice.'

'And you could buy me an ice cream.'

'Certainly!' said Jamie, ever the gentleman. Realism intervened. 'One of the smaller ones,' he said.

'I suppose so,' said Aisha.

They found their way into one of the little summer houses. Inside, they were concealed from everyone else. Everywhere there was the squawking of birds, especially the raucous shouts of the parakeets, who seemed to be having a debate of their own.

'Did you say the Pasha was going down to Atbara?' said Aisha suddenly.

'Yes. He is probably on the train now.'

'That's funny,' said Aisha. 'My father is going there, too. Probably on the same train,'

'My father isn't!' said Jamie, aggrieved.

'Lucky him!' said Aisha.

'I don't like the Sudan,' said Leila. 'There is a lot of nothingness there, and it's very hot.'

'Oh, I don't know!' said Jamie loyally.

'Why is your father staying here?' asked Aisha.

'Something to do with trains,' said Jamie.

'Oh!'

Aisha lost interest.

'Let us look at the hippopotamus,' said Leila.

They walked over to the hippopotamus's pool.

'What an ugly brute!' said Aisha.

Leila clapped her hands. 'He's like an elephant!'

'Except that he hasn't got a trunk,' said Jamie.

'With his trunk cut off,' amended Leila.

There was certainly something in common between the hippopotamus and the elephant. Close up, their skins were very similar: grey and wrinkled and dusty in the folds. They seemed to fit loosely over their bodies, as if by giving them a tug you might pull them off.

'So the Pasha's away,' said Aisha.

'Aisha,' said Leila nervously. 'I don't think that just because he's away, this would be a good time . . .'

She stopped.

'Yes?' said Aisha.

'A good time to run away,' finished Leila in a hurry.

'Oh, I don't know,' said Aisha relentlessly.

'I don't think the Pasha would like it,' said Leila, worried.

'The question is,' said Aisha sharply, 'would *you* like it?'

'Oh, yes,' said Leila hastily, 'I would like it. Of course. But . . . but perhaps not this afternoon.'

'Tomorrow?' said Aisha ruthlessly.

'I – I think that may be a bit early.'

Aisha turned away.

'I think I'm going home.'

'Oh, no, please don't, Aisha!' said Leila. 'I really do want to run away. Sometimes. But . . . not just now.'

'You've got to think about it first,' said Jamie. 'Where would you run to, for a start?'

'You're always raising practical questions,' said Aisha.

'I know!' said Jamie. 'You could come down to our house. I'm sure my mother wouldn't mind.'

'In Atbara?' said Aisha incredulously.

'In *Atbara*?' echoed Leila.

It *did* seem a bit impracticable.

'I suppose someone might see you on the train,' he finished weakly.

'Yes, the Pasha,' said Leila, eager now in support.

Aisha now turned definitely away.

'So what have you been doing this morning?' asked Mr Nicholson.

He was chatting to the Mamur Zapt.

'I was talking to Aisha.'

'Oh, yes? That's nice.'

'Not very,' said Jamie. 'She's a bit fed up.'

'Oh, why?'

'Her mum wants her to marry.'

'A bit young for that, isn't she?' said Mr Nicholson.

'Not in Egypt, it isn't,' said Jamie.

'I still think she's a bit young,' said his father.

'Do you think you can do anything about it?' Jamie asked Owen directly.

'Me? Not really. It's not the sort of thing I usually—'

'Aisha is very bothered. She says her mum wants to marry her off to some fat Pasha.'

'I'm afraid these things have to be left to parents here. Why doesn't she talk to her father? He seems a sensible bloke.'

'She has.'

'I'm afraid that in that case—'

'She says he won't listen to her, which is most unlike him. He's got something on his mind, she says.'

'I can believe that,' said the Mamur Zapt.

'And, anyway, he's going to Atbara.'

'Yes,' said Owen.

'And the Pasha, too.'

'The Pasha? The Pasha Hilmi?'

'Yes. Our Pasha.'

'Are you sure, Jamie?' said his father. 'Because the last time I spoke to him I gathered that that was about the last thing that he was likely to do.'

'Leila says so.'

'Leila?'

'The Pasha's sort-of wife.'

'Are you sure?'

'Yes. He went off this afternoon.'

'Well, that's very interesting!' said Owen. 'Do you mind if I make a phone call?'

Georgiades was waiting on the platform when the train arrived.

So were several other people, and he noted them with interest. There was Selim, the Young Croc, not in the background this time but at the forefront, talking as an equal to a group of elderly men with an air of seniority. Among them was a very old, white-turbaned man supported by two anxious boys. Selim went across to the old man and knelt respectfully and then embraced him. Georgiades guessed that he was the Old Croc.

One of the men who got off the train with the Pasha Hilmi was Aisha's father, Yasin al-Jawad. He bowed respectfully to the Old Croc and to several of the other elderly men, but then pulled aside. A little later, Georgiades saw him talking familiarly to the Young Croc.

The party of seniors left the station on foot. The Old Croc, sprightly but with his boys nervously in attention, went with them. The Young Croc, with Yasin, left a little after, while the senior party went straight to a house in the outskirts of Atbara. Yasin and Selim broke away to a little restaurant in the side street. As was often the case in hot countries like Egypt and the Sudan the restaurant was partly underground and therefore cooler as it was shielded from the sun.

Georgiades, not for the first time in his life, wished there were two of him. After thinking about it, he left Yasin and Selim in the restaurant and went to the house the others had entered, but remained outside sitting in the shade of a house round the corner. From there he could keep an eye on comings and goings. Sometime later Yasin and Selim appeared, knocked discreetly and went in.

Georgiades continued to sit.

A man came up carrying a covered basket. The door was opened by a woman in a blue burka whose face was unveiled and lined and worn. She took in the basket. A little later the smell of cooking was in the air.

Much later there was the sound of voices raised in anger from inside.

The two Crocs, the older and the younger, appeared in the doorway arguing.

The Old Croc gave the younger a cuff, which Selim accepted submissively. Then the Old Croc went back inside and the Young Croc walked away.

Again, Georgiades didn't know whether to follow or stay. After a moment's resolution, he followed.

He realized after a while that he was on a familiar road. He hung back and when Selim knocked on the door of one of the houses and went in, he took up position in the shade, from where he could keep a watch.

It was not so long this time. The door opened and Selim emerged. He shrugged his shoulders and went away.

It was the house of the Sayyids, where Georgiades had been before.

He allowed time to pass and then knocked. The door was flung open and the mother of the drowned man came out angrily.

'Is it not enough—' she began, and then stopped.

'I come at the wrong moment,' said Georgiades, humbly.

'Well, you do,' said the woman, but nevertheless invited him in.

'You are angry!' said Georgiades.

'Well, I am,' said the woman. 'The man came before, when our son was not cold in his grave, and tried to make all well. But when you have lost a son, nothing can make it well.'

'I will go,' said Georgiades. 'I wouldn't have come, but I heard . . . I heard something so shocking that I *had* to come.'

'What was that?'

'It was about my friend. They say that his death was not an accident.'

'That is what I said!' said the woman.

'I could not believe it. I know that was what you told me, but then I thought, well the mother is distraught. Who would want to kill someone like my old friend?'

'Yes, who?' said the mother.

'I mean, he wasn't perfect. No one is. But he wasn't bad, so why should anyone . . .?'

'Why, indeed? After all he had done for them!'

'He worked so hard on their behalf! At least,' he said hurriedly, 'that is what I heard.'

'He was out every night,' said the mother. 'Always working for people. Much good it did him. And now my daughter has been left husbandless, and the child without a father!'

'Friends, even back in Cairo, will want to know this,' said Georgiades.

'They can do nothing,' said the father, suddenly appearing beside his wife.

'It is not right,' said the daughter, there, too. 'I am left without a man and my son without a father.'

'And that man brought money!' said the mother. 'And he was the one who had egged him on!'

'Peace, woman!' said the father. 'It can do no good now.'

'You should never have married him,' the woman said to her daughter.

'That was not what you said when he asked for me,' said the daughter. 'Then, it was, "a rich man you have got there, daughter!"'

'I thought he was rich, and so did you at the time.'

'At the time, yes,' said the daughter.

'When he wanted to move in with us, we should have known!' said the father.

'It was while we were waiting for the right house to turn up,' said the daughter.

'Which would be never!'

'I can't understand it,' said Georgiades. 'Was not your man much respected?'

'Until they knew him,' said the mother.

'That is not fair, Mother!' said the daughter. 'I don't know what happened, but at first they all respected him.'

'So I was told!' said Georgiades.

'But then they fell out,' said the daughter. 'He and that other man, who has just been here. And offered us money.'

'He has offered us money before,' said the mother.

'Not him, Mother!' said the daughter. 'The money was from the men in the office. They knew he had done much for them.'

'Who was it this time?' asked the father.

'Selim.'

'He did not offer us money when we needed it.'

'He is offering it now,' said the mother.

'But the funeral is done with!'

'That is not what he is offering us money for,' said the mother.

'What is it, then?'

'Silence,' said the mother. 'He wishes to buy our silence.'

'Why should he do that now? When it is all over?'

'Because people have been asking questions.'

'Why didn't they ask them before?' said the father bitterly.

'They did; but in a low voice, which could be disregarded.'

'Why is it different now?'

'Because the questions come from different people. People from outside. That is why they begin to be frightened. And think to buy us off.'

'The questions will not go away,' said Georgiades.

'Why did you not take the money?' asked the father.

'Because of the boy,' said the mother.

'Would not this provide for him?'

'What sort of family is it that provides for the son by selling the father?'

'It is not our father. Nor our son.'

'Shame on you!' his daughter burst out. 'It was my husband that was killed. And it is my boy that suffers.'

'It is not the same,' said the father. 'The husband came from outside. And does not the boy come from the outside, too?'

'No,' said the mother decisively. 'Whatever the man, the boy is ours. He is our daughter's child, and we do not turn our backs on him.'

'There is a husband price,' said the father doggedly. 'If they pay it, is not that the end of it?'

'Not if it is your husband,' said the daughter.

'Enough!' snapped the mother. 'We do not take money from hands that have our blood on them.'

'Money is money.'

'And shame is shame!' said the daughter angrily. 'Is it my father that I hear?'

'Enough!' said the mother. 'Enough! Go outside and fetch some water, daughter! Go! Now!'

The daughter went unwillingly.

'I too will go,' said Georgiades. 'It is not right for me to hear your pain. But there are those who will hear of your suffering.'

He followed the daughter out of the door.

She had taken up a great, vase-like pot and put it on her head. Then she walked round the corner to where there was a pump and water splashed on the ground. Georgiades waited until she had filled it and then took it from her.

'This is women's work,' she said, resisting.

'It is not just a woman's work to grieve,' said Georgiades. 'Where there are friends, the burden is on them, too. I will speak to them, and perhaps the burden of the boy will not fall just on your shoulders.'

The daughter looked at him, her eyes brimming. 'I knew we had friends,' she said, 'but when he died, they seemed to fall away.'

'But that is when friends should come forward!' said Georgiades.

'Should,' said the daughter. 'But this world is a hard place.'

'There is also justice,' said Georgiades.

'Is there?' said the woman.

'Why should they offer money?' asked Georgiades. 'For silence? But what is there to be silent about?'

'The manner of his dying,' said the woman.

'Did he not die by drowning?'

'You do not drown in a shallow pot,' said the daughter.

'The Nile is not shallow.'

'It is where he was.'

'Was he struck? Or did someone hold him?'

'We have a friend who was standing close by. He would have saved him. But it happened so very quickly and by the time it was done it was too late.'

'What was done?'

'A man came up behind him, a very strong man, who tripped him and then held him. There was no blow, so no one could be taxed afterwards. It was said he slipped but our friend said he did not slip. And, afterwards, the man moved away and my husband lay on in the water.'

'A woman should not be left to bear burdens alone,' said Georgiades quietly. 'Tell me the name of your friend.'

TWELVE

The friend had worked in the railway offices alongside Sayyid, but he was a friend not so much of Sayyid as of the family he had married into. His name was Abou and he was a distant kinsman of the mother. Because he worked all day, Georgiades did not get round to seeing him until the evening. The streets were heavy with the smell of fried onions and garlic from the evening meals.

It was an easy time of the day. The heat was no longer as relentless and the glare of the sun had softened. It would not be long before it went altogether, for twilight comes early in the Sudan. Many of the houses had little back yards where at this time of day people were sitting enjoying the cool of the oncoming evening. It was into the backyard that Georgiades was shown.

'I am a friend of the Sayyids,' he explained.

The man looked puzzled. 'You are not from here,' he said.

'No, I am from Cairo. I knew Sayyid before he came here and thought I would look him up when I visited Atbara.'

'Ah!'

'But not,' said Georgiades carefully, 'a particularly close friend. Rather, a friend of others. Who when they heard I was coming here asked me to look into the circumstances of his death. They are closer to him than I am so the suddenness of his death came as a shock. They asked me to see if there was anything they could do. For the family.'

'The family is certainly in need, yes.'

'I am to report back. And,' said Georgiades, 'certainly there seems need of a report. For – I speak in ignorance, but in good will – all, it seems, is not as it should be.'

'That is, perhaps, so,' said the man.

'I have spoken to the daughter.'

'Yes, Khadradji.'

'Who has a son.'

'Yes, a son.'

'Who, in time, will want to know how his father died.'

'He died in the river.'

'He fell from a boat?'

'No. While he was washing. As he did every morning.'

'Forgive me,' said Georgiades, 'for I speak in ignorance: but how comes it that a man should die in the river in which he washes every morning?'

There was a long silence.

'That is certainly a question which his friends will ask.'

They didn't speak.

'And some of his friends,' said Georgiades, 'are men of substance who will want answers.'

'Let them come down and find the answer themselves,' said the friend bitterly.

Georgiades picked up the tone. 'Some things leave a bitter taste,' he said.

'They do.'

'And what is Khadradji going to tell her boy?'

'Why do you ask us?'

'For the boy's sake,' said Georgiades.

'Some things are better left unknown.'

'But can they be? With so many beginning to ask.'

'It is best if we stay out of it.'

'Excuse me,' said Georgiades, 'but I find that hard to believe. A man dies, and the family seek to know how that came about; is it not the duty of his friends to say what they know? I ask in ignorance,' he said hastily, 'but I ask because others are asking.'

'Sayyid did not come from here,' said the man.

'No, but there are many here whom he helped.'

'That is true,' said the wife, speaking for the first time.

'He was not a bad man,' said the man, 'but he brought trouble upon himself.'

'By speaking up? Against the employers?'

'But that was not all.'

'Not all?'

'The employers would have sacked him. But not killed him.'

'Ah! That, too, is my question.'

'Not everyone thinks alike,' said the man.

'There were differences,' suggested Georgiades, 'among those who should have been his friends?'

'That is so, yes.' He seemed relieved that someone else had put it into words.

'Some think this, and some think that? It is always so. But differ-ences do not always end in blows. Nor do they end in killing.'

The man was silent.

'*Did* this one end in killing?' And then, as the man did not reply: 'We are friends here. There is no one to hear us. Now surely we seek only good?'

'What happened was not good,' admitted the man.

'What happened?'

'Some said afterwards that he must have slipped. But he did not slip. I was close and I saw.'

'What did you see?'

'He was held under.'

Georgiades nodded. 'So some have said.'

'It was a bad man who did it. He did not come from these parts.'

'There were words between them? Blows?'

'Not as far as I know.'

'But that makes it very bad,' said the Greek.

'It does,' agreed the man.

'Are there not those you could tell?'

'It would be bad for me if I did.'

Georgiades shook his head. 'That *is* bad,' he said. 'My friend, I feel for you!'

'Sometimes it is best to keep silent.'

'If one can,' said Georgiades.

He sat there thinking.

'It is not right that the truth should go untold. But I can see that evil should not fall on you. So tell me, and I shall be the one who tells. I am a stranger and will soon be gone. The consequences will not fall on me. Nor on you, either. This way justice will be served and the just shall not suffer for it.'

Mr Nicholson was returning to Atbara and, of course, Jamie was returning with him. As they stood on the platform waiting for the evening train to depart, the Mamur Zapt came up and said that he was going by the same train, and would they like to dine with him?

A few minutes later there was much blowing of whistles and shouting of porters and the last passenger climbed into the train. Jamie's party went straight into the dining car.

'Have you said goodbye to Aisha?' Jamie's father asked. 'They've quite got to know each other,' Mr Nicholson said to Owen. 'It's a pity, in a way, that they've both got to go off to their schools.'

Jamie grunted something non-committal.

'That is, if Aisha *is* going back to school,' said Owen. 'Wasn't there something about her getting married?'

'It is unfortunate,' said Mr Nicholson. 'She's not ready for it.'

'She doesn't want to,' said Jamie.

'She's a bright girl,' said Mr Nicholson. 'But they're the ones who suffer.'

The train drew out of the station. In a way Jamie was glad to be going back to Atbara. He had enjoyed his time in Cairo – there was so much more to it than to Atbara. All the same he would be glad to be back in familiar territory, to see his mum again and to take Bella for her early morning walk.

As they drew out of the Gare Pont Limoun, leaving the Gezira district behind them, and temporarily the Nile over to their left, he took a last look back at the city with its minarets and mosques now standing out above the houses, and felt a mild pang. There was so much he hadn't seen. The Mamur Zapt said he would have to come again.

They had a posh dinner, with ful Sudani soup, lamb chops and ice-cream, all Jamie's favourites. Afterwards, the two men talked on and Jamie said he wanted to explore the train.

The two women were sitting in an ordinary passenger coach some way up the train, a nervous Leila and a resolute Aisha. The decision to come had been made only that evening. Aisha's marriage proposals had suddenly lurched forward and Aisha had feared they would all be over and done with before her father got up and she could have one last chance of persuading him. He hadn't really listened to her when they had last spoken on the subject and she was determined that he should. He was always the weak link in the family's defences against Aisha and normally a soft touch for her persuasion. But, just when she needed him, he had gone to Atbara. Atbara, of all places! But that was where he was and she would have to go. So she opened her money box and prepared for action.

And then Leila had said, out of the blue, that she would come with her. That morning the Pasha had spoken harshly to her, he seemed to be in a bit of a flap, and Leila had decided that she could bear it no longer. She would run away with Aisha and then the Pasha would see!

Aisha was taken aback when Leila had said she would come with her. Such a possibility had never occurred to her and she was not sure at first that she wanted her to come. But then, on second thoughts, it occurred to her that it might be a good idea. She was a little nervous about how her father would receive her when she suddenly turned up in Atbara. Fathers, although usually malleable, were sometimes unpredictable and it might be helpful to have an ally. He could hardly do anything to her if there was a Pasha's . . . a Pasha's what? Wife? Mistress? Anyway, it might help. And Aisha would do all the talking.

It had seemed a good idea at the time. This evening, though, Aisha was not quite so sure. What would the Pasha say? Would she have to do the talking to him, too?

Leila, too, was beginning to have second thoughts. What would the Pasha say? What would the Pasha do? To leave the house without permission was bad enough, but to do so without a man in attendance was frightful! When Aisha had announced yesterday that she was going to follow her father to Atbara and throw herself on his mercy, Leila had been thrilled. That was the kind of thing that she could imagine herself doing. But imagining was one thing and the actual doing was quite another. In her heart of hearts she had always known that in practice it was out of the question. And now she had gone and done it!

She began to shake.

'Maybe,' said Aisha, taking pity, 'you don't need to do it *this time*. Another time, perhaps.'

'But there won't be another time!' wailed Leila.

'There may be,' said Aisha. 'Look, we'll talk about it when I get back.'

But Leila was now in a complete state of dither. She couldn't decide anything. All she could do was stand there and twitch. In the end Aisha decided that the simplest thing to do was to take her with her. Again, it had seemed a good idea at the time, but now practical considerations were beginning to creep in.

What would they do for money? Aisha's contribution from the money box was helpful but small. They certainly wouldn't stretch to fares for two people.

At that point Leila herself made an unexpected intervention. She had money, she said, and produced a heavy, beautifully embroidered and sequined purse to prove it.

But now there was another practical consideration: what would Aisha do with Leila when they got to Atbara? Where, to start with immediate considerations, was she to spend the night?

At this point Jamie came up with a brilliant suggestion: they could all go to his mother's. He was sure she wouldn't mind. They were always having visitors, the Mamur Zapt, for instance, to name but one.

But in the rapidly darkening light as they drew out of the station, even that possibility seemed less straightforward. Was it right to spring this on her? To casually turn up with two new friends and both of them girls, which suddenly seemed to Jamie an insurmountable obstacle. Jamie had never had girls to stay before. He felt that their requirements must be sort of different from that of boys. Especially with one of them being a Pasha's . . .

A Pasha's what? Wife? Mistress (another new word, but one which he certainly intended to brandish around when he got to his new school)? Daughter, even (sort of)? And wouldn't the Pasha have a view on this? Not to mention Jamie's father. Might not politics – an unfathomable word which his father used so often – come into it?

As Jamie made his way through the train with his growing doubts he came to where Aisha and Leila were sitting bowed beneath mountains of their own.

The only thing to do was make a clean breast of it. They walked back to where Mr Nicholson and the Mamur Zapt were still sitting.

'Hello! Aisha, isn't it? And . . .?'

'Leila,' said Aisha firmly.

Beneath the burka Leila twitched.

'But . . .'

'Sorry, Dad,' said Jamie.

'We are very sorry to land you with this, Mamur Zapt,' said Aisha, 'used to problems as you no doubt are. But we find ourselves in an unexpected predicament. It really goes back to my mother, who very foolishly has been trying to force a stupid marriage upon me—'

'To an old, fat Pasha,' put in Jamie.

'But the Pasha Sukri, if he is the one you are talking about, and if rumours are correct, I think he is, is not old. He is well under thirty. And not, I would have said, especially fat,' said the Mamur Zapt.

'To me, he is!' said Aisha, through gritted teeth. 'I am not ready for marriage yet.'

'Oh, it wouldn't be for some time yet,' said the Mamur Zapt. 'These things are often arranged years in advance.'

'I am not,' said Aisha, 'a parcel to be disposed of just like that!'

'No, no, of course not. There has undoubtedly been some clumsiness—'

'On my mother's part,' said Aisha, who was never going to forgive her this.

'What about your father?'

'I am not sure that he has yet taken in the gravity of the matter . . .'

'He has other things on his mind just at the moment.'

'Yes, but the essence of good management, surely, is being able to prioritise things. And my marriage is top of the pile.'

'She is too young,' put in Jamie loyally. 'She's still just a girl.'

'Thank you, Jamie! I am, actually, a young woman.'

'No one doubts that, Aisha!' said Owen.

'And I'll make up my own mind about who I marry. When the time comes.'

'No doubt, Aisha. There's no doubt about that at all. But – what exactly are you doing here?'

'I was going to throw myself at my father's feet – well, not actually at his feet, I don't believe in that sort of thing – and plead my cause.'

'And so you followed him to Atbara?'

Looking at it now, Aisha could see that was a bit over-dramatic.

'He was very hard to get hold of,' she muttered lamely.

'Hum. Well, look, I think it would be better if you left it, just at the moment. There's less hurry than you suppose. Nothing will happen for years yet. Your case would not be prejudiced by delay. In fact, the reverse may be true. Your arguments could well gain in force as events unfold.'

'And meanwhile you could stay with us,' said Jamie.

'I am sure your mother would be delighted, Jamie,' said Mr Nicholson. 'But what about your father, Aisha? Oughtn't he to be consulted first?'

'Well yes,' said Aisha. 'But his mind is on other things and he might get it wrong.'

'And what about – Leila, is it? I think we really ought to see what the Pasha says.'

'He'll probably be surprised,' said Aisha.

'He probably will!'

'Why, exactly, is Leila with you?' asked Owen.

There was a pause.

'It was, I think, a moment of impulse,' said Aisha.

'I see. And the Pasha doesn't know about it?'

'Not yet.'

'Not yet? Well, he certainly will be surprised.'

'Do you think you could put in a word for Leila, Mamur Zapt? Twist it round to make it look better? I'm sure you could!' said Aisha winningly.

'Yes, well, we'll see!'

'And meanwhile she could come to stay with us,' said Jamie.

'How many more have you got up your sleeve, Jamie?' asked Mr Nicholson.

'We know it could prove a bit tricky for you, Mamur Zapt.'

'It certainly could. It could provoke an international incident, for a start. "British kidnap Pasha's wife." I can see the headlines already!'

'I don't think she's his wife,' said Jamie.

'Or whatever. An Egyptian woman, certainly. That's how it would come across.'

'For some foul purpose,' put in Aisha.

'Thank you, Aisha!'

'We're *not* kidnapping her,' said Jamie. 'We're *inviting* her, that's all!'

'I can see problems in explaining this,' said Mr Nicholson.

'Especially for Leila,' said the Mamur Zapt.

Beneath the burka there was another twitch.

'We must stand by Leila,' said Aisha determinedly.

The burka gave a little whimper.

'You know, Nicholson, I think it might be better after all if Leila could stay with your wife. If she wouldn't mind. That would give us time to sort things out a bit.'

'She's another one who's in for a surprise!' said Mr Nicholson.

When Owen got out of the train, Georgiades was waiting for him. Owen suggested coffee. Georgiades said that Atbara was not Cairo and there weren't coffee houses all over the place. He suggested Tsakatellis's instead.

'Ah, yes,' said Owen. 'I have a letter for him.'

'A letter?' said Tsakatellis. 'For me?'

'Yes. It's from Rosa.'

'My wife,' said Georgiades. 'It will be a business letter. Ignore it.'

'But,' said Tsakatellis, 'she gave me good advice.'

'That way damnation lies,' said Georgiades. 'Ignore it.'

Tsakatellis ignored him and opened the letter. 'She says sell the olives and put the money into sesame seed.'

'This is getting worse and worse,' said Georgiades. 'Don't let her lure you in.'

'But if I do what she says and sell the olives, that will make me a twenty-five per cent profit. In about a week!'

'She will make fifty.'

'All the same . . . twenty-five per cent in a week is not bad.'

'It is what comes next,' said Georgiades. 'She will have other crazy schemes.'

'Like this? Tell me about them!'

'I have given you fair warning.'

Tsakatellis looked at Owen anxiously. 'Is he right?' he asked.

'He's right,' said Owen. 'But so is she.'

Tsakatellis looked questioningly at him.

'You'll be all right,' said Owen. 'I think. I've always found that Rosa knows what she's doing.'

'But one of these days that won't be true,' said Georgiades.

'It's been true so far,' said Tsakatellis.

'Take my advice.'

'What does he know about it?' Tsakatellis asked Owen.

'Nothing.'

'I'll think it over,' said Tsakatellis.

The purpose of the coffee was to let Georgiades bring Owen up to date on more mundane things like murder, fraud and insurrection. He told Owen about what he had learned so far.

'So there are various promising leads you can follow up,' he said. And he was very surprised when Owen said he would start with none of them.

Instead, he went to the Caracol, the little local prison, where the two camel men who had ridden off with the Pasha's briefcase were to be found.

'They've been no trouble at all,' said Crockhart-Mackenzie.

'They wouldn't be. Good food, good conditions. What more could they ask for?'

'Women,' said Crockhart-Mackenzie. 'But they can't have those.'

The two men were sitting on the floor of a large, bare room with barred windows. Owen recognized the man who had ridden his camel up to the railway line and then sat there waiting patiently.

'You were waiting for your friend?' said Owen.

'I was,' agreed the man.

'How did he know you would be there?'

'He was told.'

'This was where?' And then, seeing the man did not understand: 'Was this in Atbara?'

'In Atbara.'

'And you?' Owen said to the man he had first encountered beside the railway line. 'You had been told before, for you were to go to the railway line to meet him. Is that not so?'

'That is so.'

'Where were you told?'

'At Erkowit.'

'Back in the Red Sea Hills?'

'That is so.'

'It was a long way from there to where you were to meet.'

'That is so.'

'So you were told to meet at the railway line? But, of course, you did not know that there would be a sandstorm and that the train would be stopped. So how was the package to be passed to you?'

'It would be thrown out.'

'By someone on the train?'

'Yes.'

'And then you and your friend would pick it up and ride to Atbara with it?'

'That is so, yes.'

'And there you would give it to someone?'

'I expect so.'

'You do not wish to tell me this man's name?'

'No.'

'Even though you go to prison and he doesn't?'

The man shrugged.

Owen went on: 'The package would be thrown out of the train near where you were waiting?'

'That is so, yes.'

'How was the spot agreed?'

'It would be within a short camel ride of the water tank.'

'Where you had arranged to meet your friend?'

'We were to meet at the water tank. But if we could not, he was to ride up the railway track until he found me.'

'So when the sandstorm came and you could not, that is what he did?'

'Yes.'

'And what about the package when the sandstorm came? Was it still thrown out? Or was it given?'

'It couldn't be thrown out because the sand would bury it. I did not know what to do. But a man came up and spoke to me.'

'He was the one who was going to throw the package from the train?'

'Yes, Effendi.'

'So he gave you the package and did not throw it out on to the sand?'

'That is so.'

'Tell me,' said Owen, 'how did he know you were the man who was to be given the package? Had you met before?'

'Yes, Effendi. In Erkowit.'

'How did that come about?'

The man shrugged.

'That is where I live, Effendi. I herd camels.'

'And what did the other man do, the man who came to give you the package? Did he also herd camels?'

'Oh, no, Effendi. He was a *nas taibene*, a well-to-do man. He had been in Erkowit some years before. He had worked there as an effendi – a government official. I knew him then, for he used to carry things for me.'

'On the camel?'

'Yes. That is how they do things in the Red Sea Hills. Nowadays there is a truck, but not then.'

'So you had worked together?'

'Yes, Effendi. And then he had gone away, gone away for a long time, so when he came back a short while ago, I was surprised that he should remember me. But he did, and embraced me. "Here is a man I know I can trust," he said. "I hope so, Effendi," I said. "I know I can," he said. "I was looking for someone, and am glad I found you. For, Abou" – Abou is my name – "there is a thing I have in hand, for which I need help. And the helping will make the man who helps me rich. And I know you are a good man, Abou, so why should not it be you?" And I said: "That would be a good thing." And he said, "Well, then . . ."'

And he had told the camel herder that the package was an important one and that it should be delivered to a man in Atbara. But that it should be delivered secretly and that, in particular, no one should know that the package came from him.

'And I think,' said Abou, 'that that is why he sought me out. The Red Sea Hills are a long way from Atbara and no one had heard of Erkowit. Or of me. Why he should want to do it in this way, I do not know. But so it was. And maybe one day it will make me rich. But I have not yet had the money.'

'It seems hard,' said Owen, 'that you should go to such labour and your only reward be a time in prison. But so it will be.'

As Owen was going along the road, he saw his old friend, the Pasha, coming towards him. The Pasha saw him, too, gave a great start and then looked around for some way of getting out of this. Seeing there was none, he settled himself and then continued boldly. Owen went across the street to greet him.

'Why, Pasha, it is a great pleasure to see you here! And what brings you to these parts, I wonder?'

'Business,' said the Pasha unhappily.

'The Khedive's business again?'

'Again.'

'I thought that was all over and done with?'

'I thought so, too.'

'Not still going on, is it? I thought that now your briefcase had been returned and handed over, that would be the end of it.'

'I thought that too,' said the Pasha gloomily.

'And now here we are, both of us, in Atbara again. I wonder if we could be on the same business?'

'I doubt it!'

'Your business, no doubt, is the Khedive's business. But so is mine!'

'Extraordinary!' muttered the Pasha, looking around desperately for a means of escape.

'Will you be here long?'

'I hope not,' said the Pasha fervently.

'But if the Khedive decrees it, so it must be,' said Owen.

'So it must be,' agreed the Pasha unhappily.

'Ah, to be back in Cairo!' said Owen.

'Ah!' said the Pasha longingly.

Owen fell in beside him. 'I expect you're looking up old friends,' he said.

The Pasha groaned.

'When, no doubt, you had hoped to get away from them.'

'That is certainly what I hoped.'

'Because they are not really your sort, are they?'

'They are not!' said the Pasha fervently.

'Some of them are,' said Owen. He named one or two of the Pashas who had been at the Khartoum meeting. 'But others not.'

'Others not,' agreed the Pasha.

'And yet somehow or other you have to reconcile the different points of view. Was that what the meeting at Khartoum was about, too?'

'No,' said the Pasha.

'You were just casting an eye over the draft contracts? For the Khedive?'

'For the Khedive, yes.'

'And surely you approved them?'

'We did. But . . .'

'But?'

'Not all of us were happy.'

'Well, that's always the way of it, in my experience. Someone's always not happy.'

'But the Khedive had made it clear . . .'

'But even so, there was disagreement.'

'There was. But we thought it was agreed. And then . . .'

'It was not agreed.'

'Some people are never content!'

'Did they want more?'

'No, no. It was not like that. It was over how far and how fast we should go. There were some . . . some who wished to push on, no matter . . . no matter the difficulties.'

'Whether the British would agree, you mean?'

'The Khedive urged caution. But there were some, the younger ones, who wished to press ahead whether the British agreed or not.

Foolish, in my opinion. And in the Khedive's opinion. At the end
of the day, the British are here with their army. That is something
you cannot get away from. That is what I said, and there were others
who agreed with me. The older and wiser.'

'Ah!' said Owen. 'But the younger and less wise did not?'

'It was a mistake,' said the Pasha, 'to have them there. And now
they want to open it all up again!'

'Well, surely if it has been decided . . .'

'One would think so. One would hope so. Especially if the
Khedive has indicated his wishes. That should be enough. But there
are people for whom it is not enough, people who question his
wishes.'

'Even question the Khedive's wishes? That is going a bit far,
isn't it?'

'That is what I said. Exactly what I said! But the young . . .'

'The young were inclined to question, were they?'

'And they had support. Especially down here in Atbara.'

'In the railways?'

'In the railways, yes. They think differently from us, the young.
They are more passionate, even violent. I am not violent, Captain
Owen. I never have been.'

'And very sensible of you, Pasha, if I may say so.'

'The violence of the language! It is really shocking! And . . .
and not just the language!'

'Not just the language?'

The Pasha stopped hastily. 'I had better not say any more. I have,
perhaps, said too much already.'

'I understand your caution, Pasha. It is so easy to be misunder-
stood. Even when one is trying to do one's best.'

'Exactly! That is just it!'

'The oldest and wisest heads are not always the ones that are
listened to.'

'Well put, Mamur Zapt. Very well put!'

'And, of course,' said Owen, 'that is why you have been sent
here. That the voice of experience and wisdom should be heard.'

'That is precisely what the Khedive said to me!'

'And it is easy to see why. In a situation like this he needs to be
able to call on people he can rely on.'

'Well, yes. I hope so. Yes, I believe that is what he feels.'

'He couldn't do better.'

'It is good of you to say so, Mamur Zapt.'

'No more than you're due.'

'Well, thank you, Mamur Zapt. Thank you. One does sometimes feel that one's talents are overlooked.'

'Not by the Khedive, I assure you. He has a very high regard for you.'

'I do my best,' said the Pasha modestly.

A thought struck Owen. 'Pasha, in these difficult times, you must sometimes feel very alone?'

'Well, I do, that's very true. Very true, Captain Owen.'

'Fortunately, you have faithful friends, who care for you deeply.'

'I do?'

'I have heard – and I will not tell you how I have heard, since it was told me in confidence – that one at least has become so concerned about you that she is prepared to sacrifice her name, her reputation, her honour—'

'Tell me more!' said the Pasha.

'—for your sake!'

'I do have that effect sometimes,' said the Pasha.

'And come down here to give you comfort and support that you need when you are undertaking your grave and responsible duties.'

'That is very gratifying,' said the Pasha. 'Very gratifying!'

'A young girl!'

'*Extremely* gratifying!'

'Willing to lay down her life for you.'

'Well, there you are! Passion cannot always be restrained.'

'Her pure, devoted love must not be abused!' said Owen sternly.

'Quite right. Nor shall it be. Much.'

'Do not build your hopes too high. These are only whispers that I have heard.'

'Only whispers?' said the Pasha with disappointment.

'But not to be discounted.'

'Indeed not. I hope.'

'But do not set them too low, either. A faithful, pining heart is not to be dismissed. Even by a man such as yourself who can call on the favours of so many Cairo beauties.'

'Actually . . .'

Owen held up his hand. 'No, no, Pasha. I have heard whispers about this, too.'

'Well, between ourselves . . .'

'Even so, the devotion of a loving heart is not to be lightly set aside.'

'No, indeed.'

'No matter the form in which it comes.'

'Such devotion I prize above everything!' declared the Pasha. 'Er, when will I see her?'

THIRTEEN

'Hello, Mr al-Jawad! It's good to see you.'

'Good to see you, too, Mamur Zapt!'

'It's nice to see you down here again. And Aisha.'

'Aisha?'

'You didn't know? Well, she is staying with the Nicholsons.'

'Staying with the Nicholsons? But I don't know anything about this!'

'I gather she tried to tell you before you left Cairo but you were in so much of a hurry that she feels you didn't have a proper conversation.'

'But . . .' said Yasin. 'But . . .'

'A bit of a surprise for Mrs Nicholson, too, I believe.'

'But this is impossible!' said Yasin.

'Far from it, I'm afraid. That's where she is right now.'

'At the Nicholsons'? Here? In Atbara?'

'Yes. Don't worry, she's all right, and will be well looked after, I assure you, once Mrs Nicholson has recovered. She has quite a house full, you see. Now that her husband and son are back, and there's also Aisha. And Leila.'

'Leila?'

'I think the Pasha will be as surprised as you. Actually, I haven't quite told him yet, so would you give me time to break the news completely?'

'Leila?'

'His *petite amie*. I am afraid she got rather swept up in Aisha's plans.'

'Aisha must come home immediately!'

'And will. Once we've established exactly where that will be.'

'Where it will be?'

'Well, you might be in prison, mightn't you?'

'In *prison*? On what grounds?'

'Well, theft, for a start.'

'*Theft?*'

'The Pasha's briefcase. Which you stole from his saloon on the train and handed to your camel-riding accomplice. Who was then to take it on to other accomplices in Atbara.'

'This is preposterous, Mamur Zapt!'

'The briefcase contained important papers relating to contracts, so I am told. Although of course I wouldn't know. I only know that the briefcase was reported stolen by its owner, the Pasha Hilmi. And then turned up in Atbara.'

'Why would it turn up in Atbara?'

'I was hoping you were going to tell me.'

'I am afraid I can't!'

'Shall I hazard a guess? You wanted it to end up with your friends, but you didn't want anyone to know that you had given it them.'

'Why wouldn't I want anyone to know I had given it them?'

'In particular, you didn't want the Khedive to know, because he thought you were working for *him*.'

'I *am* working for him!'

'Nor would he have liked it if he had found out who it was being passed to. People he saw as his enemies.'

'This is pure speculation!'

'Not at all. I have spoken to your camel-riding friends.'

'They are *not* my friends.'

'One of them, at least, was. When you were in the Red Sea Hills. And he says that he had arranged with you to pick up the briefcase and deliver it to your Atbara acquaintances.'

'He is not to be believed!'

'His cousin, the man who was with him, corroborates his story.'

'He would! He is his cousin.'

'You were the one who was seen talking to him. Now, Mr al-Jawad, enough of this. You will have an opportunity to challenge the evidence in court. I want to know about your Atbara friends. Because there are one or two things about them that puzzle me. I know who your friends are, of course. I have been following your meetings. In particular the one last night, at which, I sense, there was some disagreement?'

Yasin seemed stunned.

'What was the disagreement about? You are unwilling to say? Well, I think you should say. It is in your own interest to do so. It affects the nature of the charge to be proved against you. Theft, simply? Or murder?'

'Murder!'

'Of Mr Sayyid. Who was, I believe, a member of your group.'

'That was nothing to do with me!'

'Were you there when it was discussed?'

'No!'

'We need to be clear about this, because it affects your own position. With respect to the charges made against you. Did you participate in the planning of the murder?'

'No, no! Definitely not. I was strongly opposed to any such action!'

'So you did discuss it?'

'Not really, no. It was merely touched upon.'

'But it was touched on?'

'Only in passing.'

'Murder? Touched on in *passing*? What sort of man are you, Mr al-Jawad, when you treat a man's death so casually?'

'It wasn't like that. We were divided. Some of us could not believe what we were hearing. It was new to us. I mean, the thinking was new to us. We don't . . . we don't think like that!'

'Some of you evidently do!'

'Yes.'

'Yes? But not all of you? You are going to have to be more specific. As I say, it will affect the nature of the charges made against individuals. Including – perhaps especially, in view of your actions in connection with the briefcase – you.'

Yasin al-Jawad was silent for a long time. Then he said, 'We were divided. We were divided from the start. It was, perhaps, a mistake to try to combine us. But I thought there would be advantages if we worked together.'

'We?'

'My Atbara friends. And my Cairo friends. We were two separate groups, you see. But we had aims in common. Or I thought we did. We both wanted reform, change. And we were both opposed to the British.'

'And the Khedive? Were you opposed to the Khedive? You seem to have been working both for him, in theory, and against him.'

'I was trying to use him. Both of us, the Atbara group and the Cairo group, wanted change. Revolution, if you like, but I don't think most of us wanted to go that far. I certainly didn't. But when the Khedive asked me to serve on his working party on the railway contracts I saw, or thought I saw, how we could use it. To do what we wanted to do. And that was true for both of us, both groups. The Sudan group had a particular interest in the railways; it was where their support was strongest.

'Sayyid, of course, was especially interested in the railways. That was where he worked. So I thought we could, well, work together on this. But there were differences between us right from the start. We were different people, we wanted different things. We in Cairo wanted to change the government at the centre. Those in the Sudan were less interested in Cairo; what they were interested in was bringing influence to bear on the government in the Sudan. So we had different aims. And . . . and . . . were prepared to go about it in different ways.'

'Ah! Now we're getting to it. You mean that they were more ready to use violence than you were?'

'Yes. At least, some of them were. But they themselves were divided.'

'And why did they think it was necessary to kill Sayyid?'

'He was a railway man and he thought he could get what he wanted by concentrating just on the railways. He wanted to use the railways to bring pressure on the government. But some of them hated the British so much that they didn't want to change things, they wanted to smash things. And Sayyid fell foul of the ones who wanted to smash things and I think they thought he would betray them.'

'So they thought he had to die?'

'Yes. And they went ahead and . . . well, they did it. Without consulting us. Or rather they consulted us in passing, but they had already made up their minds.'

'Their names? Come, Yasin, you have to give me their names. So that the charges are not made against *you*.'

As Owen was making his way through the great railway complex, he saw Crockhart-Mackenzie striding ahead of him. The sun gleamed on the metal of the engines and the lesser carriages and warmed and blistered the woodwork of the saloons. Even the woodwork was scaldingly hot to touch, although not as hot as the metal work, which, when it had been in the sun, was almost red-hot and when it had been standing in the shade still retained the heat long after. Even in the evening it was hot to the touch.

Crockhart-Mackenzie saw him and slowed. 'Been making the rounds,' he said. 'I do every morning. Making sure that nothing's happened overnight.'

'Good for you!'

'But now it's time for a snifter. Care to join me?'

'Delighted.'

As they left the railway precinct they saw a man sitting in the doorway of one of the engines. He raised a hand as they went past. Crockhart-Mackenzie waved in return.

'It's Selim,' he said. 'The Young Croc. That's what we call him. His grandfather was the Old Croc. He'll be somewhere around. Selim keeps an eye on the trains, and his grandfather keeps an eye on him!'

'And you keep an eye on both of them?'

Crockhart-Mackenzie laughed.

'Not much of an eye,' he said. 'But I usually have a word as I pass by.'

They left the railway behind them and went into the Sports Club. It was a big flat field where the English played football and hockey. Not rugby: with the ground so hard there had been so many injuries that the Consul-General had decreed that rugby was banned – to the chagrin of the Welsh, of whom there were quite a few in Atbara. The Welsh Fusiliers were stationed in the Sudan and had brought their practices with them.

The attraction of the Sports Club for many, sporting and non-sporting alike, was the facilities, most notably the bar. There were tables in the shade and turbaned waiters to bring your refreshment to you. In the afternoon they brought tea and the memsahibs joined you, but at lunch it was mostly men, dropping in for a drink after the day's work was done. For the working day started early in the Sudan. It began soon after five, when the day was still cool: On the other hand, it finished early too, soon after two, when it was common to drop in for a quiet aperitif before going home to lunch, and usually a nap, before returning in the afternoon to bash a ball around.

Crockhart-Mackenzie led Owen to his favourite spot in the shade. A gin and tonic was brought as soon as they sat down.

'And for you, Owen?'

'A whisky, please. And ginger.'

Crockhart-Mackenzie was now prepared to expand.

'That boy, Selim, the Young Croc – I've known him since he was a lad, when his father first brought him to Atbara. That was just after I came from India. You know India?'

'Served there,' said Owen. 'In the army.'

'On the north-west frontier, eh?'

'That's right.'

'Hell of a place!' said Crockhart-Mackenzie. 'Was there only for a month myself but that was enough. As it was for India, too. Exchanged into the Sudan, and have never regretted it!'

'Me, too,' said Owen. 'Only I went to Egypt not the Sudan.'

'Well, you'd probably done your share of fighting by then,' said Crockhart-Mackenzie. 'Ah, those were the days! Did I ever tell you about the Khalifa's last stand?'

'I think you may have mentioned it. But carry on.'

'I will. Because it's a story worth telling. You see, after the big battle of Omdurman, when the Mahdi's army was wiped out, a few of them escaped and retreated south. Wingate went after them and caught up with them at Umm Dibaykarat. That night, the Khalifa decided to make his last stand. He knew the game was up. He gathered what was left of his army into a circle and got them all to sit on their *furwas* – have I told you this before by any chance? – and face Mecca. All through the night Wingate's army was coming towards them by moonlight. It was hard going. The grass was very long, head-high, and they had to cut their way.

'Just before dawn they reached a ridge from which they could see the Khalifa's army. They took up position along the top of the ridge. And then they opened fire with Maxim guns and cannons.

'The *mulazemin* – that's the Khalifa's bodyguard, all crack troops, and brave men – charged them at once. But, of course, they were mown down.

'They charged again, or what was left of them did, and were mown down again. And yet again and again. They were brave men, I will say that. Wonderful fighters, too. But, of course, there could be only one end to it, and by the time the sun had got well up, it was all over. What was left of them crawled away through the long grass.

'Now, the point is: the Old Croc was one of them! He was one of the *mulazemin* and had fought with the Khalifa at Karari – that's what they call Omdurman, it's the Arab name for it. And then retreated with the Khakfa to Umm Dibaykarat. With the Khalifa to the end, he was! Well, that's the Old Croc for you! That's the sort of man he was.

'He got hit early on, got up and fought on, but was hit again. And this time he lost consciousness. Lying there in the long grass they missed him when they went through afterwards, finishing them off. Well, you know what war is.

'So he lay there all day, and then when it got dark, the women came to look for them. The Old Croc's wife was one of them, with her child at her breast. Imagine that! The man we saw sitting on the foot plate of the engine! He was there. Although I don't imagine he remembers much about it!'

He chuckled, but then caught himself.

'Well, I say that, but I think the Sudanese do. For them it was the end of their dreams of independence and a Muslim kingdom beside the Nile. You'd think they'd bear a grudge, but they don't, you know. I've talked to them both. To the Old Croc and to young Selim, and they don't. The Old Croc says it was a long time ago, and Selim says we've got to look forward and not back. All the same, I wonder, sometimes.' He wiped his hand across his mouth. 'You've got to respect them, you know,' he said. 'The youngsters who come out these days, they've forgotten all that. If they ever knew. But they were wonderful men, wonderful!'

Owen was beginning to wonder if he had got to the maudlin stage, but didn't want him to stop just yet. 'Another one?'

'Well, don't mind if I do!'

A repeat gin and tonic and whisky and ginger appeared on the table as if by magic. The waiters knew Crockhart-Mackenzie of old.

'Someone like you must have seen a lot of changes,' said Owen. 'I have, I have!'

'Things were very different when you first came out here, I'll bet.'

'They were!'

'Slaves, still?'

'We got rid of them.'

'We did.'

'A good thing, too.'

'The Old Croc was one of the *mulazemin*, I think you said?'

'I did. He was. One of the Khalifa's crack troops!'

'Paid in slaves in those days?'

'Some of them. Slaves were highly valued. And some of them were very young. Grew up in the family. One of the family, you might say.'

'Did the Old Croc have any slaves?'

'Oh, certainly. One of the elite like him.'

'Has he still got any?'

'No, I don't think so. It's illegal.'

'I know, but some stayed on.'

Crockhart-Mackenzie reflected.

'I think one or two stayed on. The Old Croc was a big man in his time. But most of them would have left when the slaves were generally released. Actually, they were often at rather a loss what to do. Some went to Egypt and worked on the dams.'

'Did they come back?'

'Oh, yes. You'll find some of them here working on the railways.'

'There's always a demand for big chaps. And I expect a lot of slaves came from the south.'

'Oh, that's right. Dinkas, Shilluk, Nuer generally.'

'Shilluk, you said?'

'That's right. Very popular as slaves, they were.'

'Did the Old Croc have any Shilluk slaves?'

'Oh, yes. Bound to.'

'Do you remember any particular ones?'

Crockhart-Mackenzie stared into space.

He sat like that for so long that Owen began to think that he had dozed off.

Then he awoke with a start.

'There was one,' he said, 'one especially. Grew up in the family. Close to Selim. I remember them as little boys running around together. But then Selim went into the railways and Lukudu . . . went off somewhere. To Egypt, I think.'

'What did you say his name was?'

'Let me think a minute. Yes, I'm almost sure that's what it was. Lukudu.'

It was very early the next morning, so early that there were only a few people washing themselves in the river. Jamie appeared at the top of the steps running down from the Nicholsons' garden. Bella, their dog, brushed past him and ran on down to the water. Aisha this morning was coming with them and now appeared beneath the jasmine arch.

They walked along the river bank together, with Bella nosing ahead of them. The few Sudanese didn't seem to mind but Jamie called her back and they went higher up on the bank where the dog's presence couldn't offend people.

The water sparkled in the sun. Some bunches of *um suf* with their white fluff still in them came spiralling down in the current. Every day, thought Jamie, there seemed to be more of them. Pollock, often his companion on these early walks, said that higher up the river was being choked by water lilies and reeds. The feathery *um suf* was the biggest culprit.

Across the river a rickety boat with a patched sail had pushed out from the opposite bank and was coming across loaded with black burka-clad old women bringing onions and vegetables to market. Some chickens were running around, or would have run if there had been room. Instead they pushed at the passengers' legs and pecked up grains which had fallen from the old ladies' baskets. One old lady put her foot over the side of the boat and let it trail in the water.

On this side of the river the bank had filled up quite a lot now and people were splashing into the water. Another burst of people arrived and it became quite crowded.

Bella was nosing around at the top of the bank, giving the goats a wide berth. Aisha came down to the water's edge and took her sandals off. She put a toe in the water, shrank back from the cold-ness and then boldly put it back in again.

'That's where he fell off,' said Jamie, pointing further out.

'Who did?'

'The man who was drowned. Or got eaten by a crocodile.'

Aisha hastily withdrew her foot.

'They don't usually come this side,' he reassured her.

A lot of people were now milling around.

'Hey!' said Jamie indignantly. 'There's that man! The one who pushed me!'

One or two people looked up.

'Him!' said Jamie, pointing.

A man in the crowd began to move away.

'Him!' said Jamie, going up to him and pointing again.

The man turned on him and caught hold of him.

'Help!' said Jamie.

And then, suddenly, a lot of things seemed to be happening at once.

The man let go of Jamie and tried to push away through the mess of milling people. But then a large, fat chap, a Greek, caught hold of *him* and held him. The Greek looked rather flabby and slobby but must have been very strong because he held the red-eyed man as if he were an infant.

And then there were the Mamur Zapt and Crockhart-Mackenzie pushing through the crowd towards them and Crockhart-Mackenzie produced some handcuffs and put them on the man the Greek was holding. He seemed to have him in some sort of policeman's lock, because the man couldn't do a thing.

They went back to the house and told Mrs Nicholson about it. Leila was still asleep in one of the beds under the orange tree. Mr Nicholson had gone off to his office hours ago.

'I hope no one was hurt!' said Jamie's mother.

'I hope they *were* hurt!' said Jamie, still shaken.

'God be with us!' said Aisha, who didn't often use Muslim expressions. Still, this was a special occasion. And, if the truth be told, she was a little shaken, too.

Mrs Nicholson was just putting the grapefruit on the table outside on the veranda. They always had breakfast outside and that included Bella, who had a bowl of watered chocolate under the table.

'Where were you?' Jamie said to her severely, 'When you were needed?'

Leila emerged from under the oranges and had to be told everything. She hadn't got her burka on and put her finger nervously to her mouth.

Mr Nicholson appeared. He went in to work very early and then came home for breakfast. Then he would go back to the office. There was a lot to tell him and he was very interested.

'So you were right, after all, Jamie, about the red-eyed man!'

Leila slipped her hand nervously into Mr Nicholson's and didn't remove it until breakfast was over, which both Jamie and Aisha thought was really feeble. To be a Pasha's mistress and yet need to hold a grown-up's hand!

'She is very young,' Mrs Nicholson defended her later.

'Aisha's not much younger and yet she—' began Jamie.

'Actually, I am quite old,' said Aisha, looking daggers at Jamie.

'I thought it was pretty good of that Greek chap,' said Jamie. 'I wonder if he would teach me how to put a lock on people?'

The Young Croc was sitting in his usual place on the engine foot plate when Owen and Crockhart-Mackenzie walked across. He looked up when he saw Owen.

'I thought you would be coming soon,' he said.

Owen went to squat on the sand in front of him but the Young Croc made room beside him on the footplate.

'I have taken Lukudu,' said Owen.

Selim nodded. 'It was bound to happen,' he said. 'But I am sorry.'

'It was the English boy who identified him,' said Owen. 'On the river bank. Where he had gone to wash. He had attacked the English boy there in the past. Before he attacked Sayyid, I think.'

'I did not know that,' said the Young Croc.

'It didn't seem a serious attack,' said Owen. 'It could even have been an accident. A push in the crowd. But the boy knew it was meant. Why was that, do you think? The boy was just a boy. Lukudu didn't know him. There was no reason for him to push him like that.'

'What is a push?' asked the Young Croc.

'Nothing. Except when it occurs on the river bank, near where the bank slopes down sharply, and where you would drown if you couldn't swim. Why should he suddenly pick on an innocent boy?'

'He wasn't innocent. He was English.'

Owen looked at him. 'You don't believe that, do you?'

'No. But it is an argument.'

'A child?' said Owen.

Selim said nothing for a moment. Then: 'It is not good. I know. I just give the argument.'

'I find it hard to understand, you see. The rest, I can understand. Even the attack on the train, which might have led to someone's death. But the random attack on the boy?'

The Young Croc was silent again. Then he said: 'Sometimes you are walking along beside the river and you come upon a piece of wood. You think it is a log. And then it opens its jaws and seizes you. It is not a log but a crocodile. It is not looking out to kill you; you are just the one who passed by. It was like that with

Lukudu and the boy. Lukudu is full of anger and sometimes it bursts out. He did not mean anything by his attack on the boy.'

'Why is he full of anger?'

'Because his master had lain in the long grass while the English hunted for him with bayonets.'

'I understand the grudge, but it is a long time to bear it.'

'Our family lost fifteen men.'

'A long time ago.'

Selim shrugged.

'The pain lasts for a long time.'

'And you, do you still feel the pain?'

'Mine is a larger pain. It is the pain of seeing my country under the heel of the British.'

'You were not yet born.'

'My father was. He was a baby when my grandmother went looking for her husband's body after the battle. He was taught to remember, and the memory was passed on to me. As I say, my pain is wider. But the sting came from there.'

'And Lukudu still feels the sting? After so many years?'

Selim hesitated. 'The whole family feels the sting,' he said. 'Even after so many years.'

'But only in Lukudu's case does it come out?'

'It comes out in all our cases. But in different ways.'

'It is a general sting. Why should it lead to Sayyid's death?'

'It is a general sting and a general war which we are all fighting. And Lukudu and Sayyid are part of it.'

'No,' said Owen.

'No?'

'There is a more particular reason for Sayyid's killing.'

Selim did not say anything for quite a time. Then he said: 'Sayyid did not agree with all the moves in the battle. We were afraid he would betray us.'

Owen sat thinking for a while. 'It is usual not to agree with all the moves in a battle. I speak as someone who has fought battles. Not in the Sudan but in India. And I certainly did not agree with everything that my superiors did.'

Selim looked at him, surprised. 'You were a soldier?'

'Yes. In India. Before I came to Egypt.'

'Why did you come to Egypt?'

'Because I did not agree with those above me.'

The Young Croc shook his head and laughed incredulously. 'Mamur Zapt,' he said, 'you and I must do some talking!'

'And so we shall. Although it will be difficult, with you in prison here and me in Cairo.'

The Young Croc stood up. 'You are about to take me to prison?' he said and smiled. 'For being an enemy?'

Now it was Owen's turn to shake his head. 'For Sayyid's murder. And I am not sure you did it.'

Selim was taken aback. 'Lukudu was just the tool. I gave the order.'

'But did you?'

After the Young Croc had been taken away by Crockhart-Mackenzie, Owen went back to the Nicholsons. He had hardly got there, and was having a cup of tea on the verandah with Mrs Nicholson, when they heard hurried footsteps in the yard, and a man came running.

'Effendi! Mamur Zapt!'

Owen put down his cup.

'Yes?'

'You have taken Selim to the caracol.'

'I have, yes.'

'You are to wait.'

'Who says?'

'My master.'

'Who is your master?'

'He will be here. He cannot come as fast as I.'

'Better sit down and have another cuppa, Gareth!' said Mrs Nicholson, picking up the tea pot.

A surprisingly short time after, a very old, frail man came up to the verandah.

'You are the Mamur Zapt!' he said to Owen.

'I am, and you?'

'Selim's grandfather.'

'Ah! The Old Croc! So I am told they call you.'

The old man smiled. 'I bite still,' he said.

'Will you sit down, Sheikh?' asked Mrs Nicholson, giving him the courtesy title.

The old man disregarded the chair she offered him and sat down on the steps leading up to the veranda.

'What he said was not true,' the old man said.

'You do not know, Father, what he said,' Owen pointed out.

'I am not stupid,' said the old man. 'I know what he said. He said that he was the man who killed Sayyid.'

'He did say that, yes.'

'I killed him.'

'Forgive me, Father, but I know you didn't. I have spoken to a man who saw the killing.'

'I gave the order.'

'And why did you give the order?'

'Because they are all too weak. Sayyid had to die because he had betrayed us.'

'He might have been going to, but he hadn't yet.'

The old man made a gesture of dismissal. 'He would have. It is the same thing. Once the face turns from you, it had turned. And then you have to act fast. Otherwise, all is told.'

Owen nodded. 'And so you bade Lukudu to kill him?'

'Lukudu is a good servant. But,' said the old man, looking at Owen sharply, 'he is a servant no more. I am the master.'

'And not Selim?'

'Not Selim, no.'

'He feels as you do.'

'He feels as I do. But as yet he lacks the cutting edge.'

'It may be that it is a different cutting edge that he seeks to apply.'

The old man snorted. 'Delay too long and the edge burns blunt.'

'Act too quickly and you cut the wrong man.'

The old man looked at him sharply. 'Sayyid was not the wrong man.'

'That is not what the wife thinks.'

The old man snorted again. 'Women!' he said dismissively.

FOURTEEN

After breakfast Mrs Nicholson needed someone to go down to Tsakatellis's. The cook had already gone out to the market so she asked, as she normally did, Jamie to go down for her instead. Jamie liked Tsakatellis's. It was cool and full of interesting smells from the dried fruit, the dates, the pickles and exotic Greek foodstuffs. He was quite happy to go down and he took Aisha and Leila with him. Leila, full of guilt after running away from the Pasha's house in Cairo, insisted on wearing her burka. Jamie had got used to her now and barely noticed. Aisha didn't approve but this morning, after hearing that her father had been one of those taken into custody, was lying low and was unusually silent. Jamie had intended to take Bella for her usual walk along the river bank but his mother for some reason jumped on him particularly ferociously and wouldn't hear of it. So Tsakatellis's seemed a good idea.

Georgiades, mission completed, was sitting outside the shop having a cup of coffee. He beamed when he saw the children (he considered Leila a child, and wasn't far wrong). They reminded him of what he would find when he returned to his own house the next day. Jamie, having delivered his mother's order, and encouraged by the beam, sidled up to the table where Georgiades was sitting.

'That was a pretty good arm-lock you did yesterday,' he said. 'Could you show me how to do it?'

'Sure!' said Georgiades, and got down to showing Jamie, while the onlookers at the other tables watched admiringly. Aisha, used to the big Cairo shops, had hardly been in a small grocer like this before, and poked around interestedly. Leila tried to make herself even more invisible by standing behind a crate of empty bottles.

The telephone rang in one of the back rooms and Tsakatellis went to answer it. 'Really?' he said. 'Up twenty-five per cent? Sell? Is that a good idea, do you think? I mean, twenty-five per cent, in less than a week . . . All right, all right, you know best, Chief. I just thought the twenty-five per cent, well, you know. Thirty per cent if I shift them quickly? Well, you know the Cairo markets . . . all right, all right, I'll do it this afternoon. This morning? If you say so, Rosa . . .'

'It's my wife,' Georgiades said to Jamie. 'She's doing it again!'

'And while you're doing it . . .' said the voice on the phone.

'Hold on!' said Tsakatellis. 'Get me a pencil.'

The voice at the other end of the phone called out, speedily, a list of numbers. 'Molasses, fifteen per cent, grain eighteen, garlic twenty-six, sesame seed . . .'

'Just a minute, just a minute!' said Tsakatellis.

'Salt up thirty per cent, saffron fifteen . . .'

'Hold on, hold on. Not so fast!'

'Look, it's changing all the time, you've got to keep up.'

'I'm doing my best, but—'

'Let me do it,' said Aisha.

'Cooking oil twenty; chillies fourteen . . .'

'You want me to mark up all those, Rosa?'

'Yes. There's a strike pending in the docks.'

'But, Rosa, I won't sell anything!'

'You will. There's going to be a shortage of everything.'

'But what if I sell out?'

'Cover yourself by buying forward.'

'What?'

'Put in orders for everything you are likely to sell. Delivery in three weeks. The strike will be over by then and they'd have to deliver at the old price.'

'But, Rosa . . .'

'Once she's got the bit between her teeth,' said Georgiades, 'there's no stopping her!'

'You shut up!' said the voice on the other end of the phone. 'Where was I?'

'Chillies,' said Aisha.

'Thank you.' Pause. 'Who are you?'

'I'm Aisha.'

'Oh. I know. My husband was telling me about you. You're quite bright, the Mamur Zapt says.'

'Does he?' said Aisha, pleased.

Tsakatellis came over to the table, mopping his brow. 'It's a bit fast for me,' he said to Georgiades.

'It's a bit fast for everyone,' said Georgiades. 'That's how she does it!'

'And put in an order, *now*, for tomatoes. Two hundred kilos,' said the voice on the phone.

'Two *hundred*? Isn't that a mistake?'

'No. The price will double by next week.'

'I think – I think – I am as far in as I want to go,' said the fainting shopkeeper.

'Dead right!' said Georgiades. 'Get out while you can!'

'Well, all right, but you're missing out on fifty. Gum arabic—'

'Gum arabic? But I don't *sell* gum arabic!'

'Yes, but if you did, you could double your money.'

'But I haven't *got* any gum arabic!'

'That's not the point,' said Aisha in a moment of sudden illumination. 'You don't actually have to have the gum arabic if you've covered yourself by buying forward.'

'At least there's someone down there who's got a grasp!' said Rosa. 'What did you say your name was? Oh, I remember: Aisha.'

Aisha grabbed the telephone.

'Rosa, can I have a word with you?'

In all his years of dealing with court cases, Crockhart-Mackenzie had never seen anything like it. Three defendants, and all of them pleaded guilty! But two of them had been nowhere near when the crime took place. And the third, on learning that he hadn't done it, became so confused that after a moment he gave up and lapsed into silence. The Young Croc said that he hadn't done it, and hadn't agreed with it, but nevertheless accepted the responsibility. And the Old Croc said that he agreed with it one hundred per cent and had, indeed, ordered it, so the responsibility was his!

The bewildered young judge, fresh from England, looked around desperately for help.

Fortunately, the Mamur Zapt was standing right beside him.

All three, he said, were plainly guilty. But Lukudu, the Shilluk, the one who had actually committed the crime, had done so under instruction from someone he was bound to by an oath of allegiance, so under Sudan custom was not fully responsible. Although murder was a capital crime, there was a case for a reduced sentence. He suggested ten years, with the additional proviso that the Croc family should pay compensation to the Sayyids and undertake to pay for the raising of Sayyid's son. The Old Croc was sentenced to a long term of imprisonment, which was suspended, however, in view of his years, provided that his family agreed to keep him indoors and pay no heed to his instructions in future.

This last point was the sticking one for the Croc family but the impasse was resolved by the Young Croc, who seized the leadership of the family and undertook to see that the provisions were carried out. From his prison cell. The Mamur Zapt assured the bewildered young judge that this was actually, in the Sudan, a stronger guarantee than any the government could provide.

The Young Croc himself received a reduced prison sentence and was obliged to give certain undertakings, which he did unwillingly after negotiation with the Mamur Zapt, but adhered to them scrupulously, was re-employed after serving his time by the Sudan Railways, and thereafter rose speedily to major positions of responsibility.

Since her father was otherwise engaged and her mother was recovering from the shock of it all in Alexandria, Aisha stayed on at the Nicholson house in Atbara, from where she could visit her father every day and have a conversation with him which was, in her view, acceptably fruitful. In between she helped Tsakatellis in his shop. With Rosa's distant guidance, and Aisha's mathematical and growing administrative skills, Tsakatellis's business boomed.

There came a time, however, when Aisha's mother had recovered sufficiently to make the long journey down to Atbara, where she collected her daughter and took her back, protesting, to Cairo and school. No Paris, then, this year, nor for several years to come!

Yasin served a short prison sentence. After a little while, with the Mamur Zapt's discreet, behind-the-scenes guidance, he was able to exchange to a prison in Cairo. Aisha then encouraged her mother to go back to Alexandria, while she stayed in Cairo, nominally under the supervision of her father but actually supervising him.

At the weekends and in the school holidays Aisha worked for Rosa, which she enjoyed greatly, particularly after Rosa advanced her some money and she was able to strike out on her own.

One unexpected and unwelcome consequence of this was that she was so successful that she now had to fend off suitors from all over Cairo. However, as, with her new wealth, she now had the whip hand in her family, this she was easily able to do.

She called regularly on Leila, who was blossoming happily with the Pasha. Marriage to a – or the – Pasha was exactly what Leila wanted, and she soon secured this. As a married woman she of course enjoyed more freedom. She could go to the zoo as much as she liked, and in the English school holidays, when Jamie was around, they could meet up with Aisha and inspect the hippopotamus.

Jamie quite liked school in England but liked the holidays more and usually spent them in the Sudan. Indeed, increasingly in Cairo. His eyes were now beginning to be fixed on the Sudan government's excellent schemes for training young recruits.

As the years went by and he rose in the railways he began to see more of the Young Croc. In the fullness of time, when the Sudan became independent and Selim the Minister for the Railways, the two worked closely together.